THE REPRISE OF 1 THE SPEAR HERO

Aneko Yusagi

THE CHARACTERS:

I'm Raphtalia. Nice to meet you.

I'm the Shield Hero. The name's Naofumi Iwatani. Dammit, why do we have to do this again?

Stop being a grouch, Mr. Naofumi. We've been given the very important task of introducing the characters here. Now let's jump right in!

Motoyasu Kitamura

The Spear Hero

The protagonist of the story. 21 years old. Male. Summoned from Japan to serve as the Spear Hero.

At the time of his summoning, he was stubbornly biased and always chasing after women—his weakness. Now, however, he has developed an extreme devotion and affection that places him firmly in the realm of eccentricity. Due to a certain incident, he developed an intense distrust of women. Ever since, he perceives them (particularly those with a nasty personality) as pigs, although this doesn't seem to trouble him. He has a genuine love for the bird-type monsters known as filolials, and he refers to himself as the "Love Hunter."

Motoyasu started out as your typical hot-blooded skirt chaser, but now he's got more than a few screws loose, and in more ways than one.

The sad thing is I can't really argue with that comment.

Filo

Monster (Filolial)

The Shield Hero's Companion.
A bird-type monster called a filolial. Loves nothing more than pulling carriages.
She can transform her appearance into that of a young girl. She is naïve, with a child-like innocence. An excellent singer, she thoroughly enjoys carrying cargo and eating. Motoyasu's love for her is one-sided and a source of significant annoyance for her. She finds herself kicking him almost purely by reflex from time to time. She is extremely fond of the Shield Hero, since he hatched and raised her.

Naofumi Iwatani

The Shield Hero

Male. Summoned from Japan to serve as the Shield Hero. Filo's master.
He has a gentle nature, but his talent for business can make his comments and decisions seem dispassionate and calculating at times. He is the protagonist of the original The Rising of the Shield Hero series—the story that spawned this one. Due to the fact that he raised Filo, Motoyasu refers to him as "Father."
In this series, he sometimes appears in Motoyasu's mind as "the Father I remember" to explain details of the story. This is the Naofumi from The Rising of the Shield Hero series, hence the warped personality.

Filo is also a filolial queen candidate, by the way.

She sure doesn't act like a queen, though.

The Mr. Naofumi in this story looks a lot nicer than the Mr. Naofumi I know.

Yeah, he seems pretty naïve.

Deep down, I'm sure you both have the same kind heart.

FALLING IN LOVE WITH FILO-TAN
THE UNTOLD STORY OF
HOW THE LOVE HUNTER WAS BORN

With a party full of women, the Spear Hero had basically built a **harem** for himself. However, the day would come when they would **betray him and leave his side**. Well, actually, their lack of feelings for the hero was readily apparent to pretty much everyone around except for the hero.

The Spear Hero was **deeply hurt and more vulnerable than ever**. It was at that time that Filo attempted to **cheer him up** on a whim. "What's wrong? You're usually a lot more energetic. This isn't like yooou," she told him. She then sung him a song and gave him some of her food, after which the Spear Hero **fell madly in love with Filo**.

FILO-TAN IS AN ANGEL!!!
BY MOTOYASU

When Motoyasu hugged Filo, she let out an ear-piercing scream. She had a look of horror on her face, like some kind of venomous insect had latched on to her.

At long last, my eyes were opened to true love! All of those times that Filo-tan kicked me, she had simply been reprimanding me for my foolish behavior! (We'll omit the remainder of Motoyasu's passionate commentary, which continued for approximately five hours.)

ONE PAGE JUST ISN'T ENOUGH FOR THIS STORY, I SAY!

NO TIME IS A BAD TIME TO SEE FILO-TAN, I SAY!

Table of Contents

Prologue: Before Traveling to Another World..........................10

Chapter One: The Reprise of the Spear Hero........................20

Chapter Two: Repaying Kindness...68

Chapter Three: Leveling...82

Chapter Four: Time Reversal..106

Chapter Five: Trap..112

Chapter Six: Dungeon..127

Chapter Seven: Gerontocracy...137

Chapter Eight: Aiming..147

Chapter Nine: Filolial Farmer..181

Chapter Ten: Hallucinations..209

Chapter Eleven: Camping Out..223

Chapter Twelve: Finesse...251

Chapter Thirteen: Peeping...281

Chapter Fourteen: Fitoria-tan..301

Chapter Fifteen: Church of the Faux Heroes..........................322

Epilogue: Arrival at Siltvelt...341

SUMMARY OF THE RISING OF THE SHIELD HERO

Twenty-year-old university student Naofumi Iwatani suddenly found himself **summoned to another world**. This happened when he went to the library and began reading a book titled *The Records of the Four Holy Weapons*.

He suddenly appeared inside of a castle that looked like it was straight out of an RPG set in Medieval Europe and was taken to see a king, who informed him that he had been summoned there to serve as the **Shield Hero.**

It was a country named Melromarc that had summoned Naofumi—a country in a world being **threatened with destruction**. The source of this threat was a phenomenon that resulted in monsters pouring into the

world through fissures that opened in the skies. The legends referred to these phenomena as "waves," and these waves were feared by all.

The world's strategy to overcome these waves was to **summon heroes from other worlds**. And so, four young men were summoned to Melromarc: Ren Amaki as the Sword Hero, Itsuki Kawasumi as the Bow Hero, Motoyasu Kimura as the Spear Hero, and Naofumi Iwatani as the Shield Hero.

These four young men had actually been summoned to this new world from four separate modern-day versions of Japan—parallel universes. This new world bore a striking resemblance to games that each of them had played in their own worlds, and because of this, they chose to behave as

if they were in a game, without really giving their situations a serious thought. The country of Melromarc provided the heroes with party members, and they each set out on an adventure to save the world.

However, several days afterward, the Shield Hero, Naofumi, was apprehended for **forcing himself onto** his female companion, Myne. Naofumi himself had no recollection of doing any such thing and vehemently **insisted upon his innocence**. But for some reason, **no one would listen**. Even the other heroes reacted with surprise and harshly denounced Naofumi after hearing the accusations. This was particularly true for Motoyasu, to whom Myne had fled seeking help, and Itsuki, who had an overly strong sense of justice.

Word of the scandal involving Naofumi spread throughout the country like wildfire, and there seemed to be no end to the people's criticism of him. However, this incident, which made Naofumi the object of public contempt, was actually **a plot Myne had devised**. She had deceived Naofumi and completely fabricated the story of his misdeed, **shattering all trust in him**.

Unfortunately for Naofumi, the state religion of Melromarc was the Church of the Three Heroes, which worshipped the Sword, Spear, and Bow Heroes. As a result, the Shield Hero was not well-liked in Melromarc to begin with. The king and many of the country's nobility were also involved in the church, which only served to make Naofumi's position even worse.

As a result of this incident, Naofumi developed **a deep-rooted distrust of others** and an intensely suspicious disposition. With his reputation destroyed, hardly a penny to his name, and practically no offensive capabilities, the Shield Hero left the castle.

Empty-handed, it was a fierce struggle just to survive. Because the people looked down upon him, it was difficult for him to even manage buying the things he needed. Thrust into such a desperate situation, Naofumi found his first companion in **a young slave girl named Raphtalia**.

But even after such a bitter experience, when the first wave came, **Naofumi didn't attempt to turn the tables by defeating the most powerful enemies and chase fame and glory**. Instead, he **focused on saving the people who were actually in danger**. As a result, he gradually began to gain recognition among the country's citizens. And afterward, he gained yet another new companion in a **bird-type monster named Filo** and went on to continue slowly building personal relationships.

Meanwhile, intoxicated by their own power, **the other heroes caused numerous problems with their thoughtless behavior**. The Spear Hero relied on his own insight to break the seal on a legendary seed in order to put an end to a starvation crisis. But when he did, he failed to read the cautionary note left behind. The plant grew rapidly and overran the town's dwellings. Not only that, it even began mutating and producing monsters. The Sword Hero defeated a dragon and left the corpse to rot, causing an epidemic of disease. The Bow Hero spoke with people from a poverty-stricken country and believed them without question. That led him to overthrow the king, who was actually trying to help the people. As a result, the remaining nobility, who were unconcerned with the citizens' well-being, rose to power and established a corrupt government that caused the citizens to suffer even more.

The other three heroes were behaving as if they were playing a game. They **only thought of themselves, and that was the real cause of these problems**.

As this continued, Naofumi went **about cleaning up the other heroes' messes**, using food he had gathered and herbal medicines.

Regardless, the other heroes continued to show no interest in adjusting their attitudes. Furthermore, the other heroes' arrogance was only intensified by the wicked Myne, who manipulated them with her silver tongue and used them to her advantage. But ultimately, **Myne betrayed the other heroes**, just as she had done with Naofumi. Having hit rock-bottom, the Spear Hero developed a **deep mistrust of women**, the Sword Hero became a **bandit**, and the Bow Hero **completely lost himself**.

It was around this time that the Spear Hero, Motoyasu, **began to perceive women as pigs**. To him, not only did women look like pigs, but he could hear nothing but squeals when they talked. This was also around the same time that Filo was kind to Motoyasu. As a result, **he developed a love for her and all other filolials**.

Naofumi needed the cooperation of the other heroes to overcome the waves. It was also in his nature to look after other people in general, so he ultimately **dedicated himself to getting the other heroes back on their feet**.

The king and Myne, who had caused Naofumi so much suffering, were punished. Their names were changed to Trash and Witch, respectively. Later, a great battle would result in **Trash (the king) and Naofumi making peace.**

The heroes finally began to work together, but the enemies they faced also grew progressively more powerful. There were even times when the situation grew so difficult that there were casualties among the heroes' companions.

As Naofumi continued to investigate the source of the waves and search for Witch, he developed ties with other worlds and became aware of a presence pulling the strings from the shadows. And so, the heroes' fight would continue on.

Because it was a member of the opposite sex who had murdered Motoyasu in the first place, when he arrived in the new world, he made it his goal to **create a harem of women who got along with both him and each other**. The reason he thought such a naïve idea might work was because that new world seemed so similar to a game he'd once played. So he approached this situation as if it were a game, as well.

However, due to the accomplishments of the Shield Hero, the reputations of the other heroes took a turn for the worse **and the women in Motoyasu's party betrayed him**. Members of the opposite sex had forsaken him once again. And on this second occasion, **Motoyasu developed a full-blown distrust of women**. Of course, part of the way things turned out had been his own fault too.

Motoyasu's spirit was broken, and **it was Filo that saved it**. He'd always been fond of Filo (despite the fact that she always kicked him) because her human form looked like one of his favorite characters in a game he'd once played. But even when Filo turned back into her filolial form in an attempt to get away from Motoyasu after he had clung to her, he persisted in holding on. Filo had completely captured the Spear Hero's heart.

Ever since, Motoyasu **has continued to shower both Filo and all filolials with an abnormal amount of affection**. He has pushed forward bravely to **fight for world peace** (in his own way) as the **self-proclaimed "Love Hunter."**

Prologue: Before Traveling to Another World

"Motoyasu, do you like me or Ikuyo more?!"

"Huh? Umm . . . Oh! My cell phone is ringing! I'll be right back!"

Momiji had just confessed her feelings for me. I gave her the shake and got out of there.

"Wait! Motoyasu!"

After all, I liked her and Ikuyo pretty much the same at that point, so I still couldn't really decide between the two.

Momiji had come over to my place to talk that evening.

I just couldn't bring myself to dislike Ikuyo, who sat next to me in class at school, even though I'd heard that she was encouraging others to bully Momiji behind my back. Ikuyo was supposedly their ringleader. Actually, it *was* true that Ikuyo was bullying Momiji. But it wasn't that she was the ringleader. It was just that others around Ikuyo had noticed and joined in without her knowing, and so it snowballed into a particularly nasty case of group bullying. It was all just a matter of bad timing.

But talking and hanging out with each other is something girls are supposed to just naturally do, right? I wanted them to all get along. Bullying is disgraceful. That's why I addressed the issue head-on. That should have resolved it. The other girls admitted they had been wrong and apologized to Momiji. That should have fixed the issue. So why had things turned out this way?

Would it have been better to date my friend, Ikuyo, or the sheltered princess, Momiji?

—Ikuyo (classmate)
—Momiji (princess) ◄——

But I wanted to be with Ikuyo too. As a third-year university student, I'd dated my fair share of girls. I fully realized that this was my most complicated romantic situation yet. I'd just naturally gotten along with girls during my time in junior high and high school. And of course, I'd never seen them fight with each other like this. Everyone got along. They all respected each other.

But when it was time to go to university, I turned over a new leaf and moved to Tokyo. There, I started my new life—new romances. I'd yearned for new experiences, but now I missed the girls that had seen me off so graciously after high school.

It was one of those girls that had introduced me to online games too. And I ended up getting into them way more than she ever did. There was another game called The Magical Lands that got me really hooked too. It had an angel girl in it that I absolutely loved. Sure, angels might not have been real, but they were still my ideal type. Girls were all angels, right?

Those were the good ol' days. Why was romance so much more difficult now than it had been back then? I sighed. On days like this, I just wanted to spend all day absorbed in online games to relax and destress.

"Is it so selfish of me to want to enjoy spending time with everyone?"

The problem with the friend, Ikuyo, was that she was too pushy. She made me think of the kind of women who force guys to marry them. She would show up at my place and start cleaning. And she'd throw away my stuff without even asking. I'd found one of my things she'd told me she'd thrown away once when I went to her place, though. When I asked her about it, she said she took it home because throwing it away would have been a waste.

On the other hand, the princess, Momiji, always seemed to just happen to show up at places I went. Something about it made me feel like she was stalking me. It was probably just my imagination. Yeah, it was definitely just my imagination! Neither Ikuyo nor Momiji was the type that would do something like that!

"Oh no! I'm going to be late!"

I took off running to the place where I was supposed to meet someone.

After I'd finished my classes for the day, I went on a date with some girl I'd hit on recently. Then I headed home. I lived in an apartment by myself, but when I got to the entrance, I could hear some kind of commotion coming from inside.

"What are you doing in Motoyasu's apartment?!"

"That's what I want to ask you, Ikuyo!"

I heard a loud crash, like something was breaking. I opened the door in a hurry to see the two of them right in the middle of a scuffle. I was sure I'd locked the place up, so how had they gotten in?

"A rich girl like you can get plenty of guys other than Motoyasu! Just give up, Momiji!"

"I only have feelings for Motoyasu! He's my prince! You could never make Motoyasu happy!"

"That's not up to you to decide!"

"Stop it, you two!" I shouted.

I stepped in and pulled them off of each other.

"Motoyasu?!"

"Motoyasu!"

Having finally noticed that I had shown up, they both seemed to calm down.

"Motoyasu, you tell Ikuyo! Tell her that we're dating!"

"You're wrong! Motoyasu is dating me!"

Oh, come on! Why were these two always fighting?! If they kept acting like this, I'd never be able to take all the girls out on group dates! They were way too assertive. I couldn't handle it!

"Let me make this clear. I'm not ready to devote myself to dating any one, single person. I don't even want to think about that kind of thing at this point."

"No way."

Momiji was at a loss for words. She backed away several steps. Ikuyo's eyes opened wide when she noticed Momiji was off guard and she grabbed a knife from the kitchen.

"What are you doing? Stop!" I yelled.

"This is your fault, Motoyasu! It's your fault things turned out like this for me! In that case—"

Ikuyo turned and ran toward Momiji. I was ready to grab the knife from her. That's when I felt a stabbing sensation in my side.

"Huh?"

I turned around to see Momiji holding on to a knife sticking out of me. I felt a sharp pain, and an unbelievable amount of red liquid came gushing out of my side.

"Ha! I'm sure you just got back from a date with some other girl anyway, right? If Ikuyo or some other girl is going to steal you, then I might as well just kill you. Then I can die too, and we can be together in heaven! Ahahaha!"

Momiji laughed like some kind of broken toy and slowly pulled the knife out of my side. Ugh. The wound felt like it was on fire. I could feel myself gradually losing strength.

"Ikuyo, help—"

I immediately turned to Ikuyo and asked for help. She had been standing there dumbstruck, but she came back to herself and rushed over to me. Then she thrust the kitchen knife into my chest.

"_____"

I let out an inaudible scream. My body trembled as blood gushed out. I could feel the warmth inside of me dissipate and slowly turn to coldness.

It . . . It hurts! Somebody . . . help me!

"If anyone is going to be with Motoyasu in heaven, it's me! You can feel free to die and go to hell, Momiji!"

"You're the one that's going to hell, Ikuyo!"

"You think so? Just so you know, I'm the one that killed him."

"He's still alive! Hold on, Motoyasu! I'll put you out of your misery!"

Momiji thrust her knife toward my neck.

"I won't let you interfere! I'm the one who's going to be with Motoyasu!" Ikuyo shouted.

"Do you really think you can beat me?!"

The two of them continued their scuffle, now with knives in hand. I held a trembling hand to my chest and reached out with my other hand in vain as my eyes glazed over.

Was I . . . going to die? Why? Why had things turned out

like this? All I wanted was to get along with everyone and have a good time! All of the girls I had dated before had stuck with me in the end. We'd all gotten along and enjoyed our schooldays as friends, and I did my best to make sure everyone was happy. So why? Why had it turned out like this? What had I done wrong? What had been different this time? And then it hit me.

The Ikuyo I knew wouldn't have done this. Momiji was kinder than this too. But I hadn't let myself believe they felt so strongly for me. I should have made it clear to them. I should have told them I had lots of female friends and that all of them trusted me, and I trusted them. I should have told Ikuyo and Momiji to trust in me too so that we could all just enjoy life.

I messed up. I really messed up. If I ever had another chance, I would choose to believe. Girls were all angels. It was my fault for failing to gain their trust.

All of this happened just before I was summoned to another world, which turned out to be nearly identical to an online game that I had played obsessively.

ABOUT FATHER'S EXPLANATIONS

In this series, Father will be explaining some of the details for those who aren't familiar with the story!

Well, Motoyasu is terrible at explaining things, so I don't really have a choice.

We'll do our best to make sure all of the readers can keep up.

It's all thanks to Father that I get to share my own adventure like this!

I can't help but worry about any adventure of yours.

We'll be explaining things like this from time to time, so we hope it helps you enjoy the story even more!

Explanation of Explanations

I really wish I didn't have to, but I'll be explaining things in a space like this every now and then. Just like I am right now.

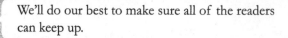

Aultcray Melromarc XXXII (Trash)

King of Melromarc

Something about this king gives one the impression that he is cunning. Despite being the king, he comes in second place, since the queen is the highest authority in Melromarc. The queen is currently away from Melromarc while she visits other countries.

ACTUALLY QUITE SHREWD.

Myne (Malty Melromarc, a.k.a. Witch)

Adventurer; First Princess of Melromarc

The source of all evil and the one who deceived Naofumi. Using her good looks and silver tongue to skillfully manipulate men, she is a wicked woman who acts only in her own self-interest. In The Rising of the Shield Hero, she often showed up wherever Naofumi went and constantly caused him trouble.

BEWARE OF THE WICKED WOMAN.

Ren Amaki

The Sword Hero

From the very beginning, compared to the other heroes, he was less inclined to treat Naofumi unfairly. However, he is terrible about cooperating with others and his solo-player tendencies frequently cause problems. Hopelessly unable to swim.

SOLO PLAYER.

Itsuki Kawasumi

The Bow Hero

A high school student with a seemingly mild disposition. Has an amazing ear—perfect pitch, in fact. In the beginning, he constantly behaved recklessly as a result of his excessively strong sense of justice. In addition to being egotistical, he also has a tendency to look down on others. His refusal to listen to others caused problems on several occasions.

JUSTICE CRUSADER.

Chapter One: The Reprise of the Spear Hero

All of that was a long time ago.

My name is Motoyasu Kitamura! I have a feeling I might seem a bit different now, but I don't care! I'm the Spear Hero, meant to save the world, and I've sworn to protect Filo-tan and all the filolials! Alas . . .

"Gahhh!"

I was faced with an inordinately strong enemy and I was defeated! I wanted to at least look my enemy in the eye, but I couldn't even manage to do that. My vision grew blurry, and everything started to fade to black. Alas! It was the second time I'd died, but dying never gets any easier.

Now that I thought about it, getting stabbed by a pig was how I ended up in this world. Back then . . . Ah, yes, I remember. There were two girls that I liked, but I could never make up my mind which one I wanted to be with. One of the girls began bullying the other viciously, perhaps because she didn't like my indecisive attitude. I stepped in to help the other girl, who then decided she wanted me all for her own.

In the end, I ended up with two selfish girls coming at me with knives, both trying to force a fake double-suicide on me! Which one had stabbed me first, again? I couldn't remember.

Wait. Did I say girls? I misspoke. Those were pigs, I say! I couldn't even remember what those pigs looked like anymore! When I tried to recall their voices, all I heard were squeals.

But more importantly than all of that—Filo-tan! Such a glorious angel! I had shown up in the game world that I knew and loved, and I naïvely set out to create my own harem, intent on keeping my relationships with the pigs uncomplicated at the time. It was Filo-tan who was gracious enough to try to beat some sense into me. I would be walking along with my pigs in tow and she'd suddenly come running like a bat out of hell and kick me off into outer space. And it was all because she cared about me, I say!

And then there was Witch—the crimson swine. She was the former princess of the country that had summoned me to this world. She deceived Father and then took advantage of my cluelessness to make me treat him like an enemy. Eventually, Father raised Filo-tan, which then led to our fateful encounter!

A lot happened after that. Unaware that I had been deceived, I went chasing after the pigs that had abandoned me once I could no longer afford to spoil them. I did my best to try to win them back again. But then I finally realized what a clown I'd been and fell into hopeless despair. And when I did, it was Filo-tan that tried to make me feel better! "Cheer up," she said! I'll never forget the way she looked at me that time, I say!

In the end, my gaming knowledge and my experience with

getting along with pigs didn't help me much. But my encounter with Filo-tan genuinely made me a new man! After that, I decided to fight to save the world for the sake of Filo-tan and all the majestic filolials. Being able to devote myself to that cause, until the very end, is all I could have asked for, regardless of how things turned out!

That's what I wanted to say, but I had to admit it probably wasn't completely true. I wished I could see Filo-tan's smile again. I wished I could still be with Filo-tan. I wished I could do more to help Father. I didn't want to die! At the very least, I wanted it to be after I married Filo-tan!

And then everything went black.

"Oh wow."

When I came to, I looked up to see men in robes in front of me, looking back at me in awe, and apparently speechless.

"What's all this?"

"Huh?"

Whose voice was that? It sounded like Ren. Was I dreaming? I looked around to see Father, Ren, and Itsuki standing there. They didn't seem to know what was going on. Below us was one of the magic circles they used in this world. It was a rather large one too. I'd seen these brick walls before. And this altar. I'd seen it all before. Everything looked exactly the same as it had when I was first summoned to this world. The whole situation was just like it had been then too.

"Where are we?"

Ren turned to the castle mages and spoke. Ah, this must have been a fond memory of that day—the day I first arrived in that new world.

"Oh heroes! Please save our world!"

"What?!"

Father, Ren, and Itsuki all responded in unison. Ah, yes, that's right. I'd responded the same way, right along with them. The flashback seemed so real. But what was this spear in my hand?

Minute Hand of the Dragon 0/300 LR
<abilities unlocked> equip bonus: ability "Time Reversal"
equip effect: diverging worlds

I figured I would try opening my weapon book to check. What was this "Time Reversal" listed as an equip bonus, anyway? Even I had finally gotten it through my head that my knowledge of games wasn't going to help, so . . . Wait. Had I gotten it through my head? I couldn't remember. Hmm . . . I could remember up until the point that Filo-tan cheered me up, but I was having a hard time remembering anything after that. The rest was all a haze.

My fragmented memory was a bit disconcerting. But there

was something I could never forget, and that was this boundless love I felt for Filo-tan and all filolials! I didn't know if I was dreaming or if by some stroke of good fortune I'd gained a skill that had sent me back in time, but there was only one thing for me to do. I would fight for the sake of the world!

"I wonder how much you're willing to consider our wishes here," Ren said.

"Depending on how the conversation goes, keep in mind that we might end up enemies of your world," Itsuki continued.

I'm pretty sure those had both been my lines the last time we were summoned. Father's expression looked like he felt he was somehow losing to the others.

"Yes, well, we would very much like you to speak with the king. He will discuss future compensation with you in the throne room."

The castle mage, who was in charge, opened the door and motioned for us to follow.

"Whatever."

"Fine."

"Come on. Let's go," I said as I extended a hand toward Father.

"Oh, umm, okay."

Something about Father's face was more cheerful—or perhaps childlike—than I remembered. There was an innocence there. I wondered if he would grant me his daughter's hand if I asked now. But wait! If I really had returned to the past, wouldn't that mean that Father hadn't raised Filo-tan yet?!

I considered that possibility while we were being led into the throne room. Ah, there was Trash. Just as his name implied, he was a real piece of trash. He was reclining on the throne.

"Huh, so these kids are the four holy heroes?"

He was staring at us. It sent a shiver down my spine. The old man was a real troublemaker, he was! I could only imagine just how much Father had suffered because of him.

"My name is Aultcray Melromarc XXXII, and I rule these lands. Heroes, show me your faces!"

Ah yes, that was his name, wasn't it? I had completely forgotten. What had I been thinking around this time back then? I was pretty sure it was something like, "I've traveled to a parallel universe! Hell yeah!" I remembered getting even more excited when I realized I already seemed to know how things worked here.

Then they explained the waves to us. The waves were actually . . . huh? I couldn't remember anymore. That was strange. I remembered it being some kind of incredibly grave problem. Was this a side effect of Time Reversal? It must have been. My memories of my dates with Filo-tan were slowly starting to disappear too! No! This was the worst mistake I'd ever made!

"Like they said, we don't have a responsibility to help you.

If we dedicate our time and lives to bringing peace to your kingdom, do we get anything besides a 'thanks and see you later'? I mean, I guess what I really want to know is if there's a way for us to get home. What can you tell us about that?" Father asked.

"Hmm . . ." the king responded with a groan.

The sound of Father's voice brought me back to reality. I was busy thinking about other things and had stopped paying attention. This really wasn't the time to get distracted. But it wouldn't be a problem, since I still remembered this part.

Besides, I had a much more serious problem on my hands—my memories of Filo-tan were disappearing! Those were supposed to go to the grave with me! What could I do to make myself remember? But when I really thought about it, I didn't actually have to remember. I could just create new memories! I could imagine them now! My new memories would be even more glorious than the ones I'd lost!

"Hey."

Father gave me a little jab with his elbow.

"Huh? What is it?"

"Your introduction."

"Oh. My name is Motoyasu Kitamura. I'm twenty—"

How old was I again? I was currently in my 21-year-old body. But I wasn't sure how many years I had been fighting now.

"Twenty years old?"

"No. I'm 21, I say!"

I puffed my chest up and told Father the simple truth.

"'I say'? Umm, what's your occupation?"

"I'm the Love Hunter!"

"Huh?"

Winning Filo-tan's heart was the reason I chose to fight. I'd ridden myself of boring titles like "Spear Hero." I was the Love Hunter, now and forever!

"He's clearly unemployed."

Itsuki apparently felt the need to comment. He could say whatever he wanted! My love-filled days with Filo-tan were much more than an occupation, anyway.

"Now then. Ren, Motoyasu, and Itsuki, correct?"

"Don't you forget Father's name!" I roared.

"Huh?!"

To think he would forget Father, of all people! Ah, yes, that reminded me! Trash was the father of that crimson swine, wasn't he?! I would bring them both to justice!

"'Father'?!"

Whoops! Saying something like that in our current situation made me seem suspicious. First impressions were everything with people. I needed to do my best to make a good impression on Father or he wouldn't give me Filo-tan's hand in marriage.

"Oh, my bad. You look just like the father of the girl I love, so it just came out like that unintentionally."

"Oh, uhh . . . Do I really look that old?"

"Not at all! You look quite young, just like him!"

"Just how old does that make the girl you like?!"

"Let's see . . ."

How old was she? I tried to remember how old Filo-tan had been for a moment but then decided to just go with what was true at the time.

"She's not born yet!"

"You're quite the character, huh?"

"You think so, Father?"

"Is that what you're going to call me from now on? I'd really prefer if you didn't."

"Heroes, please keep the personal conversation to a minimum."

A rather inconspicuous government minister reprimanded us.

"Back to what I was saying, then. Father's—"

"Umm, Kitamura, right? Please stop calling me 'Father.'"

"As you wish! I'd like the king to apologize for intentionally failing to state Naofumi's name."

"Intentionally?!" the others responded in unison.

"That's right. Trash here is intent on trying to cause the downfall of the Shield Hero. He has all sorts of dirty tricks in mind to—"

"Oh! I'm sorry! That was my mistake, Spear Hero! Please! Calm down!"

Hmm . . . Trash seemed to be genuinely apologizing. The four holy heroes must have still had their full authority at this point.

"Just who do you think you are, calling the king 'trash'?" asked Ren suspiciously.

Huh? Had I said something strange? The king's name was Trash, right? He'd just told us his name, but I'd already completely forgotten what he'd said. It wasn't worth remembering, after all.

"I'm the Love Hunter!"

". . ."

Ren's gaze suddenly seemed to grow very cold. Had I said something strange?

"Ahem . . . We got a bit off track there. Heroes, please confirm your status and give yourselves an objective evaluation."

"Huh?"

As if I didn't already know! I checked my status screen. Oh? I was stronger than I remembered being the first time. That meant a new game in god mode?! This would make things too easy! The first wave would be laughable—I wouldn't have anything to do.

"Excuse me, but how are we supposed to evaluate ourselves?" asked Itsuki.

"You mean to say that you all haven't figured it out yet?

Didn't you realize it the moment you arrived here?" asked Ren.

He was acting like he knew everything. He sighed and was about to start explaining. Yes! This was my chance to show off in front of Father!

"I mean, hav—"

"Haven't you noticed any weird icons hanging out in your peripheral vision? Just focus your mind on those!" I interrupted.

"Huh?"

Ren was standing there dumbstruck after I beat him to the punch. He looked like a complete fool.

"Level 1? That makes me nervous."

"What is all this?"

"Do these things not exist in your world, heroes? You are experiencing 'status magic.' Everyone in this world can see and use it, I say."

That wasn't me speaking. That dirty minister must have been trying to mimic me, I say!

"Really?"

Ah, I'd forgotten there was a time when Father acted like this. The Father I remembered always looked menacing, said terrible things, and got mad at everything. It was a relief that this Father seemed much more reasonable.

Oh? I imagined the Father I remembered looking at me with his icy gaze and saying, "You're the one who's unreasonable!" Hahaha! What a jester! Of course I was a sensible guy!

"And what are we supposed to do? These numbers seem awfully low."

"Yes, well, you will need to go on a journey to further polish your abilities and to strengthen the legendary weapons you possess."

"Strengthen them? You mean these things aren't strong right from the get-go?"

"That is correct. According to the legends, the summoned heroes must cultivate their legendary weapons by themselves. That is how they will grow strong."

I stood there silently. Father was thinking hard about something with a worried look on his face for a while before he began to speak.

"Even if they are legendary weapons, mine is only a shield. Wouldn't it probably be best if I used a sword or something?"

Ah, Father didn't know yet.

"It seems that's not an option. You can't use other weapons while possessing a legendary weapon, I say."

"Huh?! Really?!"

"Yes. You'll just have to rely on your companions, Fa—Naofumi."

"Are we going to form a party? The four of us?"

"That's not allowed, either."

"Huh?"

"The legendary weapons interfere with each other and

prevent us from gaining experience. We can share the materials used to strengthen them though!"

"Wait just a mom—"

"Hm?"

I interrupted the minister and he fell silent. Was there some kind of problem?

"You seem unusually knowledgeable about all of this, Motoyasu," said Itsuki.

He was looking at me suspiciously.

"That's because I come from the future, I say!"

"I see."

He believed me quite readily. Everyone was still so good-natured this early on! I thought it would have been best if I explained things before they all got stuck in their ways.

"So you were saying?"

Itsuki was trying to get the minister to talk. Had he not been listening to me? It seems like he hadn't believed me, after all.

"Well, what the Spear Hero says is accurate, more or less. The weapons will interfere with your growth if you form a party with each other."

Father seemed to be looking at something on his screen. Was he reading the help files? Impressive, as usual!

"I guess it's true. So you think we should try and form our own parties?" Father asked.

"I will attempt to secure travel companions for you all. Regardless, evening draws near. Heroes, you should rest for the night and prepare for departure on the morrow. In the meantime, I will find companions for you," Trash replied.

Hmph. He was clearly plotting something. I'd have to stay on my guard, no matter what.

"Thank you very much."

"Thanks."

"The Shield Hero deserves to be treated the same as the other her—"

"I know! I'll find someone! I promise I'll find people willing to be his companions!"

Trash snapped at me to shut me up. He clearly didn't know his place. Whatever. Maybe everything would be alright now.

Back in the chamber provided for us, everyone except for me was closely inspecting their weapons and reading the explanations on their status screens. We'd all had such high expectations at first. But we would end up going through so much hell. What miserable fates! It would happen to Father sooner than later too.

"Hey, this is just like a game, don't you think?"

"It does seem like a game, but it's not quite—"

"This world is from a console game."

"No, it's a VRMMO."

"Huh? VRMMO as in virtual reality MMO? That sounds like something out of the future."

"Huh?! What are you talking about?!"

"Wait a second!" I called out to stop them from arguing.

The answer was right there in front of them.

"Ren and Itsuki. Naofumi. Listen carefully."

"Huh? What is it?"

"All of us here came from different worlds. We're all from Japan, but our Japans are completely different. I want you all to remember that."

"Huh? Really?"

"Yes. If I remember correctly, Itsuki's world is . . ."

Hm? I knew there was something characteristic about it, but I couldn't remember what it was.

"My world is . . . what?"

"I can't remember."

"Anyway, you seem to be unusually knowledgeable about all of this. What's the deal with you?"

"I told you. I come from the future."

"Yeah. Okay."

Ren brushed me off. Just who did he think he was, ignoring such important information?

"Regardless, what the self-proclaimed time traveler said does make some sense. Let's go over what we know for sure."

They ignored me and just went ahead with their

conversation. Hmm . . . Did that mean they wouldn't believe me? It was useless, then. They had just been transported to a parallel universe! Surely they could believe in something paranormal like time travel. Either way, I would still tell Father what I knew.

"I'll stay up all night and fill you in since you don't know anything, Naofumi."

"Umm, thanks. You sure are considerate, Kitamura."

"Don't mention it! And no need for formalities. Just call me Motoyasu. In return, I'll take the liberty of calling you Father!"

"Please don't!"

Father looked really displeased when he refused. Uh oh. That was not the response I was going for.

"Mutual trust between the heroes makes our weapons stronger. Knowing the power-up methods that Ren, Itsuki, and I use will make you more powerful too. Ren and Itsuki might tell you that shielders are weak, but don't worry. You can become incredibly strong! That shield has just as much potential as our weapons."

Back then our hearts had all been in different places and we made things difficult for Father. But it didn't have to be that way this time!

"I want you to hear this too, Ren and Itsuki. The things I know might not match up with the things you know. But trusting each other will reveal the power-up methods."

"Okay, sure," Ren replied with a sigh.

"Uh huh," said Itsuki.

Their responses weren't very enthusiastic. They didn't seem to believe me. What could I do to make them believe me?

"I guess I wouldn't mind hearing more."

Father never failed to impress! He had a thirst for power, after all. I was just about to start explaining when . . .

"Heroes, we have prepared a meal for you."

Someone came to take us to eat.

"I'll explain it all after we eat."

"Thanks."

Afterward, I stayed up all night explaining the weapon power-up methods to Father. More specifically, I mimicked the Father I remembered and told him what that Father had told me. Believing those words and staying faithful to them would produce results, I say!

‖ The Power-Up Methods ‖

There are several different methods to power up the legendary weapons. Information about those methods is sealed away and hidden in ruins, manuscripts, and within the weapons themselves. The legendary weapons can only be equipped by those who are chosen to do so, so the information found within a weapon can generally only be seen by the weapon's owner. That's why sharing information is so important. Through cooperation, the heroes can come to understand each other's methods for becoming stronger. But that means telling a potential rival your secrets to getting stronger. That's why a mutual relationship of trust is important. If a hero just sees the other heroes as competition to be defeated, they'll never be able to use these methods.

After the Father I remembered finished explaining, he faded away like a fog lifting. I took my time and went on carefully explaining the power-up methods to Father, and eventually he began nodding off. I looked over and noticed Ren and Itsuki were already asleep. I tucked Father into his bed, and then I went out for a nighttime walk.

The scenery looked a bit different than I remembered. There were no Spirit Tortoise mountains in the fields outside of the castle town.

I pinched my own cheek to make sure I wasn't dreaming. What in the world was going on? Had I really gone back in time? I started thinking about what I should do if that were true. Of course, the answer all came down to Filo-tan. Filo-tan had asked me to bring peace to the world.

‖ Filo's Wish ‖

This refers to a line that Filo used to brush Motoyasu off when he kept making advances on her, after he'd lost control, when she tried to talk some sense into him. I think the line was, "You can follow me around once the world has truly become peaceful!"

Motoyasu apparently took her words to heart. He believes that achieving world peace is Filo's dearest wish. But I doubt the time will ever come when the world is truly at peace. It's scary to think that even if the waves come to an end, Filo's conditions will probably never be met.

What are the Spirit Tortoise mountains? Answering that requires some explanation about the Spirit Tortoise first. The Spirit Tortoise is one of the guardian beasts collectively known as the four benevolent animals. Its body is so massive that there is even a mountain range on its shell.

The four benevolent animals were originally meant to protect the world from the waves and were each sealed away in different regions of the world. They have the ability to form a powerful barrier around the world, but the sacrifice of countless souls is required in return. The beasts could eliminate the threat of the waves, but there would be no point if it meant sacrificing the people of the world.

Naofumi was preparing to defeat the Spirit Tortoise when a woman who claimed to be a familiar of the Spirit Tortoise appeared in front of him. She revealed that someone had taken control of the Spirit Tortoise and was using it to their own advantage. Unable to serve its original intended purpose, it ceased to have meaning as one of the four benevolent animals and instead became a weapon of mass murder. The woman had come to tell Naofumi that the Spirit Tortoise itself wished to be defeated.

It was a young man named Kyo who had taken control of the Spirit Tortoise. Like Naofumi and the other three heroes, he had originally been summoned from another world. This made him feel special and he let that go to his head. He liked to insist that he was much more powerful than he seemed and was simply holding back. His ultimate objective was to show off his superiority.

Kyo had been taking advantage of the Spirit Tortoise's ability to accumulate power, which was originally meant to be used to form a barrier. But when Naofumi and the others defeated the Spirit Tortoise, he fled. At that time, it was still almost entirely unclear just who Kyo was and what his motivations had been.

The Spirit Tortoise mountains were what remained after the battle. They were a reminder that the area had served as a battlefield.

On a related note, the other three heroes also set out to defeat the Spirit Tortoise but went missing somewhere along the way. It turned out that, due to their own selfish decisions and brash behavior, they had each been driven into a corner and then Kyo captured and took them hostage. Having publicly made fools of themselves, their reputations only worsened after the Spirit Tortoise had been defeated.

Aye, it was I, Motoyasu Kitamura, who would make Filo-tan's wish come true! Oh, how I yearned to see Filo-tan again! Wait a minute. Father hadn't met Filo-tan yet. If things went right, I could probably become even closer to Filo-tan than before, right? I felt a sudden surge of motivation!

I was walking around the courtyard thinking about such things when I caught a whiff of the scent of majestic filolials! I followed my nose toward the origin of the scent, where I found a stable of filolials.

"Gweh!"

"Gweh!"

It was late at night, so the filolials were already asleep. Ah, that scent! It was irresistible! Now that I thought about it, since arriving in this world, I had gone more than half a day without smelling the scent of a filolial. I was probably on the verge of exhibiting withdrawal symptoms.

"Good evening, I say!"

"Gweh?!"

I walked into the filolial stable and greeted the filolials. They woke up, surprised. They seemed to be looking at me somewhat warily. How embarrassing!

"Please don't be alarmed, my lovely filolials!"

"Gweh?"

They didn't make a "kweh" sound. Oh, how I missed Filo-tan! But they were still majestic filolials! They deserved to be fed some more!

"Come, I shall offer you some feed!"

I took some dried meat from the nearby storage shed and offered it to the filolials. They were certainly interested in the offering. The filolials all rushed at the meat and began gobbling it up.

"In return, I hope you don't mind me taking the liberty of petting you all!"

They all seemed to be in good spirits.

"Gweh!"

"You have my sincere gratitude!"

I started petting the filolials and running a comb through their feathers while thoroughly enjoying their fragrance. Before I realized it, I had fallen asleep there in the stable with them.

"Is it just me or do you stink, Kitamura?"

The next morning, I'd woken up refreshed and gone to meet the others.

"'Stink' is a bit rude. This is the fine fragrance of the majestic filolial, I say!"

"Filolial?"

"Filolials are filolials!"

"That doesn't explain anything."

"They are bird-type monsters that pull carriages," added the minister assigned to us.

"Oh. Those."

Father must have understood, because he nodded. A few moments later, we were called for.

"The heroes enter!"

When we arrived at the throne room, there were a bunch of pigs and men waiting there. There were twelve of them in all. We were supposed to bow to Trash. I didn't like the idea of that. But since Ren, Itsuki, and even Father all bowed their heads, I had no choice but to play along.

"As we discussed yesterday, I have called for others to assist you in your journey. Apparently my call did not go unheeded."

I was pretty sure, last time, I had been wondering if the women would choose to come with me. But there were no women here now. Only pigs, I say! More than that, I was worried about Father. I couldn't let him end up all by himself!

"Now then, gathered adventurers, please choose the legendary hero with whom you will travel."

Ren, Itsuki, and Father all looked surprised. Ah, that was right. It was the adventurers that did the choosing. The adventurers came over and gathered around the hero they wanted to group with.

Four people stood before Ren.
Three people stood before Itsuki.
Three people stood before me.
And two people stood before Father.

"I seem to be one short," Father mumbled discontentedly.

He'd been chosen by exactly zero adventurers last time, so this was a big improvement! And it was all thanks to me, I say!

"Ren, give him one of yours!" I said.

Ren's companions (?) started hiding behind him. I was surrounded by pigs. It was sickening. I felt like I might throw up.

"Oink oink!"

"Oink oink oink!"

I had absolutely no idea what they were saying. *Speak human words, you swine!* Blech! There were two pigs in front of Father too. There were so many pigs. How annoying! What was Trash thinking, gathering up all of these pigs?

"Naofumi, I'll give you three of my herd if you like," I said.

"Really?! But then you wouldn't have anyone left, Kitamura. Wait, 'herd'?"

Just as expected of Filo-tan's father! So humble! To think he would be worried about me! I was deeply touched, I say!

But the Father I remembered shot me a spine-chilling, cold glare. He was in my head now, telling me, "Don't try to push your trash off onto others." That glare of his was nice, but the kind eyes of this Father sure were swell too, I say!

"Heroes, please stop trying to trade adventurers without their consent."

"Hmph."

Going on an adventure with a bunch of pigs is not something I wanted to do.

"Now then, heroes, I have set aside these funds for you. Please accept them."

A money pouch was placed in front of each of us. I could hear something heavy and metallic rattling inside of them. I seemed to remember there being 600 silver pieces inside.

There was a red pig over near Father that caught my attention. It was difficult to tell one pig apart from another, but I had a feeling that was my nemesis, the crimson swine. Ah, so that was what happened. She must have noticed the vigilant look in my eyes and gone straight to Father from the start.

"Heroes, I have given each of you 600 pieces of silver. Please take these funds, equip yourselves, and begin your journey!"

"Yes sir!"

I could hear pigs squealing! Did they really think this bunch was going to help us save the world? What a joke!

After taking the silver and getting ready to begin my journey, I tried to go speak with Father, but the pigs got in my way.

"Oink oink oink oink!"

"Oink oink oink oink oink!"

I had absolutely no idea what they were saying. Just what kind of joke was this, trying to force me to go adventuring with this bunch?! There were lots of things I needed to do to help Father, before anything else.

"Oink oink oink oink!"

"You're a nuisance! Out of my way!"

I shoved the pigs out of the way and started to approach Father, but they got right back in front of me. Persistent swine! The pigs of this country had no discipline!

"Oink oink oink oink!"

"Umm . . . Spear Hero, I'm not sure you should be treating your companions like that."

One of the castle soldiers scolded me.

"I couldn't care less. They're all fired, effective immediately!"

"Oink oink oink oink?!"

"Stop your annoying oinking!"

"Please calm down, Spear Hero!"

"Let go of me! There are things that I need to tell Father—"

But Father disappeared while I was arguing with the soldiers. Immediately afterward, Trash called for me and lectured me about treating my companions with respect. His words went in one ear and out the other.

"Hmph. You're just playing king while the real boss is out. Stop acting so big!"

"Ack! Just how much do you know?!"

"Out of my way, nuisances!"

I ignored the pigs and Trash and went to search for Father.

In the end, I didn't have any luck due to the soldiers' continued interference and my self-proclaimed companions clinging to me the whole time. I was going to murder them if they kept that up! But I restrained my urge to kill them and decided to figure out what I needed to focus on.

It was the day after we had been summoned. Where had Father gone and what was he doing? Now that I thought about it, I had only been concerned with myself at the time. I was regretting that now. I decided I should give up for the day, since I wasn't going to find him. I was sure my chance would come!

That reminded me! Why not go ahead and buy a filolial? I could buy Filo-tan! I had plenty of money, so I decided I should go see the monster trainer. I sprinted off into the back alleys and lost the pigs and soldiers. Surely they didn't expect a hero to be strolling around the back alleys. They would probably be searching for me on the main road.

"Welcome! Yes sir!"

I'd made my way to the gentlemanlike monster trainer's place of business. His monster trainer business was a cover for being a slave trader, I think. He got along well with Father.

"You are a new customer, I see. What brings you to our humble little shop?"

"Filo-tan."

"Huh? Oh, umm . . . Do you mean a filolial, perhaps? Yes . . . sir."

"Filo-tan."

NAOFUMI AND FILO'S ENCOUNTER

Naofumi had known the Melromarc slave trader for some time before learning that he also operated a monster trainer business as a front for his shadier dealings. In addition to needing to prepare for the coming battles, Naofumi had gotten the itch to do some buying and selling, and so he decided to participate in a monster egg lottery.

When the egg he'd won from the lottery hatched, a bird-type monster, called a filolial, with peach-colored feathers came out. Filo had been born.

Since most filolials tended to be docile and enjoyed pulling carriages, the monsters had become a familiar part of people's day-to-day lives. Like those other filolials, Filo also loved pulling cargo and running around. Since

Naofumi still had very limited options for travel, Filo made an excellent ally. Her powerful kick and keen sense of combat also contributed greatly to Naofumi's offensive capabilities.

But when filolials were raised by a hero, they could actually exhibit a special pattern of development that allowed them to transform into a human form. When not raised by a hero, filolials would forever remain a bird-type monster. Naofumi did not know this, of course, and he ended up with a filolial that could transform from a bird into a young girl at will. Filo was an insatiable glutton who could speak human

languages. But there were times when her cheerfulness and innocence helped save Naofumi too.

Controlling a monster meant imprinting it with a monster seal, which was similar to a brand. One of the merits of this was that a monster with a monster seal was regarded as a party member, which meant its combat duties and party placement could be assigned via the status screen. This was extremely convenient when managing increased numbers of companions or organizing parties.

I'd heard that this was the shop where Father had gotten Filo-tan. Oh! I just realized that I should even be able to become Filo-tan's owner!

"We don't have anything called that . . . I'm afraid. Yes sir."

"Umm . . ."

What was Filo-tan again? *Come on, brain cells! Let me remember!* I was trying to remember her species. Ah, yes, that was it!

"I'd like to buy an aria-type filolial egg!"

"Understood."

"I have 100 pieces of silver to spend."

I was pretty sure Father had paid 100 silver pieces for the egg. The memory was hazy. There were a lot of things I didn't know about Filo-tan and Father's relationship.

"Very well. I'd be happy to oblige."

And then a mountain of around thirty eggs was brought out. Oh no! Which one was Filo-tan?!

"Which one will have pink feathers when hatched?"

Filo-tan had white feathers with pink tips in the beginning. I could still remember our first meeting! It was at a village just outside of the castle town called Riyute. Father was with her then. It was a predestined encounter, I say!

"I'm afraid there's no way to know until they hatch. Yes sir."

The monster trainer had a puzzled look on his face. I suppose that made sense. I'd raised tons of filolials and even I couldn't tell what color they would be before they hatched. But I was feeling lucky. I chose like my life depended on it!

"This one!"

I went with my gut feeling and chose an egg. I was sure it was Filo-tan!

"Thank you for your business. What would you like to do about the monster seal registration and incubator?"

"You just need a drop of blood for the registration, right? And I suppose the incubator is sold separately?"

"Correct."

"I'll take one!"

I gave the slave trader 130 pieces of silver and bought the egg that I thought was Filo-tan and an incubator. If it wasn't Filo-tan, I could . . . No, I could never sell off a majestic filolial! I would just keep buying more eggs until I found her! I didn't really need to level or unlock any weapons, anyway. I would just focus on earning money and producing Filo-tan for the time being!

And so, having purchased the filolial egg, I left the monster trainer's tent and headed out.

When I thought about it some more, I realized that Father had likely gone to the fields outside of the castle town on the second day. I'd meet up with him there! That's what I thought, but taking the main road led to my doom. That's where the pigs found me, unfortunately.

"Oink oink oink oink!"

"Oiiink! Oiiink!"

The pigs were making a fuss and it was making my head hurt! They dragged me into a tavern, where the master lectured me about needing to find more companions.

"Companions? There's no one even worth considering around here!"

That went for the adventurers at the tavern too. The pigs were clearly out of the question. They were all just riffraff.

"If I run around with companions like this, I won't be able to accomplish anything!"

Maybe in their next life, if they were lucky enough to be reborn as filolials!

"You scumbag! You surround yourself with women and you talk like that?!"

"Surround myself with women? You mean these pigs?"

"P-pigs?!"

The adventurers in the tavern started gathering around me for some reason.

"Hey, you bastard! Show these women some respect!"

"Pigs are pigs, regardless of what you might say. I'd happily take a man over a pig, I say!"

"You hear this guy?! Pretty boy is gay!"

"Don't get the wrong idea! I only have feelings for filolials!"

"He's a deviant!"

"Oink!"

"Say what?! The Spear Hero?! This creep?!"

"That's right! My mission is to fight for the sake of the world, I say!"

"Lies! A deviant like you?!"

"Whether you believe it or not is of no concern to me. I shall save the world for the sake of Father, Filo-tan, and all the majestic filolials!"

I knew what was important. I didn't care if everyone in the world called me names! If it meant bringing peace to Father, Filo-tan, and all filolials, I would overcome any hardship!

"Of course, I shall save the other inhabitants too. That includes all of you!"

"Who does this bastard think he is?!"

"Stop screwing around!"

The adventurers started trying to pick a fight with me.

"Allow me to show you the difference between my strength and yours!"

I swiped at them with my spear. I held back since I was likely to kill them if I swung too hard.

"Wahhh!"

My spear had only brushed them lightly, but they went flying through the air and smashed into the tavern wall. They were a bunch of useless weaklings.

"How the hell?! That bastard! He barely even swung his spear!"

"Is this the strength of the heroes?!"

"Give up already, I say!"

I had put the adventurers in their place, but it seemed to have caused a commotion.

"I'm getting annoyed, so that's enough for today. Farewell then, I say!"

I left the tavern. I went and searched for Father for the rest of the day. I tried keeping an eye out near the castle town gates for a while before it got dark, but in the end, I never found him. If that red pig really was who I thought it was, then Father was in danger. I asked at all of the inns after that, but they claimed guest information was confidential and refused to tell me if he'd checked in.

Why had my sway as a hero lost effectiveness? Was it because I caused a commotion at the tavern? Damnit! All of these obstacles were causing me a lot of trouble! It was a gamble, but I had one last idea. I would wait at the tavern where I met the crimson swine!

"Oink!"

It was the crimson swine! There was no doubt about it. That red pig was her, I say! She was carrying a suit of chainmail and came over to me. How thoughtful.

"Oink oink oink oink?"

If I remembered correctly . . .

"Oh? Is that you, Mr. Motoyasu?"

I think that's what it had been.

"Oink oink oink oink."

"I would love to join you, if you don't mind."

I seemed to remember that's what she'd said last time, while acting all cheerful. I'd happily obliged and the two of us hit it off. A short while later, the crimson swine gave me the chainmail as a gift and then left. And then later that evening, she came rushing into the inn where I was staying and asked me to rescue her.

"Sure, I guess we can talk for a bit."

"Oink oink oink oink."

I had no idea what she was saying! All I could do was just randomly nod and smile. Everything would be fine. That's the kind of animal pigs were. All you had to do was nod here and there and they would carry on the conversation themselves. The content of the conversation didn't actually make any difference. Thinking back on my time in Japan, I could see that clearly now.

And then finally, the red pig tried to give me the chainmail.

"I know you stole that. You will return it to its owner, pig!"

"Oink?! Oink oink oink?!"

"Don't think you can frame Naofumi! I won't let you, I say!"

"Oink! Oink oink oink oink!"

She was really mad now. I didn't know what she was saying, but she was making the face that pigs made when they got mad. Pigs were such selfish animals! They pretty much always responded like this when they didn't like an answer. Filo-tan and the other filolials, on the contrary, just puffed up their cheeks and whined. They were so cute! It was rude to even draw a comparison.

The crimson swine must have realized I wasn't going to budge, because she spun around and stomped out of the tavern.

"Now then, it's about time I get some sleep!"

I'd rejected the stolen goods and kept my guard up. I was sure things would work out better now. I wasn't going to be an accomplice to the false charges against Father this time, I say! I'd managed to squash them preemptively.

I went back to the inn and fell asleep while sniffing (what was supposed to be) Filo-tan's egg.

That night, I had a nightmare. Or perhaps it was more accurate to call it some kind of lingering memory of the past.

Bam! Bam! Bam! It was in the wee hours of the morning, before the sun had risen, and I was still asleep. I heard a loud banging on the door of my room at the inn.

"It's too early! Who is it?!"

I opened the door and looked with sleepy eyes to see who it was.

"Oink oink oink!"

Let's see . . .

"Please save me, Mr. Motoyasu!"

I could remember the crimson swine crying and begging for me to rescue her. Her clothes were all torn for some reason. I'd instantly snapped out of my half-asleep daze and asked her, "What happened to you?!" I'd thoughtlessly assumed that she had gotten caught up in some terrible incident and took her into my protection last time.

"Oink oink oink! Oink oink!"

Sob… Sob… "The Shield Hero drank too much, and he came bursting into my room. He held me down and said, 'The night is still young, baby.' Then he started to rip my clothes off. I was so scared! I screamed as loud as I could and ran from the room. That's when I came to ask you for help, Mr. Motoyasu."

The crimson swine had completely fabricated the whole story. It was a complete package, with messy clothes and a dramatic delivery. But at the time, I assumed everything she said was true and got so mad that I started shaking.

"That otaku bastard! I'll never forgive him!"

In a fit of rage, I'd stormed into to the castle, explained the situation, and then had the heroes summoned. I had Father brought in and denounced him, absolutely certain that I was doing the right thing.

Had I been thinking normally, I'm sure it would have been obvious. Someone who had just been summoned to a parallel universe, with no one to rely on, wouldn't have tried something so dangerous. That would only ruin their reputation and make things hard on them if people found out.

And regardless, I should have listened to Father's side of the story too. Without doing that, there could be nothing just about what I'd done. That would reduce justice to a simple matter of speaking first, whether it was truth or lies.

"What are you talking about? I went to bed right after we finished eating!"

"Liar! If that were true, why would Myne be crying like this?"

"Why are you speaking for her? And just where did you get that shiny new chainmail of yours?"

Of course I knew now. The crimson swine had stolen it. But back then, I . . .

"Last night I went to the bar for a drink. I was sitting there, alone, when Myne came running over. We had a couple drinks together, and she gave me this chainmail. She said it was a present."

Ugh . . . I was wearing the chainmail in the nightmare. It made me sick. That wasn't mine! It was Father's. I had taken something from him that I would never be able to return.

After that, Father quickly realized what had happened and his expression gradually turned to one of hatred for the whole world.

"You! You had your eyes on my money and equipment, and so you made all this up to get your hands on my stuff!"

Everyone around us suddenly disappeared and Father was standing there, pointing at me and glaring.

You're wrong! You're wrong, I say! Father! I . . . I . . .

"Ah!"

I jumped up and looked all around. Now I was certain that I really had traveled back in time. But I still hadn't rescued Father! I would save him for sure, no matter what, I say!

I woke up early that next morning and headed for the castle. I had to make sure that things had changed drastically! Surely the future would change if I hadn't become an accomplice to the crimson swine and didn't denounce Father.

"Please wait, Spear Hero!"

"Out of my way!"

I'd been left out. Ren and Itsuki had already gathered at the castle. Ugh . . . Did that mean I hadn't been able to stop it? If I remembered correctly, they were preparing to condemn Father for crimes he hadn't committed!

The soldiers were standing in front of me to keep me from entering, but I kicked them out of the way and walked into the throne room. They probably realized it would look suspicious to the other heroes if they tried to keep me out for no reason, because they didn't try to stop me after that.

Itsuki was standing there wearing the chainmail. The crimson swine was standing next to him with her arms folded. The other pig that had been with Father was standing next to him too. I guess if I didn't play accomplice to the setup, then

Itsuki would. Was this the power of history to correct itself? I felt like the universe was laughing at me and telling me that there was no way to avoid Father being framed, even if I didn't play the part.

"O-oh? Kitamura? What are you doing here so early?"

Trash was playing dumb, but I knew what was really going on!

"You!"

That filthy crimson swine! I'd turned her down, so she just went crawling to Itsuki!

"I heard about what you did, Motoyasu. You called Myne a pig, didn't you? What kind of person are you?"

"Whatever. When I look at her, all I see is a pig, and I hear nothing but squealing coming out of her mouth. It's because her heart is as black as coal, I'm sure!"

"Your behavior is a disgrace to the very title of Hero!"

"You have no right to say anything! You're an accomplice to a crime and you're wearing stolen goods like it's only natural!"

"Stolen goods? What are you talking about?"

"That chainmail that you have on."

"This was given to me by Myne."

"And I'm telling you that it's stolen goods."

"Stop making things up. Do you have any proof?!"

"I do! The weapons and equipment in this country are magically imprinted with—"

The memory was vague, but I remembered! Weapons and equipment in this country were magically imprinted with the creator's name and an identification number. I remembered Ren saying something like that. He'd spent time helping with blacksmithing at a weapon shop. I don't think Father had been there at the time.

Itsuki and I continued going back and forth, and Father was brought in wearing nothing but his underwear. How humiliating! He needed to be given something to wear immediately!

"Myne!"

Trash, Itsuki, and Ren all glared at Father.

"Huh? What's with those looks?!"

Seeing the situation left a bitter taste in my mouth. I wouldn't make the same mistake this time!

"You mean you really don't remember?"

"What do you mean? Remember what? HEY!"

Father stood there dumbstruck, pointing at Itsuki.

"So it was you! You thief!"

"Who's a thief? I didn't know you were such a scoundrel, Naofumi!"

"A scoundrel? What are you talking about?"

"Wait!" I shouted.

If I didn't stop this, no one would! After I realized I'd been deceived by the crimson swine, I don't know how many times I'd looked at Father and wished I could take it all back.

And now, by some miracle, I'd been given the chance to do just that! I had no intention of ever falsely accusing Father again. I wanted to help! I would prove his innocence no matter what, I say!

"King, I—"

"We will now hear the charges against the Shield Hero."

Damn it! It was clear they intended to completely ignore me! Several soldiers came and stood in front of me so that Father couldn't even see me. They must have known that I would try to protect Father.

"Charges? But . . . but I—"

"Oink oink . . . oink . . . oink oink oink."

"What?"

"Oink oink oink oink!"

She'd completely deceived me last time. This was her little performance. That filthy crimson swine!

"Oink oink oink oink!"

"Huh? What are you talking about? I went to bed right after we finished eating!"

"Liar! If that were true, why would Myne be crying like this?"

"Why are you speaking for her? And just where did you get that shiny new chainmail of yours?"

"Father, I—"

"Last night we all went to the bar for drinks. Myne stopped

by the tavern too. We had a couple drinks together, and she gave me this chainmail. She said it was a present."

They clearly had no intention of letting me talk in the first place. If that's how they wanted to play, I had other options. I was just about all out of patience. And now that I thought about it, I wasn't the type to act with discretion like this.

"That's it! Your Highness! I've been robbed! My money, clothes, equipment—everything but my shield has been stolen! Please bring the person who did this to justice!" Father shouted.

"Silence, scoundrel!"

Trash! That bastard! He was determined to go through with his plan! Should I just kill him? No, it would put Father in a bad position if I did that. Father was still low-level. I couldn't risk doing anything that might get him killed.

"Any act of sexual aggression committed against the people of my kingdom against their will is barbaric and unforgivable! If you were not a hero, you would be put to death immediately!"

"But this is all a mistake! I didn't do it!"

Father was still trying to be polite. He still believed in Trash and the people of this world. But then Father's expression started to fill with anger. *No, Father! You mustn't!* More than anyone else, I wanted Father to have love for this glorious world that Filo-tan would be born into!

Thanks to Filo, Father's face had eventually grown kind and he began working hard for me and for everyone else. But

I knew he still had trouble trusting people. He was constantly fighting off doubts and suspicions and was always on his guard. Seeing Father like that was painful at times.

I didn't want to let him end up like that again! The world may have been a cruel and merciless place, but if nothing else, I wanted to make the part of it around Father a kinder place. I had been given a second chance, and there was no way I was going to let it slip through my fingers!

"You! You had your eyes on my money and equipment, and so you made all this up to get your hands on my stuff!"

Father was always quick to grasp the situation. That was one of his finer points! If I'd shared such a fine trait back then—even if only a bit—then perhaps I would have been able to stop myself before I had denounced Father.

"Ha! Who would believe the words of a sex offender?"

"You come to another world and treat your companions this way? You're trash," Ren interjected, coldly condemning Father.

"Stop screwing around! You had your eyes on my money and equipment from the start! You and your little friends had a meeting about it, didn't you?!"

The soldiers were still blocking my way to try to keep me from talking. But they better not think that was all it took to stop me!

"You're in my way! Brionac!"

A beam of energy shot out from the tip of my spear toward the soldiers blocking my way. Of course, I throttled the power so that it would only knock them out of the way and not kill them.

"Gahhh!"

Everyone was left speechless and the room fell silent when they saw the soldiers go flying through the air. I seized my chance and pointed my spear at Trash, the crimson swine, and Itsuki.

"Huh?"

"I believe Father. He didn't do it. This is all a conspiracy, I say!"

Father wasn't sure what was going on. I gave them the bare facts while glaring at Trash.

"You seem intent on doing something thoughtless while the real boss is out, but if you're going to try to harm the Shield Hero, then I—the Spear Hero—will not allow it, I say! It goes against that which is love!"

I pointed my spear threateningly at the soldiers who were restraining Father.

"Let go of Fa—the Shield Hero, I say! I don't care who you are. I won't forgive anyone that interferes!"

It felt like there'd been a fog that had settled over part of my mind, and now it began lifting away as I awakened to a clear picture of what it was I wanted to achieve. I glared at Itsuki and Ren next.

"That goes for you two, as well. You two are no match for me in your current state."

I held my hand out to Father, who was now free of restraint, and bared my soul. This was my chance. Once I'd realized the truth, I thought I'd have to live with the regret of what I'd done forever. This was a once-in-a-lifetime chance to put things right. I had no intention of making the wrong decision again, I say!

I'd been summoned to another world to serve as a hero. I decided that—that time for sure—I would believe in this world's angelic women no matter what, and I would gain their trust. And so I did my best, in my own little way. I helped everyone level up and I cooked for them. I fought bravely against the waves and reigned victorious. I bought everyone the accessories they wanted because I thought it would make them happy. I did so many things out of devotion for them.

But that determination had been a mistake! No matter how devoted I was, they were still pigs at heart. Being spoiled by others was only natural in their eyes. Whenever things didn't go their way, they started squealing up a storm. They mistakenly believed that they belonged to the privileged few. When they didn't get the response they wanted, or when people didn't go out of their way to satisfy them, they would get bent out of shape and resort to violence.

Those were no angels! Angels were compassionate. They lent a helping hand when someone was about to stray from the path. Pigs that thought of no one but themselves were not angels. Nothing good would come from believing in pigs! I should have believed in the angelic Filo-tan, or Father, who displayed compassion befitting a god.

But I had foolishly chosen to believe that pigs were angels. Whenever Filo-tan saw me, without fail, she would come over and give me a reproachful kick before running away. In the beginning, I didn't understand that she was being compassionate, so I grew wary of her. I just thought of her as a savage bird-monster that kicked me whenever she saw me. I even wanted to kill her!

It pained me to recall how long it took to realize that—from her angelic appearance to her pure, innocent character—she was the perfect embodiment of an angel in my eyes. When I realized that the crimson swine had deceived me and fell into despair, it was Filo-tan who cheered me up. It then became crystal clear that everything she had done prior to that had simply been tough love!

If hurting me was all she wanted to do, she wouldn't have tried to cheer me up. That's right! A true angel had been right there all along! She might not have been blue, but Filo-tan was the bluebird of happiness, I say! When I was acting foolish, it was Filo-tan and Father who stopped me from straying even further from the path than I already had. I would protect them, no matter what, I say!

Chapter Two: Repaying Kindness

"Come! Let's go!"

Father reached toward my outstretched hand. He took my hand into his and stood up.

"Motoyasu, you . . ."

At a loss for words, Itsuki glared at me. He could glare at me all he wanted. I wasn't going to back down! I would continue fighting—for world peace, for Father, and for Filo-tan! It didn't matter if my opponent was Itsuki, Ren, or even a god! I wasn't going to lose!

"It's best not to believe anything that crimson swine next to you says, Itsuki!"

"Crimson swine? Judging from the way you worded that, I'm guessing you mean Myne, right?!"

"That's right. She's a fat, ugly red pig. Thus, 'crimson swine.' Think about this carefully, Itsuki. Would a person truly guilty of trying to rape someone let themselves get dragged in looking like this?"

"I . . . I don't care what you say! Look at Myne crying!"

"Deceived by a pig's tears! It's like looking at my past self. Pathetic!"

"What did you say?!"

Itsuki clearly didn't believe that I had come from the future at all. Ren seemed undecided and was looking back and forth at me and Itsuki.

"Wh . . . what are you waiting for?! Men! Put an end to the Spear—"

I emitted a palpable wave of malice like I'd learned from Father and glared at them. I focused the pressure on Trash, Itsuki, and the crimson swine. That's all it took to make the three of them—even the crimson swine—think twice about speaking.

"Don't make me laugh. I'm in a good mood today, so I'll let you off the hook for now. But you better think long and hard about this and choose to do the right thing."

Yes! I had been able to atone for one of my sins! It was a beautiful day, I say!

"Come then, Father. Let's go!"

"Oh, umm, okay!"

I took Father's hand and we headed out of the castle, leaving the group of slandering conspirators behind.

"Thank you, Kitamura!"

After we left the castle and came to the plaza, Father graciously expressed his gratitude. I had saved him from the crimson swine's plot. I was on cloud nine! Coming to this world and successfully managing to save its people couldn't even begin to compare to this feeling of pride and bliss!

"Kitamura . . . To be completely honest, I felt a bit uncomfortable around you before today. But you really do believe in me."

I'd never seen Father look like this. He blushed slightly and scratched his head while thanking me.

"I'm the Love Hunter and I've come from the future! It goes without saying that you would be telling the truth!"

There was no greater honor than to be thanked by Filotan's father! Come hell or high water, I would never forget this day!

"Now then, Father. I have a favor to ask of you."

Now that I thought about it, Father had originally called me by my first name, Motoyasu, from the first time we met. Having him call me by my last name felt awkward.

"Please dispense with the formalities and call me by my first name, Motoyasu."

"Umm . . ."

Father had a troubled look on his face. But I was his son-in-law, so it only made sense for Father to call me by my first name, I say!

"Is something wrong?"

"No, it's just that . . . It feels strange treating the one person that believed in me without due respect."

"Don't let it bother you! It'll make me happy if you call me Motoyasu!"

"Oh, really? Okay then, Moto . . . yasu."

"Come on! Don't worry about it!"

"Umm . . . I'm sorry. I'll try, but it will take some time to get used to."

Father looked embarrassed when he replied. Hmm . . . I would have been happier if he addressed me in a more abusive manner. As I mulled over it, I took a long, hard look at Father. He was in his underwear.

That's right! He'd been stripped of all of his possessions by the crimson swine! I'd gotten Father to safety, so I wondered if I should go kill the crimson swine and take his stuff back now. Yes! That was what I needed to do. I was sure that would make Father smile and praise me. I'd make the crimson swine pay for her sins with her life! That's what Father would have done.

"Please wait here for a few minutes."

"Huh? Where are you going? That's the way to the castle!"

Father called out after me when I started to head back toward the castle. His expression was a mixture of confusion and worry.

"Is something wrong?"

"Why are you going back to the castle?"

"Ha! Ha! Ha! What do you mean? I'm going to go slaughter that red pig and get all of your stuff back, of course! If Itsuki or Ren try to interfere, I'll beat them to a pulp, but I won't kill them. I do have principles, you know!"

"What?! Umm, uhh . . . Motoyasu, you don't need to do that! Please! Do I need to beg you?!"

Father had an expression of shock on his face and a distant look in his eyes as he spoke. He was incredibly kind, but he seemed a bit too soft. He certainly didn't seem like the same person that would eventually have the names of Trash and the crimson swine changed to the ones they deserved.

I guess this incredible kindness was Father's true nature. It was no wonder that Filo-tan had turned out to be such a magnificent angel. But it would take more than this to stifle my urge to kill that crimson swine!

"Are you sure? If we act now, I can slaughter them in an instant. Trash and Witch are a curse upon this world, I say!"

"Just forget about them. I understand that you're incredibly strong and you believe in me. But . . . let's just let it go."

"You're so kind! Your compassion moves me to tears, Father!"

"Umm, please don't do that when there are so many people around!"

I was crying and bowing my head to Father. The people walking by kept looking at us with confused looks on their faces. I might end up embarrassing Father if I wasn't careful.

"But, Father, we can't have you running around in your underwear."

"Yeah, but all of my money was stolen."

"Worry not! Please, use mine!"

"Huh? Are you sure?!"

I gave Father my money pouch. My assets were Father's assets, I say!

"Anything of mine is yours! And anything of yours is yours too!"

"You're making me sound like a bully!"

Father opened the pouch and responded in disbelief. I had used some of the money to buy the filolial egg, but there was still a good amount left.

"What are you saying? This is us we're talking about!"

"But what are you going to do if I take this money?"

"Ha! Ha! Ha! That's not a problem!"

"No, seriously, what will you do?"

"Ha! Ha! Ha!"

"Stop trying to avoid answering by laughing. Umm . . . Well, thank you. I'll borrow half, then."

Father took half of the money and returned the pouch. Just as expected of Father! He was so humble.

"Let's go buy you some equipment then!"

"Y-yeah."

I took Father and headed into the castle town. The fresh morning air filled my lungs.

There, we ran into the owner of the weapon shop. Father

had been on good terms with him the first time around.

"Hey there, shield kid."

"Umm . . ."

Father had a troubled look on his face. The weapon shop owner was glaring at him. Without hesitation, I stepped forward to protect Father.

"I heard that you tried to take advantage of your friend. Come over here and let me give you a hard smack," the weapon shop owner growled.

"You're wrong, I say!"

"Huh? Who are you? Judging by that spear, I'm guessing you must be the Spear Hero."

"I am, indeed! But you have one thing wrong. Father has tried to take advantage of no one!"

"I wasn't talking to you. I was talking to the kid, there."

"I . . . didn't do it."

Father averted his eyes when he responded, as if he were upset. The weapon shop owner continued glaring at Father for several moments and then sighed. His face softened.

"I figured as much. You don't seem like the type to try something like that right out of the gate."

"You believe me?!"

"What can I say? That woman was acting a lot more suspicious than you were. You get a good sense for these things after years of dealing with customers."

"It's such a relief to hear that, old guy."

"Besides, I doubt you would look like that if you really had been guilty. I'm sure you would have known what was coming and made a run for it before they caught you."

"Yeah, you've got a point there."

"So what now? Don't you need some clothes?"

"We'll pay with this!" I said.

I handed the money pouch to the old weapon shop guy.

"Please take this money and give us some equipment that would be good for Father."

"But that's your money . . . Motoyasu . . ."

"Ha! Ha! Ha!"

"Stop trying to avoid answering by laughing."

"You two . . . I'm glad you seem to have found a friend, kid."

The weapon shop owner seemed to be in a good mood. He went back inside of the shop and started to choose armor that would be good for Father.

"How does chainmail sound? You've had some bad luck, kid, so I'll throw it in for free."

"No thanks. I'll pass."

There was a hint of annoyance in Father's voice. He pushed the chainmail away and put on some leather armor instead. He probably didn't like the idea of wearing something that looked like the equipment that was stolen from him.

"You sure?"

"Here . . . Motoyasu. This is your money."

The shop owner gave Father his change and Father politely handed it to me.

"Don't worry about it!"

"I am worried about it."

"So what now? What are you two planning on doing?"

"I'm already strong enough, so I'm going to help Father get stronger!"

"I thought the legendary weapons would clash if heroes fought together," Father said.

"That's right. But I told you we can share materials for the weapons."

"Oh yeah, you did. Does that mean I can get strong enough to put up a fight if you gather materials for me and then I use the power-up methods you told me about?"

"I do believe that should work for now!"

"Okay. Let's stick together for a while, then."

"Understood! As you wish!"

I bowed my head in a show of loyalty to Father. A troubled expression came over his face and he backed away several steps.

"Seriously, Motoyasu, stop that!"

"Your friend sure is weird, kid."

"This is only going to create more misunderstandings," Father mumbled with a sigh.

We all stood there chatting for a moment and then I felt the incubator I'd been keeping warm in my pocket start shaking.

"Oh?"

I pulled the incubator out and sat it on the shop counter.

"Huh? Did you buy a monster egg?" the owner asked.

"I did indeed! It's a filolial egg, I say!"

"Those are the birds that pull the carriages, right?" Father asked.

"It's the same divine bird that Filo-tan is!"

"I see. You really do love those monsters, don't you?"

"I do!"

We stood there watching the egg shake for a moment and then the shell cracked open.

"Chirp!"

The filolial peeked out of the egg and chirped cheerfully. It was a . . . black male filolial. As a connoisseur of filolials, I'd developed a discriminating eye. Identifying their sex was no problem for me!

"Chirp!"

I had already registered the monster seal to myself. Monsters meant to be raised by people had seals applied before birth. The seal was basically an imprinted pattern that served as a bond between the filolial and its owner.

"Wow! It's so cute! Umm . . . Motoyasu? Why do you look so disappointed?"

"I'm not disappointed!"

The filolial clearly wasn't Filo-tan. But there was no use crying over spilled milk. I reached a finger out toward the filolial and brushed his neck gently.

"Chirp chiiiirp!"

"What should we call you? Let's see . . . How about Kuro?"

"Because it's black and 'kuro' means black? That's not very original."

Father didn't seem to appreciate my choice. I would probably have to buy tons of eggs before I found Filo-tan. I'd never be able to make all the names original. He was a black filolial, so it made sense. The name just felt right to me. But if Father didn't like it, then I was willing to choose a different name.

"If you don't like that, then how about something like Black Thunder?"

"I'm not so sure about that. It'd probably be better to stick with Kuro."

"Chirp!"

That settled it. This little fellow would be named Kuro. I was certain he would grow up to be a lively angel.

"Now we have one more companion!"

"He's not just a pet, then?"

"Filolials are extremely reliable companions! No, they're family, I say!"

"You never cease to amaze me, Motoyasu."

"Anyway, helping Father and raising filolials is what I'll be doing!"

"Well, good luck with that, both of you," the old guy said.

"Thanks. We'll do our best."

"And we're off, I say!"

"Chirp!"

The filolial jumped onto the palm of my hand and we made our way out of the castle town.

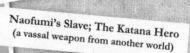

Raphtalia

Naofumi's Slave; The Katana Hero
(a vassal weapon from another world)

A demi-human female. Ears and tail resemble those of a tanuki or raccoon. Naofumi's first companion and the person that understands him best. Fights with swords and katanas. Because Naofumi's primary role is defense, she began serving as his offense in battle from early on. She has a secret crush on Naofumi but does not openly pursue it since he has an aversion to women in any sort of romantic context. She's like a big sister to Filo, who joined Naofumi some time after she did. Because of this, Motoyasu refers to her as "big sis." In other words, Motoyasu sees the three as the father, Naofumi, the big sister, Raphtalia, and the little sister, Filo.

ACTUALLY BELONGS TO THE IMPERIAL BLOODLINE OF A CERTAIN COUNTRY.

S-secret crush?! D-does it really need to be stated so directly?!

Hm? What's wrong, Raphtalia? What's written on that piece of paper?

It's nothing, Mr. Naofumi! Let's get on with the story!

Erhard

Weapon Shop Owner

Runs a weapon shop in Melromarc. Good at judging people's character. He believed in Naofumi from the very start, when no one else would. He looks scary, but he takes good care of people. Also, he's quite skilled at his craft.

A GOOD GUY WHO BELIEVES IN NAOFUMI.

???

Monster Trainer (Slave Trader)

A merchant who sells monsters in Melromarc. Off the record, he is also a slave trader. Naofumi came to rely on him relatively shortly after being summoned, since he couldn't find any normal party members and had to turn to slaves and monsters for companions. He also recognizes Naofumi's knack for business and acknowledges that it surpasses even his own.

A MERCHANT, FOR BETTER OR WORSE.

Chapter Three: Leveling

We passed straight through the fields and went to the neighboring village.

"Yesterday I just barely managed to defeat that weak monster called a 'balloon.' What am I going to do?"

"As a general rule, you can't put up a fight without companions to assist you."

"Yeah, I get that. But how am I supposed to find companions? No one wants to join someone who's been accused of rape. This country hates the Shield Hero too, right?"

Oh yeah. Father was supposed to have big sis, Raphtalia, with him! She was supposed to be his most trusted companion. I was pretty sure she had been a slave. I wondered what to do about her.

"In that case, how about buying a slave and having the slave fight for you?"

"A slave?!"

An expression of shock came over Father's face.

"Y-you mean to tell me they have slaves in this world? I guess that's fairly common in fantasy settings, though."

"If you work them like a horse, you'll both level quickly!"

"No thanks. I couldn't do anything that horrible."

"Oh? That's strange. I remember you owned a whole horde of slaves."

"Just what kind of savage am I in the future?!"

Oh? Father hadn't doubted my words. In that case, I would only tell him the bare truth from now on!

"You taught your slaves how to defeat monsters with a smile on your face!"

I could remember Father bragging and saying something like that. The village that he rebuilt stunk of pigs, but it was a really nice place to live and a great place overall. The slaves there all went about their work with smiles on their faces too.

"That's terrible! There's no way I could do something like that!"

Father was such a kind person by nature—the kind of person that felt a strong aversion toward using slaves. But suffering the hardships of a cruel world and being deceived on top of that had left him apathetic. I was sure the crimson swine and I were to blame for that too. I had to protect this innocent face of his from such a harsh reality.

"Why did I do such a terrible thing in the future anyway?"

"This will be tough for you to hear, but the role that Itsuki is playing now was originally played by me. In other words, no one was there to help you."

"Huh? What do you mean?"

"All three of us heroes were thoroughly deceived. We were

all convinced that you were guilty."

"Oh, I see. I guess that means I was stuck fighting all by myself in a whole new world with no one to believe in me."

"I'm so very sorry! It was the greatest mistake of my whole life!"

"But you were deceived too, right? So there's nothing you really could have done. You believe in me now, and you rescued me too."

I was so happy to hear those words. Father's compassion was deeper than the ocean. I bowed my head as a sign of my gratitude.

"And what did you not helping me have to do with me having slaves?"

"You had no allies and there was no one you could trust. I'm guessing that forced you to adopt a savage mindset and you came up with the idea of using slaves."

"That makes sense. I guess I could see that happening if I didn't have anyone on my side."

"But things are different this time! I believe in you unconditionally!"

Actually, saying I worshipped him wouldn't have been an overstatement. But he was Filo-tan's father, after all, and I owed him my life.

"Thanks. But I'm still not comfortable with having slaves."

"Then we'll just have to make do without. Kuro!"

"Chirp?"

"We're going to level you up in a hurry! Then, once you're stronger, you can help Father level the same way!"

"Chirp!"

"Oh, now I see. You're thinking I can make Kuro a party member once he's stronger, right? And since you're so strong, you can power-level Kuro."

The term "power-leveling" was online gaming jargon. It was when a high-level player did everything in their power to help rapidly level up a new player. A little bit of power-leveling could spice things up and make a game more enjoyable, but it was also a double-edged sword. Too much of it would take away from the fun! But power-leveling Father would be a good thing in our case.

"That's right! First, I'll get Kuro to around level 30. Then Kuro will help you level."

In the meantime, I would focus on earning some money by looking for work at the adventurers guild. Or I could hunt some bandits that seemed to be doing well for themselves. Getting my hands on Filo-tan would require money, and the more of it I had the better.

Plus, filolials were the treasure of the world! Every single one I could bring into the world would make it a richer place. That was my lifelong goal, I say! Viva filolial paradise!

"What should I do while you're doing that?"

RAPHTALIA AND NAOFUMI

At a time when he had no companions, a slave trader approached Naofumi and he ended up with his first slave. The slave he chose was considered a leftover—sickly and defective. That young demi-human girl was named Raphtalia.

Not only was Raphtalia frail, but she was absolutely terrified. Naofumi fed her and taught her how to fight. Despite being rather tactless, Naofumi also displayed a kindness that encouraged Raphtalia to open up to him. No matter how much she cried at night or how expensive her medicine was, Naofumi never turned his back on her.

Before long, the two developed a strong bond of trust. Not only did Raphtalia become a powerful offensive force, but she also took on the role of the person who admonishes Naofumi when he starts to act a bit too slimy (?).

Raphtalia was originally from a small village of demi-humans at the outskirts of Melromarc. Her village was destroyed by a wave of destruction, but Naofumi gained ownership of the territory and built a new village. It was a peaceful village with no racial discrimination. Over time, it developed into a place where many lived, and the residents all acted responsibly and showed each other respect.

By that time, Naofumi had been successful in countless battles as a hero. Despite most of the villagers being his subordinates, it was Naofumi's nature to take care of others, so he often found himself cooking large meals for everyone. When Naofumi cooked, his primary consideration was the person who would be eating the food, and everything he made was absolutely delicious.

On a related note, Naofumi had experience running a large guild in a game back in his own world. According to him, being good at taking care of others was a result of that experience and had nothing to do with being kind.

"Hmm . . . Might I suggest you enjoy an exquisite cup of tea, perhaps?"

"What kind of suggestion is that?!"

"Well, there's no way I could order you around!"

"Okay, that's fine. I'll figure out what to do on my own."

"Excellent. We're headed off to level, then! We'll meet you back in this village later tonight!"

"Okay, got it."

"Chirp!"

Kuro chirped loudly and the two of us headed out!

After leaving Father, Kuro and I hurried off to a mountain range where there were powerful monsters. I had high-level stat adjustments and I could always use my portal skill to return to the village in a flash. I wanted to level Kuro up as quickly as possible! The only problem was securing food for him. But that shouldn't be an issue if he just ate the monsters we defeated. Filolials were the ultimate angels and happily ate anything, after all!

We headed deep into the mountains and entered a region where powerful dragon-type monsters lived.

"Brionac! Ha! Ha! Ha! Weak! You're all too weak!"

I fired off one skill after another and mowed through the dragons and other monsters that lived there in the mountains!

The Father I remembered started to explain about dragons.

‖ Dragons ‖

It wouldn't be a proper fantasy world without these quintessential creatures, right? As a species in general, filolials don't get along with dragons. That's also why Motoyasu doesn't like them very much. All of the dragons I've met have been really quirky and tough to deal with.

After he finished speaking, the Father I remembered disappeared.

Dragons were natural enemies of filolials! That meant they were my natural enemies! I went about attacking as if I was set on annihilating the whole species. They must have realized that they were no match for me, because after fighting for a while the dragons started to avoid us.

But I didn't care! It would still be a while before Ren or Itsuki would show up around here to hunt. There were places with even more powerful monsters, but I would've needed more than one day to go hunt in those places. So this was really my only option! I couldn't wait to see how strong I could make Father in the month we had before the next wave!

I kept fighting until the sun set. Kuro had hit level 32 in no time. I'd collected plenty of food for him and a bunch of materials too. I would give Father some of those later. My work for the day here was done, so I used my portal to return to the village, where I was supposed to meet Father.

"Welcome back. How much progress did Kuro make?"

"Cheep?"

"Whoa, he's a lot bigger."

Kuro came walking up with me. He had made the transformation from a chick to the next stage of filolial development. He was shaped like a fluffy dinner roll and stood at around the height of my thigh. He would probably be a normal, full-sized filolial by tomorrow. I'd collected a massive amount of food just for Kuro, so that wouldn't be a problem.

"Cheep . . ."

The poor little guy's stomach was constantly growling. I needed to prepare a meal for him at once!

"Aww . . . You're so cute, Kuro!" I exclaimed.

"Cheeeep!"

I gave Kuro a snuggle and he squinted his eyes happily. There was no mistake about it. Filolials were the treasure of the world!

"Yeah, he is. And he's growing super fast. So? What level is he now?"

"Level 32, I say!"

"Already?! You said something about only being able to get him to level 40, right?"

"That's right. He'll need to class up to level higher than that!"

"But the dragon hourglass is under the country's control, right? After fighting with the nobility like you did, you won't be able to use it, will you?"

"That's not a problem! If we go to another country, I'm sure they'll let us use theirs."

"Oh, so Melromarc isn't the only country with an hourglass. In that case, I guess I need to get strong enough to venture off to a neighboring country."

"Ha! Ha! Ha! We have busy days ahead!"

"Yeah. Oh, that reminds me. After thinking about whether there was something I could do, I went to the river and did a bit of fishing."

Father showed me some fish. He must have been good at fishing, because it was quite the catch!

"I'll cook those up for us back at the inn!"

"Actually, would you mind if I did that? That's about all I can really do, after all."

"Ha! Ha! Ha! Father's cooking is superb! I look forward to it!"

"My cooking is nothing to brag about, really. Or are you talking about the future again?"

"Indeed. Everyone loved your cooking!"

"Really? Well, I'll do my best."

His countenance and behavior were different, but in the end, Father was Father. If there was something he could do, he did it, without fail. Come to think of it, Filo-tan absolutely loved Father's cooking. I was sure Kuro would enjoy it as well.

Back at the inn, Father got permission to use the kitchen (I threatened the innkeeper when he tried to refuse) and cooked for us. It was delectable, I say! There was no way I could ever produce such immaculate flavors! But Father's cooking was better in the future. That probably had to do with his shield's abilities and being able to use life force, though.

"That really was superb, I say!"

"I'm glad you liked it. I tried using some of the seasonings in the kitchen, but this is a different world, after all. Other than the salt, none of them are quite the same as what I'm used to."

"Humble, as always! Okay, I'm going to sleep in the stable with Kuro. You sleep in our room and make sure to keep the door locked."

"You're going to sleep in the stable? If anyone should sleep in the stable it should probably be me, since I'm borrowing your money."

"Ha! Ha! Ha! Kuro can't sleep in the inn, so this is just how it will have to be."

"Oh? Okay. I'll let you hold on to my valuables, then. I'd hate to have them stolen while I was asleep."

Father handed me his money and armor. This was a sign of his trust! Now was the time to prove my loyalty!

"I will protect the items you've entrusted to me with my very life!"

"Umm, thanks."

"In return, I'll give you some of the materials I gathered. You should absorb them into your shield."

I gave Father all of the materials I'd brought back for him and had him absorb them into his legendary weapon. His level was probably still too low to use them, but they would come in handy later.

"Oh, wow. It keeps saying something about level and conditions not being met, though."

"That's just the way it is. It's fine. You still want to keep gathering materials bit by bit and absorbing them into your shield."

"Materials? Like what?"

"You can use anything for materials! Even rocks, plants, or branches. In the future, you would break down the monsters you defeated and absorb the bones and meat into your shield."

Doing so would unlock even more weapons!

"Break down, huh? So in addition to just absorbing things whole, you can split them up into separate materials too. That makes sense. It seems like a pretty intricate system. Alright, I'll do my best."

"Kuro should be able to fight as your bodyguard come tomorrow, I think. Then we can start making some real progress!"

"Yeah."

"Cheep!"

And so we settled down for some R&R at the inn. Kuro got hungry a few more times during the night, and each time I fed him some of the food I'd brought back. Then, while sniffing Kuro's scent and listening to the sounds of his body rapidly developing, I drifted off to sleep and dreamt about meeting Filo-tan once again.

"Gweh!"

"Wow, he grew that much in one night, huh? Monsters sure can do some amazing things."

The next morning, Father was looking up at Kuro with an expression of surprise on his face. Kuro had reached the second phase of his development, making him a normal, full-sized filolial.

"Okay, Kuro. Now you're going to take Father to fight monsters nearby and get him experience!"

"Gweh!"

"Umm, how do I form a party? Oh, there it is. That must mean those women were planning on deceiving me from the very start," Father mumbled.

After a few moments, he sent Kuro a party invitation.

Those weren't women. They were pigs! Every now and then, Father's face looked like he wanted to kill someone. It brought back fond memories of the Father I remembered!

Suddenly a message popped up on my screen asking if I wanted to permit Kuro to join Father's party. Monster seals had a feature that requested the owner's approval. I approved without hesitation and a party was formed with Father and Kuro in it.

"Kuro, let Father ride you and go fight!"

"Gweh!"

"So I should ride him? Alright."

Kuro squatted down, and Father climbed up onto his back.

"Okay, Father, please be safe out there!"

"Umm, I'll try. Thanks for everything, Motoyasu."

"Don't mention it! Now off you go!"

I waved at Kuro and he dashed off energetically with Father on his back.

"Whoa! He's so fast!"

Kuro sprinted off into the distance, and before I knew it, the two of them had disappeared. Now then . . . What was I going to do next? I had collected a good amount of material, but I felt uneasy having so little money. That had never really been an issue before coming back to the past, but I had something big to accomplish now. I had to find Filo-tan! Not to mention, if I got lucky, I might even end up being her master this time!

"That's it!"

I'd decided what I would be doing that day. It was time to make some money! I would try looking for jobs at the adventurers guild. If that didn't work, I would sell some of the materials I gathered! And if I still didn't have enough after that, I would go look for some bandits and take their money. That was something that Father had done often!

And so, I returned to the castle town and made my way to the adventurers guild.

"I'm very sorry, but we can't offer you a job, Spear Hero."

That was the response I got at the adventurers guild reception desk. I'd tried asking a male clerk who could speak human words. I quietly pointed my spear at him and gripped it hard, making it shoot sparks. That was a secret intimidation technique passed on to me directly from Father. (That's what I liked to say, anyway.) Then I tried asking one more time.

"Don't tell me that. Surely you have some lucrative jobs for me, right?"

"Oink!"

The pig standing behind the male clerk started squealing about something. It was hurting my ears. I wondered if I should kill her. I had no plans of going easy on pigs! Filthy barn animals had no place making a fuss about anything, I say!

"D-despite what you may say, the country simply will not allow us to offer you work."

"Is that an order from Aultcray? The crimson swine . . . The princess has a part in this too, I suppose?"

The male clerk averted his eyes and just kept asking me to leave repeatedly, like a broken record. I was sure Trash and his minions had threatened him.

"If the Queen of Melromarc happened to hear about this, what do you think she would do?"

"Ugh."

I was pressuring the clerk when a pig approached him from behind. The pig was holding a missive, which she passed to the clerk. This was just a guess, but she was probably a member of an organization of operatives referred to as "shadows." The organization couldn't be trusted unconditionally, but they *had* been allies of Father.

Oh? The Father I remembered appeared and began to explain again.

‖ Shadows ‖

Commonly referred to by this name. These covert forces sometimes employ disguises when carrying out operations. There are supposedly multiple organizations and factions spread across a number of different countries. The shadow member that I knew disguised herself as the queen and played an active role behind the scenes during the Church of the Three Heroes mess.

After he finished explaining about the shadows, the Father I remembered disappeared.

"I see. Understood. It seems I can offer you some work, Spear Hero."

"I'd prefer something that can be done quickly and has a large payoff. If there's something with payment in advance, that's even better!"

"U-understood. This should fit the bill."

I accepted the work from the adventurers guild. Just as I'd thought, mentioning the queen would make people more willing to compromise. I decided I'd throw her name around everywhere I went after that.

"Spear Hero! Prepare yourself!"

As soon as I stepped out of the adventurers guild, several adventurers surrounded me and began to attack.

"Windmill!"

Without a word, I immediately used an area-of-effect skill called Windmill to make quick work of the attackers. It was a skill that produced a tornado when I swung my spear around horizontally. The tornado that I created sucked the adventurers up and sent them flying through the air.

"Gaaahhhh!"

"What's the idea, attacking me all of a sudden? Pulling a stunt like that will get you killed, I say!"

I wasn't going to stand by and let these mosquitoes eat me up! I'm sure they were just some of Trash's thugs, after all.

"Ugh. You're just a mock hero who's aiding the Shield Demon!"

I'd heard a line like that before. Ah, yes! They must have been from the Church of the Three Heroes. That was it. That bunch was still alive at this point. It was a sorry excuse for a religion that Father had helped destroy. I was pretty sure it had been the official religion of Melromarc. I'd forgotten all about them!

"Mock hero? Say whatever you like. I'm the Love Hunter and I live for love! If you're going to cause Father trouble, then perhaps I should just head to the Three Heroes church now and slaughter the whole congregation."

I held the tip of my spear against the cheek of one of the adventurers and grinned. They were a scourge that would make Father suffer. I contemplated what I should do.

"D-demon! You're a demon! Don't think you can get away with something like that!"

"Surely humiliating Father . . . the Shield Hero for completely unjustified reasons isn't something that someone should get away with!"

Their religion worshipped the Spear Hero. But I wasn't acting the way they wanted me to, so they were probably trying to get rid of me somehow. They had called us imposters when things stopped going their way the first time around too.

"Take this as a warning from one of your gods! If you try to harm us, I will exterminate you without hesitation. You've been warned. Ha! Ha! Ha! Ha!"

I laughed boisterously as I walked away. Of course, I'd taken the wallets of the foolish religious fanatics who'd attacked me too. I would be able to buy a new filolial now!

"You're just a demon pretending to be a hero!"

I could hear the riffraff hurling insults once I had left the area. I couldn't have cared less. After that, I took different sorts of random material to sell to a vendor. I threatened to kill the vendor if he tried to take advantage of me when I sold him my stuff.

I swung my money pouch around and listened to the clattering sounds as I made my way to the monster trainer's tent. The monster trainer wiped the sweat from his brow with a small towel when I arrived.

"W-what can I do for you today? Would you like another filolial? Yes sir."

"I would, indeed! I'd like several this time!"

It occurred to me that there was no need to buy only one filolial at a time. That's why I planned to spend all of my current surplus of money on new filolials! It went without saying that I would save enough money to buy Father equipment. I'd take back plenty of monster material with me too.

"H-here you are, then."

Once again, the slave trader presented a box full of eggs. I picked several of them out and made my purchase.

Now then! I still had tons of things to do! I went straight to work taking care of the jobs from the adventurers guild, and before I knew it, the sun had set.

"Oh hey, Motoyasu. Welcome back."

I returned to the village after finishing up the guild jobs. Father and Kuro were waiting for me there.

"How did it go?"

"I managed to make a fair bit of money."

I showed Father my money pouch.

"Whoa, that's a lot."

I'd used some of it, so there really wasn't that much. But the guild had given me a job to clean up some monsters nearby that was supposed to be quite difficult. That alone had earned me a nice bundle. The job required a minimum level of 70. I probably would have been able to handle it even before I knew about the power-up methods, but having implemented them all now, it was a breeze.

"I'll be using this to help raise more filolials, I say!"

I showed Father the filolial eggs that I'd brought back from my travels. Father seemed surprised at how many I had bought.

"Kweh?"

Kuro looked confused.

"And what level are you now, Father?"

"Umm . . . I made it to level 15."

"Not bad at all."

"All I did was watch Kuro plow through the monsters. Also, Kuro seems to gradually be getting even bigger. The filolials that were this size at the castle were already fully grown, right?"

Father petted Kuro and he squinted happily. It was a heartwarming sight.

"Kweh!"

"That's right. He should be able to speak by tomorrow night!"

"Huh? Filolials can speak?!"

"They can, indeed! Filolials are absolutely amazing, filolials are!"

"Wow. That's exciting. We didn't have talking animals back in my world. That makes it seem like anything is possible. That's just like what I'd expect from a parallel universe. Alright, I guess we should go ahead and have dinner."

"Indeed!"

Father treated us to his home cooking once again that evening.

And then it happened the next morning. I found Father talking with some strangers in front of the inn reception area.

"Oh hey, Motoyasu."

"What's going on?"

Father called out to me when he noticed me.

"Umm, these people say they want me to come with them. Maybe you know who they are."

There were two pigs and one man. I looked over at the man. He appeared to be a demi-human. His ears looked like fox ears.

"We are emissaries from Siltvelt. I'm guessing you are the

Spear Hero. Please hear what we have to say."

"I'm listening!"

Siltvelt? I was pretty sure that was a country where demi-humans were the majority. I'd heard something about relations between Melromarc and Siltvelt having been hostile for a very long time. But what would emissaries from Siltvelt want to talk to us about?

It wasn't like I knew every little detail about the future. There was a lot that I couldn't recall, and I didn't even know where Father was when he'd gone to Siltvelt. I was busy secretly protecting the village in his territory from the shadows at the time, so I didn't know much about what happened to him there. I'd have to hear the emissary out before I could make any judgments.

Oh?! The Father I remembered seemed to want to say something!

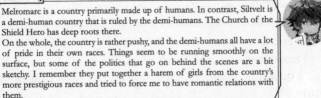

Siltvelt

Melromarc is a country primarily made up of humans. In contrast, Siltvelt is a demi-human country that is ruled by the demi-humans. The Church of the Shield Hero has deep roots there.

On the whole, the country is rather pushy, and the demi-humans all have a lot of pride in their own races. Things seem to be running smoothly on the surface, but some of the politics that go on behind the scenes are a bit sketchy. I remember they put together a harem of girls from the country's more prestigious races and tried to force me to have romantic relations with them.

I see! Oh? Father disappeared when he finished talking.

"Thank you. Please do join the conversation, Spear Hero. We would very much like to welcome both of you to accompany us back to Siltvelt."

This was what the man told us. When Siltvelt got wind that the four holy heroes had been summoned, they sent these emissaries to retrieve Father from Melromarc, where he would be persecuted.

"So what do you think? I've leveled up a bit now, so I was thinking it might not be a bad idea. There's no reason I have to stay here and fight for Melromarc, right?"

"Hmm . . ."

We had originally based our activities out of Melromarc, but going to another country this time might not have been a bad idea. But I still had aspirations of becoming Filo-tan's new master! I was pretty sure that Father had purchased Filo-tan from the Melromarc monster trainer. The eggs I'd bought recently would hatch later that day. If none of them were Filo-tan, I would need to stick around here for a while.

"The Shield Hero said that he wanted to ask your opinion before deciding, Spear Hero. We hope that you understand our good intentions."

"I figured it would probably be best if I wasn't constantly relying on you. They seem to respect me as a hero in Siltvelt, so I was thinking I'd have a better chance of succeeding there. What do you think?"

"It does make sense."

I couldn't argue that Father would have a tough time in Melromarc. But I still had just too much unfinished business here to leave yet!

"In that case . . ."

"I hate to say goodbye, Father, but I look forward to hearing about your success in Siltvelt!"

Father seemed to be satisfied with my answer. He nodded.

"Yeah, this is for the best. I can't just keep letting you spoil me forever. This is my chance, so I'm going to take it."

"Have you decided then, Shield Hero?"

"Yeah. I think I'll accept your offer to go to Siltvelt."

"Very well! Thank you for your cooperation, Spear Hero!"

"Not at all! It's a once in a lifetime chance! Don't hesitate to get in touch if you ever need anything, Father! I'll come running to the ends of the earth, I say!"

"Kuro . . ."

"Gweh?"

Kuro was standing at the entrance of the inn and peeking inside. Father waved to him.

"It's probably best if he stays with you, I guess," he said.

"Gweh!"

Kuro looked back and forth between me and Father several times as if he were trying to make up his mind and then nodded. After that, the carriage prepared by the emissaries arrived and Father climbed inside.

"I'm guessing money won't be a problem," I said.

"Not at all. We will be happy to provide any funds that the Shield Hero might need," the emissary answered politely.

"Thanks for everything, Motoyasu. Make sure to stop by and say hi if you ever find yourself near Siltvelt. You're welcome any time."

"Understood. I'll come and join you as soon as I achieve my goal!"

"Umm, yeah. Okay. Thanks to you I was able to avoid losing my humanity. You saved me, so . . ."

The carriage began moving. Father stuck his head out of the window, waved at me, and continued.

"Thank you! It's a harsh world, but I'll do my best! And I promise to return the favor!"

"We shall meet again, I say!"

Kuro and I waved as we saw Father off. Thinking about what had happened the first time, I was sure he would be much happier going to Siltvelt instead of staying and fighting in Melromarc. The conditions would be much better for him there.

Now then! I still had lots of work to do! It was my mission to become Filo-tan's new master. Later that evening, Kuro began talking and gained the ability to transform into an angel. The next day, the filolial eggs hatched and things gradually began to grow more and more lively.

Chapter Four: Time Reversal

Two days had passed.

"Moto! I want to run some more!"

Kuro was in his angel form and was helping me raise the other new filolials.

"Are you going to buy more new eggs today?"

"I am, indeed!"

"You already have a whole flock!"

"It's not enough, I say!"

I had more than seven filolials in all now. But only Kuro and three others had become angels so far. I needed more!

"After you buy more eggs, let's go running and have some fun defeating monsters!"

"Of course! And don't forget about defeating bandits!"

I needed to take Kuro and the other filolials to another country and have them complete their class-ups! I just had to make sure the timing was—

All of a sudden, four icons appeared on my screen. There was a sword, a spear, a bow, and a shield. And then the shield icon turned red and began flashing.

"Moto!"

Suddenly, Kuro . . . No, the whole world turned gray and froze!

"Huh?"

I reached out toward Kuro. He was hard as a rock, as if he'd been petrified. And then it happened. My spear began shaking and making rattling sounds. An analog clock appeared on my screen and the minute hand began spinning backward.

When I came to, I found myself in a dark, familiar room with magic circles on the floor.

"Oh wow."

I looked up to see men in robes in front of me, looking back at me in awe, and apparently speechless.

"What's all this?"

"Huh?"

These lines . . . I'd heard them before!

"Where are we?"

Ren turned to the castle mages and spoke. I looked around to see a familiar sight. Everything looked exactly the same as it had when I was first summoned to this world. This was the third time now.

"Oh, heroes! Please save our world!"

"What?!"

Father, Ren, and Itsuki all responded in unison, just like before. What was going on?

"Father, I need to talk to you for a moment!"

I tried speaking to Father, but he just seemed confused and

started looking over his shoulder. His face made it look like he had no idea who I was talking to.

"Who are you calling 'Father'? Are you half asleep or something?"

Father looked at me suspiciously when he replied. This was not the kind face that I had seen two days earlier. This was the good-humored face of his from before I'd rescued him from being falsely accused.

When I didn't say anything, Father turned his back to me and went chasing after the man who looked like a mage. The man was taking us to see Trash. Father was walking alongside Ren and Itsuki as if nothing had happened. I was certain the Father who'd just recently departed for Siltvelt would not have been walking with Itsuki and acting so friendly and full of hope.

It was as if everything that had happened up until that point had been completely reset! Doubt crept into my mind and I decided to check my monster seal settings. When I did, I realized that none of the filolials I had been raising were registered to me anymore. That meant that I must have returned to the day we were summoned to this world. If that were true, then my precious Kuro had most likely been reduced back to being an egg.

But, oh? Some of the things I couldn't remember the last time began to come back to me! I could remember more details about the weapon power-up methods! I recalled that there were power-up methods used by the seven star weapons in addition to those used by the four holy weapons. I was sure I would be able to help Father and the others become even stronger this time.

But why had I gone back in time again? A complete reset was something that seemed like a one-time miracle. Had it not been? Thinking about the last time the reset occurred, I'd died and then I returned to the day of our summoning. This time I hadn't died.

But . . . Death? I thought about what had just happened. Four icons shaped like the holy weapons appeared and then the shield began flashing. The resets had begun with my death. So there was death. And then there was the shield icon. Maybe that meant . . . I decided I might as well test it out.

"Itsuki!"

"What? Hey, why do you know my na—"

"This is for framing Father! Brionac X!"

"Huh? Gahhh!"

I gripped my spear tightly and fired off a skill at Itsuki. He may have been a hero, but he was still level 1. He had no time to dodge and was blasted to smithereens.

"Huh?! What the—"

Father was standing there speechless. *Worry not! No matter what happens, I would never harm you, Father!* Suddenly, everything turned black and white. This time the bow icon turned red and began flashing. I heard that same rattling sound. The same clock appeared, and the minute hand began turning backward again.

"Oh wow."

I looked up to see men in robes in front of me, looking back at me in awe, and apparently speechless.

"What's all this?"

"Huh?"

Itsuki, whom I'd just eliminated only moments earlier, was looking over the place and having trouble wrapping his head around what was happening. There was no doubt about it now. But I wanted to make extra sure! Just for good measure, so to speak.

"Ren!"

"Huh? What? Why do you know my na—"

"Shooting Star Spear X!"

"Wha?!"

Ren let out a moronic-sounding yelp as I blew a huge hole right through him. This time the sword icon turned red and flashed. I was able to verify that the same phenomenon occurred immediately after.

"Oh wow."

I looked up to see men in robes in front of me, looking back at me in awe, and . . . Okay, I was getting tired of repeating that.

"What's all this?"

"Huh?"

Just as I suspected, this Minute Hand of the Dragon seemed to have an effect that would send me back to the time when we were summoned if any of the heroes died. That must have been what the Time Reversal ability and diverging worlds equip effect did. The red, flashing icons must have been an indication that someone had died.

That meant that Father must have died for some reason after we parted ways. I'd made the greatest mistake of my life again! I owed my loyalty to Father, and yet I hadn't been there with him when he was faced with danger!

It became clear to me that I needed to keep a close eye on the situation and protect Father if I wanted to see Filo-tan again. Fortunately, I'd figured out how the time looping worked. If my involvement meant that the circumstances could change, I would use that to bring about a better future!

Chapter Five: Trap

I put on my thinking cap! First, I needed to figure out what to prioritize. I wanted to see Filo-tan again.

I really, really, really, really, really, really, really, really, really wanted to see her. I really, really, really, really, really, really, really, really, really wanted to see her. I really, really, really, really, really, really, really, really, really, really wanted to see her. I really, really, really, really, really, really, really, really, really, really wanted to see her. I really, really, really, really, really, really, really, really, really, really wanted to see her. I really, really, really, really, really, really, really, really, really, really wanted to see her. I really, really, really, really, really, really, really wanted to see her. I really, really, really, really, really, really, really wanted to see her. I really, really, really, really, really, really, really, really, really, really, really, really, really, really wanted to see her. I really, really, really, really, really, really, really, really, really, really, really, really wanted to see her.

"Umm, are you okay?"

"Me? Why do you ask?"

I snapped back to reality. Father was peering into my face and speaking to me.

"I was just wondering because you seemed to be completely out of it. Come on, it looks like they're taking us somewhere."

"You're right. Let's go, then!"

"Yeah."

I followed Father and we walked toward the throne room. Back to what I was saying. If any of the four holy heroes died, I would loop back in time to my first day here in this world. And I wouldn't be able to see Filo-tan!

The first time it happened, I'd saved Father from being framed for rape and then wished him all the best and we parted ways. My goal was to become Filo-tan's new master, after all. But I ended up looping back in time before I could do that. I was certain the loop had been caused by Father dying sometime after we split up. That meant I had to make sure Father didn't die. But how was I supposed to do that?

"Hey."

Father gave me a little jab with his elbow. I had gotten lost in thought and hadn't been listening at all.

"Huh? What is it?"

"Your introduction."

"Oh. My name is Motoyasu Kitamura. I'm twenty—"

Things were going pretty much the same as always at this point. I introduced myself just like I had before. But I roared out in anger when Trash purposefully forgot to mention Father's name.

"Don't you forget Father's name!" I roared.

"Huh?!"

Father was standing there dumbstruck.

"'Father'?!"

Surely there was no need to continue on with this farce anymore!

"Come, Father. Let us leave this place at once and begin our journey!"

Sticking around here would just mean ending up caught in a trap again. I couldn't stand to see Father suffer anymore!

"Is 'Father' supposed to be referring to me, Motoyasu?"

"It is, indeed!"

"Why? And do you mind explaining why you're so upset?"

"Sure. I come from the future!"

"Huh?!"

"Well, I wasn't expecting that."

Ren and Itsuki were rolling their eyes and mumbling. It seemed like those two were almost guaranteed not to believe me.

"From the future? I don't believe that," said Itsuki.

"Even though you were just summoned to another world?" I asked.

"Erm . . ."

Itsuki's eyes were roaming as he tried to decide how to respond. Ren was furrowing his brow.

"Then allow me to explain. This country, Melromarc, secretly plans to persecute Father, the Shield Hero, I say! If things continue unchecked, Father will get caught in their trap and have to endure an utterly terrible experience."

My complaint was sincere. Judging by past experience, I was certain that was what would happen if things were left to their natural course. I couldn't let Father experience something like that again.

"I can tell you this because I'm stuck in a time loop and keep re-experiencing this timeline!"

I changed my spear to the Minute Hand of the Dragon and showed it to them.

"Umm . . . Are you really trying to set me up?"

Father turned to Trash and asked with a confused look on his face.

"Do you really expect him to say, 'Yes, it's true'?" Ren asked.

"Well, I guess not, but . . ."

"Time loops on top of being summoned to another world? That's just taking things a bit too far. He's just trying to draw attention to himself, I'm sure," said Itsuki.

Father and Ren fell silent. I tried to recall what I'd been thinking when I was first summoned to this world. I'd viewed Father, Ren, and Itsuki as rivals. I was friendly with them, but I considered myself to be the number one hero. In other words, they probably thought I had just come up with an impressive story to make myself stand out, even if it was all lies.

Trash tried to act unflustered. He puffed his chest up and spoke confidently.

"That was certainly unexpected. Melromarc will treat all of the heroes hospitably, without discrimination. Please calm down, Spear Hero. I am sure your memories have just been muddled a bit as a result of being summoned."

"That makes sense."

"Yeah, that's probably it."

"Umm, Motoyasu, it seems like you've gotten things mixed up."

Even Father, of all people, was doubting my words now.

"I guarantee he's lying to you!"

"Hmm . . . Perhaps we should wait until the Spear Hero calms down before continuing here. I believe that will be best," Trash suggested.

The other heroes, including Father, all nodded in response to Trash's suggestion. But they didn't seem to fully trust Trash yet, either. It only made sense that he wouldn't show his true colors in front of four heroes. I'd take this opportunity to do my best to make them believe me.

"Who knows what to believe?"

"I'll prove that you should believe me!"

"Yeah, you do that."

"First, there's Ren. He comes from a Japan with VRMMOs! And then there's Itsuki. He . . . Oh, I remember! He was summoned from a Japan where people have psychic abilities!"

"What about my world?"

Hm? Had there been anything distinctive about Father's world?

"I'm not sure. I only remember the versions of Japan that Ren and Itsuki came from, because they surprised me. I'm guessing there's nothing out of the ordinary about the Japan you come from. But I do remember overhearing Ren and Itsuki talking about it one time in the future, when you weren't around. They said it was probably like a world out of a manga about cooking!"

As far as I knew, it was most likely just a completely ordinary Japan. It was difficult to explain what ordinary meant, though.

"A world out of a manga about cooking?"

They probably said that because Father's cooking skills were so exceptional. It was no surprise that they might think that!

"That's interesting. So are there really VRMMOs in your world, Ren?"

"Why do you ask such an obvious question? Everyone knows there are VRMMOs. Mentioning that proves nothing."

"What?!"

"Huh?!"

Father's and Itsuki's voices cracked when they yelped in surprise. I'd been shocked when I first heard too!

"We definitely don't have those!" Father shouted.

"Yeah, there's no such thing," Itsuki agreed.

"Okay, then. What's this about psychic abilities, Itsuki?"

"Is that supposed to mean supernatural powers? Of course, there are people with those."

"No there aren't!"

"No way!"

"H-heroes! Please calm down!"

Trash and his attendants tried to step in.

"Hmph. I'm starting to think that Motoyasu's words might have some credibility after all."

"You mean what he said about me being set up?" Father asked.

"It's true. You're falsely accused of trying to rape your companion and then stripped of everything you own, I say!"

"Are you serious?"

I nodded. Father grew pale and looked over at Trash.

"Oink!"

And then, a red pig wearing a dress came out from the rear of the throne room. This was a new development!

"Oink oink oink. Oink? Oink oink oink oink."

"Umm, okay . . ."

"Uhh, thanks."

"Oink oink oink oink."

Father and the others suddenly grew timid and bowed to the pig. The red pig. I was certain that was her!

"That's the scum responsible for setting you up, I say!"

I pointed at the crimson swine and she grew teary-eyed. Then she put her hand to her chest and started snorting or something.

"My ears have no idea what she's saying!"

"Huh? You can't hear her, Motoyasu?"

"All I hear is a pig squealing, I say! Please tell me what she said, Father."

"Umm, could you please stop calling me that? Anyway, she said, 'It seems the Spear Hero has the ability to foresee the future. Melromarc will do everything it can to back the Shield Hero and ensure that no such thing happens.'"

That crimson swine! She was lying through her teeth! I wanted to turn her into pork chops right then and there! Pork chops, I say!

"Oink oink oink oink."

"Huh? Umm, okay. I guess that's fine," Father said.

"That's probably for the best," Itsuki agreed.

"What did she say?"

I gripped my spear tightly and got ready to attack. But fighting in this situation would have been a bit disadvantageous.

"She said that to make sure I'm not persecuted, they're going to send me to a country named Siltvelt, where I'll be welcomed," Father explained.

Hmm . . . That actually made sense. Had she had a change of heart?

"A true princess. In exchange for her graciousness, you can settle down now, Motoyasu. Apparently, you can foresee the future, but it seems your accuracy is lacking," said Itsuki.

"You have people with psychic abilities in your world, right, Itsuki? Now I see. Motoyasu must be one of those people," Ren said.

"He might be a diviner. They're usually emotionally unstable. Sometimes their predictions come true, but they often miss the mark," Itsuki replied.

"I see. So that's why he was going on like that," Father said.

Father and the others seemed to have made up their minds. They were all nodding.

"I'm not lying, I say!"

"Calm down, Motoyasu. It's not that we don't believe you. Lower your spear," Father soothed.

Hmm . . . If it was Father's wish, then I had no option but to back off. I cautiously put my spear away.

"It seems like we should probably start by getting a better understanding of our worlds," said Ren.

"You might be right, but it looks like I have to leave the country already," Father mumbled, as if he were disappointed.

"Oink oink oink oink."

After that, the red pig started squealing again. She seemed to be explaining something. It must have been about status magic.

"Excuse me, but how are we supposed to evaluate ourselves?"

"You mean to say that you all haven't figured it out yet? Didn't you realize it the moment you arrived here?" said Ren.

He was acting like he knew everything. He sighed and was about to start explaining.

"Haven't you noticed any weird icons hanging out in your peripheral vision? Just focus your mind on those!"

I cut him off and explained. Ren was standing there dumbstruck. Father paid him no heed and seemed to be busy checking his status instead.

"Level 1? That makes me nervous."

"What is all this?"

"Oink oink oink oink oiiiink."

That crimson swine! I couldn't understand anything she said! *Speak human words, I say!* It seemed to be something about how to get stronger. But there were other secrets about how to do that. The power-up methods would be ineffective if they didn't believe me, though. I would save that talk for Father only.

"Even if they are legendary weapons, mine is only a shield. Wouldn't it probably be best if I used a sword or something?"

Yes! This was my chance to steal the show and explain so that I could gain their trust! Itsuki's blabbering about psychic this and that had made them think my words were inaccurate. It would be problematic if I didn't change their minds!

"Unfortunately, the legendary weapons won't allow you to use other weapons, I say."

"Huh?! Really? Then again, you could just be mistaken, Motoyasu," Father replied.

"It's true. You'll just have to rely on your companions, Father!"

"Are we going to form a party? The four of us?"

"That's not allowed, either."

"Huh?"

"The legendary weapons interfere with each other and prevent us from gaining experience. We can share the materials used to strengthen them, though!"

"That sounds like a hassle. But I'm not sure if we can trust—" Ren started to reply.

"Exactly. Everything he says sounds so negative. Is this guy really okay?" Itsuki interrupted.

The crimson swine turned to Father and seemed to be spouting off some kind of explanation. I was getting the feeling that I wouldn't be able to gain their trust for some reason. The instincts that I'd developed while running through the mountains and fields with the majestic filolials were telling me that the way things were going could end up being very dangerous!

"Apparently he's right. I guess that means I'll just have to find some companions when I get to Siltvelt."

"Your reputation seems to be dubious in this country, so

that sounds like a good idea," Itsuki replied.

"Oink oink oink!"

"Umm, okay. That's fine, I guess. Umm, Motoyasu?"

"What is it?"

The crimson swine approached Father and said something. He then turned and spoke to me with an embarrassed look on his face.

"She said the carriage to Siltvelt will be ready for me to-morrow and we should just relax until then."

"They're going to secure some companions for the rest of us, apparently," Ren added.

"Hmm . . ."

It all seemed reasonable. If I could save Father from trag-edy without having to kill anyone, that wouldn't be half bad.

"Understood," I said.

"Very well. We will take each of you to your own private chambers," announced the minister.

Oh? We had shared a single room every other time so far. I wondered what had caused things to be different this time.

"I shan't leave Father's side, I say!"

"Umm, please don't try to come with me. I can't help but feel like you're stalking me or something. It's kind of scary."

There was a clear look of disgust on Father's face. Had I done something wrong? Maybe I had been acting a bit too familiar with him. When I thought about it, this Father had just met me for the first time. It might not have even been an issue of whether he trusted me or not.

"You can tell me all about whatever it is later, okay?"

Father had given me his orders, so there was no arguing. I'd just have to rush to his side should anything happen!

"Understood. I'll settle for the room next to Father's!"

"V-very well. Prepare the chambers!" barked Trash.

And so, I ended up staying in the room next to Father's.

The sun set. I was waiting in my room and keeping my ears open so that I could respond if anything happened when a soldier came to my door.

"Your dinner has been prepared, Spear Hero."

Oh! I would finally be able to talk to Father! If I didn't teach Father about the different methods for becoming stronger, he wouldn't even be able to dream about overcoming what lay ahead. I had to prioritize keeping Father alive over everything else for now.

I opened the door and looked at the soldier.

"The other heroes have already gone to eat. Please make haste, Spear Hero."

"Understood!"

I dashed out of my room and started running toward the dining hall.

"Hey! Hold on!"

"What is it?"

"That's not where they're eating. Please come with me."

Oh? Had the place where we would eat changed? I stopped and spun around.

"Where are they eating, then?"

I had been to the castle numerous times in the past, so I was familiar with the layout for the most part. If they just told me where to go, I could get there on my own.

"This way."

That's all the soldier would say. Ugh. What a pain! I followed the soldier. He took me straight through the castle hall and then stopped just near the entrance of the castle.

"Please wait here for a moment."

"Where are Father and the others?"

"Heh."

Hm? I had a bad feeling about this. I immediately grabbed for my spear, but I suddenly felt like I was floating. By the time I realized what had happened, I had already fallen into a hole that had opened up in the floor.

Chapter Six: Dungeon

I looked down as I fell rapidly through the air. I could see the passageway split into several different paths, like a fancy playground slide below me. I immediately thrust my spear into the wall to stop myself from falling.

"It seems I've fallen for a trap."

What fools! I considered just killing all of the Melromarc scum right then and there without hesitation. But if I started firing off skills recklessly, there was a risk that Father and the others might end up buried alive in the rubble. Using the time loop as an easy way out would be the height of stupidity.

But I wasn't the type to give up easily, I say! I wondered what I should do. Using Portal Spear inside of the castle would be difficult. If I were outside of the castle, I might be able to use it to teleport to the summoning chamber, but . . . Actually, no, I hadn't bound the summoning chamber as a portal location in the first place. That had been a mistake.

If I used my portal now, I would end up in a nearby village. And then it would take time to get back. Actually, I hadn't even tested to see if my portal bindings would remain intact after subsequent loops. I'd lost them all after the first loop back in time. I needed to spend some time looking into that more thoroughly.

Either way . . .

"I'll just have to climb out of this hole!"

I used my spear like an ice axe and started climbing back up the slide. It was dark, so I used magic to illuminate my surroundings. But the passageway was like a labyrinth, and I was having trouble telling which way I'd fallen from.

I thrust my spear into the wall and it made a hollow sound. There must have been an opening on the other side of the wall. I decided it would probably be easier to break through the wall and continue my escape from there. I gripped my spear and aimed it at the wall.

"Shooting Star Spear!"

With a loud explosion, the spear blew a hole through the stone wall and dust filled the air. A new path now lay before me, so I stepped through to the other side gallantly.

"This is . . ."

It was pitch dark. From what I could make out, I seemed to be in some kind of prison cell. I guess it only made sense that the Melromarc castle would have a dungeon. Despite having caused an explosion, there was no sign of any guards coming to see what had happened. I must have been deep underground.

I sliced through the prison cell bars and exited into the walkway. The place was rather old and dilapidated. There were little mouse-like monsters running back and forth along the walls. I turned to my left and I could hear the sound of water flowing ever so faintly. Maybe that led to the Melromarc sewer system. In that case, I would want to go to the right to head back toward the castle.

As I continued down the dungeon walkway, I began to see some prisoners. Some of them seemed to be rather well-dressed, but there were the typical haggardly looking prisoners too.

"Hey! You don't look familiar. Are you a Melromarc soldier?"

I looked over at the prison cell where the voice had come from. Several other prisoners had spoken to me before that and I had ignored them. But this voice belonged to a woman. It wasn't a man, and yet for some reason I hadn't heard the squeals of a pig.

The woman's hands were bound by shackles hanging from overhead, forcing her to remain standing in the cell. Her feet were shackled too. It was painful even just looking at her.

"What are you staring at?" she asked.

She had strawberry-blonde hair and an attractive face. I remembered seeing her somewhere before. Aha! I was pretty sure she had been the bodyguard of Fiancée (which was the nickname I used to refer to the Melromarc princess named Melty, because she was so close to Filo-tan).

Fiancée had introduced the woman to me once when Father was away. She told me, "She may be a woman, but she's a capable knight who protects me and Filo-chan." The filolials had told me she was a good, loyal person too. Also, I remember she sparred with Ren often and he stuck to her like a needy boyfriend. Apparently, she had dueled with him and saved him from complete emotional despair.

So she wasn't a pig, I say! But why was she being held captive in a place like this?

"I've never seen you before. Who are you?" she asked again.

"What in the world are you doing here?" I replied.

"Me? I was arrested for punishing some Melromarc soldiers that were hunting demi-humans. They stripped me of my knighthood, so I'm just a commoner now."

So basically, she had been thrown in prison for punishing the rotten scum of this country. What she had done was a noble deed, and yet she had been wrongly arrested for her "crime." Now I was certain that this was the woman who was big sis's good friend and Fiancée's bodyguard.

"It will all be okay if I can just stay alive until the queen returns. But that's just wishful thinking, I'm sure."

I guess she was being held captive here until the queen got back. The queen sure was useful, I say! I'd used her name during the last cycle of the time loop. Even just mentioning her name in a threat would usually get good results here in Melromarc!

"And? Who in the world are you?" she asked yet again.

I figured it wouldn't hurt to tell her what was going on.

"I'm the Spear Hero, I say! I was summoned to Melromarc earlier today."

"What?!"

Fiancée's bodyguard responded by rattling her chains and leaning forward.

"Why would the Spear Hero be down here in a place like this?!"

"Like I said, Melromarc summoned the four holy heroes today. They summoned all four of us!"

"I'll ask you again. Why would the Spear Hero be down here in a place like this?"

"The reason I'm down here is because I was tricked and fell into a trap, I say!"

"They set a trap for a holy hero? Why in the world would they do that?! What's going on in this country?!"

It would have saved me a lot of trouble if I knew the answer to that question! But I could think of several possibilities. The Melromarc scum had probably decided that having me around was disadvantageous for them. In all actuality, I did consider Melromarc an enemy, so they weren't wrong.

"You might not believe me, but I'm from the future. And in the future, Father . . . the Shield Hero is framed for rape by that pig of a princess, who then colludes with the king to denounce him. I exposed their plot today, I say!"

". . ."

Oh? Fiancée's bodyguard just stood there silently. I guess no one was going to believe me!

"Yeah . . . Knowing the king and the princess, I wouldn't put that past those two. I can definitely imagine them coming up with a rotten plan to ingratiate themselves with the other heroes while taking pleasure from seeing the Shield Hero suffer."

Her face grew even grimmer than it had been. It seemed like she might have believed me, even if only a tiny bit.

"But the demi-human countries wouldn't stand by quietly if they tried something like that. All of my father's monumental efforts to establish friendly ties with them would go straight down the drain."

"In the future I came from, Father worked hard to be successful. The Church of the Three Heroes presence in Melromarc was destroyed, and Melromarc began taking good care of Father as soon as the queen returned!"

"So that's what happens? Hold on, I must be losing my mind. How could I actually believe such foolishness? I must be hallucinating."

Fiancée's bodyguard seemed convinced I was a hallucination. I guess being locked up in a dungeon like this could mess with somebody's head.

"When I uncovered these facts, I was trapped and ended up here. And now I intend to rush back to Father's side as quickly as possible."

That's right. I was worried about Father, I say! It would be one thing if he was just having his meal like normal, but the likelihood of that being the case was slim.

"I bid thee farewell for now, I say!"

Considering what I knew about the future, she should make it out of here alive even if I left her behind. But saving her might improve Filo-tan's opinion of me since she was Fiancée's bodyguard. That said, if I didn't focus on saving Father's life right now, then I would never even get to meet Filo-tan!

"Wait!"

"What is it?"

"If this is real . . . If you're not a hallucination, then get me out of here! I have a duty to protect my territory and its people, my father's words, and the law. Leaving this cell will only make my punishment worse, but I'm willing to accept that to find the truth!"

"Understood!"

I wasn't sure if Fiancée's bodyguard would prove to be of any use. But based on my loyalty to Father, if anyone with favorable ties to him asked me to save them, I would do it, I say!

"Who goes there?!"

A soldier appeared. He was holding a hand lantern out toward us. I guess we had been speaking too loudly and drew attention to ourselves.

"You're the Spear—"

"Air Strike Javelin!"

I used a weak skill and threw my spear at him. It wasn't like I had developed a reverence for life or anything. But using a powerful skill would have destroyed the passage and just made things more difficult!

"Gah!"

The soldier passed out. I paid him no heed. My spear flew back into my hand and I swung it, slicing through the prison cell bars. Then I thrust it at the shackles binding Fiancée's bodyguard and they shattered.

"Come, now is our chance!"

"Such power. Truly fitting of a legendary hero. Perhaps you aren't a hallucination, after all."

Free from her shackles, Fiancée's bodyguard took the sword from the fallen soldier's belt.

"This way! I'll show you the way out of here."

"Understood!"

I followed Fiancée's bodyguard and we ran through the dungeon halls. This was a stroke of good luck! I'm sure I would have wandered around lost for a while if it had just been me.

"By the way, I forgot to introduce myself properly. My name is—"

"Éclair, right?"

I remembered Filo-tan calling her that. Her name always made me hungry. I remembered Father made a yummy treat with the same name, so that's what all the filolials called her.

"That's not how it's pronounced! It's Eclair Seaetto! And what is your name, Spear Hero?"

"Motoyasu Kitamura. Motoyasu is my first name!"

"Mr. Kitamura, then. In that case, I shall accompany you until I find out if what you've told me is true, Mr. Kitamura!"

"Understood!"

As we ran through the halls of the dungeon toward the exit, Éclair and I forged a partnership and our journey began!

Eclair Seaetto

Governor's Daughter; Knight of Melromarc

Daughter of a governor. Her father's territory included the village that Raphtalia lived in before it was destroyed by a wave. Extremely serious and honest. There are times when she argues with Naofumi as a result of her dislike of unfair methods, but she is also learning how to deal with her own shortcomings from observing his way of thinking and countless successes.

STRAWBERRY-BLONDE
BOMBSHELL.

She's a first-rate knight, but I'm sorry to say she has no aptitude for governing a territory.

I respect her a lot. She can be a bit reckless every now and then, but she's a really good person.

Chapter Seven: Gerontocracy

We exited the dungeon and ended up coming out at the rear of the castle courtyard.

"I know my way from here, I say!"

"Scoundrel!"

Some castle soldiers started to cause a commotion.

"And you! Eclair! You're helping the Spear imposter betray Melromarc, aren't you?!"

The soldiers had shown their true colors. If they'd acted like they didn't know any better, I might have let them live. Holding back against this scum wasn't worth the effort. I decided to use a skill that wouldn't demolish the castle.

"Shooting Star Spear V!"

"Gah—"

My Shooting Star Spear skill smashed into the soldiers running toward us and they turned into dust. Any enemy of Father and his companions was an enemy of mine. I don't go easy on my enemies!

"Wha . . ."

Éclair was standing there speechless while staring at me.

"What's the matter? We can't protect the people that need our protection if we aren't willing to protect ourselves!"

"You're right. But please try to refrain from killing people if at all possible."

"If you insist. Brionac!"

"Gahhhh!"

I used a weaker skill, Brionac, to mow down some more soldiers running toward us.

"Come! We must rush to Father's side at once!"

I dashed into the castle. Where was Father?! I ran in the direction of the room where he was supposed to be staying. I encountered more soldiers several times along the way and made quick work of them each time.

"Motoyasu! Stop this!"

"Motoyasu! What's this rampage all about?!"

"Oh, it's you, Ren and Itsuki. Do you know where Father is?"

Ren and Itsuki had shown up to see what all of the commotion was. They were trying to act friendly, but they were looking at me like I was some kind of nut just randomly attacking people. More soldiers came at me swinging and I mowed them down with an effortless sweep of my spear. Ren and Itsuki gulped.

"So strong . . . Just what level are you?"

"How did you get that strong? Aren't you supposed to be level 1?"

"I said I was from the future, didn't I? My level stayed the same when I traveled back in time."

"Say what?! T-that means . . ."

"Is this the Sword Hero and the Bow Hero? Where is the Shield Hero?" asked Éclair.

She was looking on as I stood face to face with Ren and Itsuki. She was right. Father wasn't with them. Where in the world had he gone?

"Motoyasu, why are you rampaging like this?"

"They set a trap for me and separated me from Father. This is payback, I say!"

"A trap?!"

"They used the trap to send me tumbling down underground, but I escaped and now I'm here!"

"Underground? Seriously?"

After we had been talking for several moments, Trash showed up.

"What's all the commotion about?!"

"Your Majesty!" Ren exclaimed.

"Motoyasu says that a trap was set for him. Is that true?" Itsuki asked.

"Depending on your answer, I may kill you, Trash!" I shouted.

"Trash?!" Ren repeated, flabbergasted by my response. "I realize you're strong, but isn't that a bit much?"

"Whatever you say. All I know is he better answer quickly, because I'm just about all out of patience!"

I gripped my spear tightly and it crackled and sparked. I was preparing to fire off a powerful Brionac skill. Trash might have been a seven star hero, but I was sure that if he took the full brunt of my powered-up attack, it would leave a mark. He'd caused a mess last time and now this time too, so surely running him through once or twice wasn't uncalled for.

"T-there seems to have been a misunderstanding, Spear Hero!" Trash replied in a fluster.

"Misunderstanding? Do you really think an excuse like that will work?" I asked.

"I-I don't know how they found out so quickly, but just a moment ago some emissaries from Siltvelt showed up in a hurry to take the Shield Hero. When they did, it seems that a demi-human disguised as a castle soldier used the castle's trap door to try and dispose of you for political reasons."

A demi-human soldier was brought over. The soldier was already dead.

"This is the demi-human that trapped you before trying to kill the Sword Hero and the Bow Hero. He committed suicide when he realized he was about to be captured."

"No way . . ." Ren whispered.

"You weren't in your room when we went to get you so that we could all see Naofumi off. We were looking for you," Itsuki said.

Everything about it sounded fishy. Did they really think I

would believe a story like that? After all, Filo-tan and Father were the ones I trusted! There was no way I could believe the words of anyone who was trying to deceive Father!

"And you want me to believe that?"

I got ready to release Brionac in its most powerful form. According to Trash's story, Father had already departed and was on a carriage headed for Siltvelt. I had supposedly just missed him and been set up by a demi-human emissary from Siltvelt who disguised himself as a soldier and tried to kill me. And then the castle soldiers panicked and attacked me when I came out of an entrance where no one expected to see me.

"Your Majesty! That's not a very convincing story!" Éclair stepped forward and spoke up.

"What?! Seaetto's girl?! You're a prisoner! What are you doing here?! How did you escape?!"

"I asked Mr. Kitamura to free me so that I could find out the truth and he granted my wish! It's not too late, sir. You can still put an end to your plan to trick the Shield Hero. The queen would never forgive such savagery!"

"M-my wife's intentions and my own are one and the same! Return to your cell at once, felon! I show you the grace of responding to you and you speak to me like that?!"

Éclair's shoulders sunk dejectedly for a split-second before she straightened back up and glared at Trash fiercely. Trash belonged out on the curb. He was nothing but a useless old man who used his authority to cause trouble. He couldn't be trusted one bit.

"You've made your intentions clear, sir. I shall accompany the Spear Hero, Mr. Kitamura, and we shall go after the Shield Hero now."

"Wait! Do you intend to defy me?!"

"I will accept my punishment as soon as I hear it from the mouth of the queen. Until then, I'm going to act based on my convictions! That is all!"

There was a crackling sound. Éclair seemed to be channeling magic power into her sword.

"That's enough talk. Now's the time, if you have any last words before I wipe you from the face of the earth, I say!"

I pointed my spear at Trash.

"B-before you what?! You're going to kill me?!"

I told him I would listen to what he had to say, but I never said I wouldn't kill him! That was a little trick to use when talking to people. I had learned it from Father.

"Mr. Kitamura, please hold off on doing that for now. If you defeat this king right now, it will only put the Shield Hero in even more danger," Éclair pleaded.

"I don't think erasing him would change Father's situation. We should nip the evil in the bud, I say!"

In the end, he was just an old troublemaker abusing his authority. Surely, getting rid of him here wouldn't have any real effect on the big picture.

Sensing my bloodlust, Ren and Itsuki stepped in front of the king to protect him. If I wasn't careful, I might accidentally kill the two of them. Then I would end up starting the loop all over. If there were a next time, perhaps I would try to restrain myself from causing such a disturbance after having seen what happened this time.

"Ren and Itsuki, you would do well to remember this: putting your faith in Melromarc will only bring you pain. In particular, beware of the crimson swine, I say!"

I would never give up on saving Father! I was sure I could still fix this. I couldn't waste another second. I needed to go after Father now. I decided to hold off on unleashing Brionac and lowered my spear.

"Come, Éclair! We leave at once, I say!"

"That's not how you say it! It's Eclair!"

"Wait!" shouted a soldier.

"Let them go! If you go after them now, you'll get everyone here killed!"

Ren, Itsuki, and the soldiers started to chase us, but the king called them off. I ran out of the castle in pursuit of Father.

It was nighttime, and the castle town was buzzing with life. Which way had Father gone? How incredibly annoying! They could have taken the back streets of the castle town, or they might have gone straight out into the fields. I had no idea which way the carriage with Father in it had gone!

I imagined the so-called Siltvelt emissaries were almost certainly soldiers of Melromarc. Father didn't know any better, so they tricked him and were dragging him off to who knew where. The castle gates should have been closed during the night, but I couldn't rule out the possibility that they had made an exception and opened them for the carriage.

"Mr. Kitamura! I got a lead!" Éclair said.

"What is it?"

"I was told that a short time ago the gates were opened and a carriage passed through."

"I see. It's highly likely that Father is in that carriage, then."

I ran toward the gates in a hurry. I didn't know what kind of carriage they were using, but it would be extremely difficult to catch up to them on foot. I wondered what I should do.

"Why do you keep calling the Shield Hero 'Father'?"

"Because Father is Filo-tan's father, I say!"

"Is that your loved one?"

"It is, indeed! Filo-tan is an angel that descended from heaven! She's the one who soothes my soul. She's my ultimate and my everything, I say!"

"Oh, I see. The Shield Hero must be quite old."

"He's 20 years old."

"Then what in the world does that make your loved one?!"

Éclair was becoming rambunctious. We arrived at the gates and I pried them open and took a close look at the road leading out.

"It's a stone-paved road. In that case, I guess there's no way to tell which way they went," Éclair mumbled disappointedly.

I got down on the ground and looked at the stones closely.

"Mr. Kitamura?"

I could see faint markings left by carriage wheels and hooves. It was almost imperceptible, but I could also detect Father's scent! Judging by the carriage wheel markings, they had gone . . . southwest. That was the opposite direction from Siltvelt, which was to the northeast. Judging from the dirt left by the horse hooves, I was guessing the carriage had passed through the gates perhaps twenty or thirty minutes prior.

"I've got it! They went that way!"

"Really? I know some therianthropes and monsters have heightened senses of sight and smell. Do you have some kind of special power like that?"

"I didn't do anything special. Anyone properly motivated by love and a sense of loyalty could do the same, I say!"

"I really don't think . . . Oh, never mind. We don't have time to argue right now!"

I did a quick calculation of how much time we had lost in the castle town.

"Éclair, I'm going ahead. I want you to follow and catch up when you can!"

"Understood. We're all counting on you, Mr. Kitamura!"

I took off running at full speed down the road. I'd trained

my legs well, running around with the majestic filolials! The question was whether my level and stats would give me enough of a speed boost to catch up with the carriage. I'd just have to try and find out, I say!

Chapter Eight: Aiming

I could see them! My Super Motoyasu Love-Seeking Eyes had locked on to the carriage that Father was in. It was swaying side to side as it rattled down the road.

"I didn't know we would be traveling during the night. I wonder if there are monsters out there right now," Father was saying to himself quietly.

His voice sounded relaxed and carefree. Several moments later, the carriage came to a sudden stop. It was in the middle of nowhere on a mountain road that led to the next town over.

"Huh? What's going on?"

Father peeked out from inside of the stalled carriage. The cloaked emissaries climbed down off of the carriage and began walking toward Father. One unsheathed a sword and another brandished a spear. Father must have realized what was going on, because his face turned pale.

"You bastards tricked me!" he said.

"He looked so carefree and utterly clueless! Sheesh. Why didn't the king just let us take care of him straight away without going to all of this trouble?" one of them muttered.

"I'm sure he didn't want to give the other heroes a reason not to trust him. It would be a real pain in the neck if they tried to run away because they were worried about getting killed, after all," another explained.

"Huh? Wha? S-so this is what Motoyasu was talking about!" Father stuttered.

"It's too late for you now, Shield Hero! Prepare to die!"

I had to make it in time!

"Thunder Spear!"

Sparks of electricity were leaping from my spear. I hurled it at the men who were about to attack Father. Like a flash of lightning, it went flying toward the Melromarc assassins.

"Gahhh!"

The spear turned into a crackling thunderbolt and it pierced straight through one of the enemies. But I hadn't been able to defeat them all. I was still running toward the carriage to try to protect Father. My spear came flying back into my hand.

"I haven't used this one in a long time," I said.

I focused my concentration on my spear. I was going to lock on to the enemies with a skill that offered a high level of directional control in exchange for being slightly underpowered.

"Aiming Lancer X!"

My spear flashed brightly as I threw it. In the game I'd played, Aiming Lancer was a skill with a significant hit rate boost. Perhaps slightly more powerful than Air Strike Javelin. Its strength was only average. But it was basically guaranteed to hit all targets within a specified area. Of course, that didn't mean they couldn't parry or strike down the attack, but at my current level it was more than enough to make quick work of the riffraff trying to kill Father.

"Gahhhh!"

"Urgahh!"

After I threw the spear, it split into multiple beams of light that went flying toward every enemy in my sight! Since the skill was able to lock on to multiple targets, the beams of light pierced through them all.

There had been three enemies. I'd defeated one with Thunder Spear, and the other two with Aiming Lancer.

"Father! Are you okay?!"

I ran over to the carriage and checked on Father.

"Y-you're . . . Motoyasu! Umm, yeah. I'm okay, but . . ." Father muttered.

Father stepped down from the carriage and gazed at the fallen enemies.

"D-did you kill them?"

"I couldn't afford to hold back under the circumstances."

It was true that we might have been able to make them spill the beans on who was behind all of this if we had taken them hostage. But trying to do that could have gotten Father killed too. Then we would be right back where we started, I say!

"Why would Siltvelt emissaries . . ."

"You're mistaken. They weren't Siltvelt emissaries. They

were either Melromarc soldiers or members of the Church of the Three Heroes, I say!"

"Church of the Three Heroes?"

"It's the official religion of Melromarc. They're a powerful group, but you drive them to their destruction in the future."

"O-oh, really? And you . . . saved me, didn't you? Thank you."

"There's no need to thank me! That's my mission!"

I was starting to feel overwhelmed with emotion upon being reunited with Father when Éclair came running up, looking exhausted.

"I finally . . . caught up . . ."

"Who are you?" Father asked.

Father looked at Éclair and blushed ever so slightly when he asked. She was a woman who wasn't a pig, after all. That could only mean that she had excellent looks and an excellent heart. Of course, compared to Filo-tan she was just another pig.

"My name is Eclair Seaetto. I ended up accompanying Mr. Kitamura here for certain reasons. I've come to give you my assistance, Shield Hero."

"Oh really?"

"Your life was in danger, Shield Hero. I'm not sure what would have happened to you if it weren't for Mr. Kitamura."

"Yeah, that's been made painfully clear. I guess what you said was true after all, Motoyasu."

Father finally trusted me! In that case, I decided it was probably best if I told him about everything that had happened. But before I could, Father began telling me everything that happened to him instead.

"Princess Malty came and told me that the Siltvelt emissaries had arrived earlier than expected and I would be departing right away. Everyone came to see me off. I never imagined it would turn out like this . . ."

Father looked heartbroken.

"I guess none of this would have happened if I had made an effort to go and talk with you. I wasn't really sure how to deal with you, so I just kept my distance and then left without saying anything. I'm sorry," Father went on.

"Don't let it bother you, Father!"

I hadn't been able to gain Father's trust, so I was to blame too!

"Please don't get down on yourself. Éclair and I are here for you, I say!"

"That's right. I will fight for you too, Shield Hero," Éclair said. "Rather than staying in this country, we should probably take you and head to either Siltvelt or Shieldfreeden, where they revere the Shield Hero."

Oh? There was that feeling! It was the Father I remembered again!

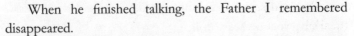

| Shieldfreeden |

A country of both humans and demi-humans. It was established as a result of discontent with the way bloodlines influenced politics so heavily in Siltvelt. To be honest, I don't know a lot about the country myself.

When he finished talking, the Father I remembered disappeared.

"Yeah, that's the cardinal rule of war. Melromarc doesn't want me to go to either of those countries. That's why they did this. And I sure don't want to sit around here and let them bully me," Father announced.

"That's the Father I know!"

"Haha . . . I just realized you calling me 'Father' doesn't even really bother me anymore. Thanks again for sticking with me."

And just like that, we managed to successfully rescue Father!

"I think it's best if we get across the border before anything else."

That was what Éclair said the next morning when we woke up after sleeping out in the fields.

"I'm sure you're right, but . . . I'm really hungry," Father replied.

We'd ended up fighting a string of battles without really eating anything yesterday. We were supposed to have eaten in the castle dining hall, but I got caught in a trap and ended up in the dungeon and Father had gotten on a carriage and left before that happened. In other words, we hadn't eaten a single proper meal since coming to this world! Considering that, it only made sense that Father would say something.

"But I guess I can wait to eat. What should we do now, then?" he went on.

We didn't have any money or equipment. With my level and power-ups, I would probably be able to put up a good fight with just my spear, but we still needed to get equipment and money. I wouldn't be able to buy any filolial eggs in our current state of financial affairs. Father and I were both wearing ordinary clothes too. I wondered if we could teleport to a village that would suit our current needs. I used my skill to check.

"Portal Spear!"

I called up my portal skill to check what locations I could teleport to. All of the locations that I had saved after the initial loop appeared to have remained intact!

"It looks like I can use my teleport skill. The only thing is, all of the portal locations I have bound right now are inside of Melromarc."

I'd been focused on raising filolials during the last cycle and hadn't gone to any other countries. But this was still a good thing.

"You have a teleport skill? These sure are handy weapons," Father replied.

"We can use my portal skill to flee if they happen to catch up to us."

"Yeah, I bet."

"I guess there's no other choice . . ." Éclair mumbled.

She walked over to the corpse of one of the soldiers still lying on the ground from last night and pulled his armor off. The carriage that they had used to transport Father was in pristine condition, so we were going to use that for transportation. Éclair had a bothered look on her face. Father looked at the money pouch she had taken and then asked her a question.

"Taking things from the dead bothers you, doesn't it?"

"Stripping the dead of their belongings goes against the principles of chivalry. But under the current circumstances, we have no choice."

I decided to try saying something that I could imagine Father saying.

"There are no rules on the battlefield! If chivalry was enough to keep us alive, then that would be fine. But right now it's doubtful whether we'll make it out of this alive. We need to protect ourselves. Or are you going to say that choosing death is chivalrous?"

A self-deprecating smile suddenly appeared on Éclair's face.

"You sure hit me where it hurts. You're right. On the

battlefield, you have to keep pushing forward and never stop fighting, even if it means walking over the bodies of your fallen comrades. Not to mention, these were men that used underhanded methods in an attempt to kill Mr. Iwatani. Surely taking their things is an acceptable compromise."

"Having an aversion to taking from your enemy . . . You sure are an earnest person, Eclair. That's so cool."

"C-cool? You shouldn't tease others, Mr. Iwatani."

"I know you're hungry, but we can just snack on the monsters I'm sure we'll run into on the way to the border. As for money . . . It seems we have a bit now, so we'll just have to buy anything we need somewhere along the way," I said.

"Yeah, that sounds good."

"Agreed."

And so we departed. An official notice posted at a village we passed said a former knight of Melromarc was running around on the loose with two dangerous criminals, one carrying a shield and the other a spear. Trash and that filthy crimson swine! They had made us outlaws!

"Hmm . . ."

I gazed at the sign from a distance and thought to myself.

"What are you thinking, Motoyasu?" Father asked.

"They really piss me off. I was thinking that maybe I should just go kill Trash, the crimson swine, and the high priest of the Church of the Three Heroes. I could capture Ren and Itsuki while I was at it."

"Huh?!"

"M-Mr. Kitamura! If you did something like that we would become wanted criminals in every country in the world! Please restrain yourself for now!"

Both of them objected, so I did my best to withstand the urge. For the time being, we would just quietly continue our journey.

Getting to Siltvelt without using filolials would probably take three or four weeks. I couldn't help but feel like that was a bit too long. But the portal locations I'd saved were all nearby places. Alas! It was one of those moments—it really hit home just how precious filolials were!

I made quick work of any monsters that appeared along the way.

"I don't get any experience points when you defeat those monsters," Father said.

"That's because of the interference when heroes fight together."

"Ah, you mentioned that before, didn't you? So this is what you were talking about."

"If I kept my distance you would be able to gain experience, but I might not be able to respond in time in the event of a sudden emergency."

Every now and then, Melromarc soldiers or adventurers would come chasing after us and attack. When they did, I had

Father wait inside the carriage while I mowed them down. It had been three days since we'd set out for Siltvelt. The latest of the repeated assassination attempts that I'd squashed was still fresh in my mind.

"That would be dangerous. Mr. Iwatani is level 1. It's too dangerous to try to level up in this country. I'm not confident I could protect him on my own."

I sure missed my filolials! I missed their soft, fluffy feathers with their healthy shine!

"At the very least, I would feel better if we had some more companions," Éclair continued.

"But could we trust them?" Father asked with a wary look in his eyes.

"That's the problem."

It was a difficult problem, indeed. We had no way of differentiating between friends and foes at the moment. That reminded me. It was about time the Siltvelt emissaries reached out to us. That said, we were considered outlaws now.

I was trying to figure out what to do when I noticed a familiar demi-human and two pigs walking toward us. Incredible. I couldn't believe they had managed to find us. Éclair drew her sword and readied herself to attack if necessary.

"We are emissaries from Siltvelt. You must be the child who Seaetto left behind. Please, lower your sword. We have no intention of fighting."

"Hrm . . . Very well," Éclair conceded.

The emissaries bowed their heads deeply to Father, as if praying, and then began to speak.

"Shield Hero. Spear Hero. We would very much like you to come to Siltvelt."

"We were already planning on going that way," Father muttered.

He averted his eyes, as if he was uncomfortable about what he was going to say.

"I find it hard to trust these people after almost being killed by those guys pretending to be emissaries. Motoyasu, what do you think? Can we trust them?"

Father had died after I turned him over to these people last time around. I wasn't sure what had been the cause of his death, but I couldn't deny the possibility that they might be fakes only claiming to be emissaries.

"I told you what happened before, right?" I said.

"Yeah. So going with them would be dangerous, right?" Father replied.

I'd told Father all about the time loops while we had been traveling. I hadn't omitted any of the details, including how he'd died after I passed him off to some people that claimed to be emissaries from Siltvelt.

"It seems your journey has been riddled with deception, Shield Hero. You have our deepest sympathies. It pains us greatly to know that you feel you cannot trust us."

"That's the thing. I really want to trust you, but . . ." Father replied.

It was impossible to trust them after everything that had happened. There was hardly anyone we could trust while we were still in Melromarc, at least.

"In that case, might I suggest you make us your slaves and put restrictions on what we can do?"

"Slaves? Actually, that's not a bad idea," I replied.

"Slaves, huh? Slaves in this world have slave curses that restrain them so that they can't defy their owner's wishes, right?" Father asked.

"They do, indeed!"

"It makes sense. But . . . slaves?" Éclair muttered with a troubled look on her face.

When Father noticed her expression, he seemed to become flustered.

"I'm sorry, Eclair! It's just that I don't think we can be too careful."

"I understand. We must take every precaution and proceed with discretion."

"How do you suggest we perform the slave curse ceremony? I do believe we'll need an ink pot to apply the curses," I said.

"We will take care of the preparations. Please give us some time to do so."

"I would like to be registered as an owner as well, just to be safe," I replied.

"If that's what it takes for you to trust us, then we would be happy to comply."

I stood guard and kept an eye on our surroundings. Several hours passed and the emissaries returned with an ink pot.

"Father, place a small amount of your blood in the pot."

"Oh, umm, okay."

Father used Éclair's sword to nick the tip of his finger and let the blood drip into the pot. Then I added some of my blood to the ink pot as well.

"Now we'll take this to our nearest associate that can complete the ceremony and then return as your slaves. Please wait here."

We hid in the forest, where people were less likely to pass, and waited for the Siltvelt emissaries to finalize the enslavement. After some time, a slave icon popped up on my screen.

"Whoa! Is this the slave status screen? There sure are a bunch of options."

"It is, indeed! Now you just need to check off all of the precautionary options, like restricting lying, hostility toward one's master, and attacking. Then we'll meet back up with the emissaries."

I adjusted my own settings and taught Father how to do the same. I was really more familiar with the monster seal settings, but there wasn't much of a difference between those and the slave curse settings.

Anyway, the enslavement had been successfully completed, so it was safe to assume the emissaries weren't fakes. Or was it?

Shortly afterward, the emissaries met back up with us.

"Is that enough to earn your trust?"

"Pardon me."

I activated the slave curse without warning. The emissaries grasped at their chests and wailed with pain. I canceled the effect immediately and nodded.

"It seems you were telling the truth."

"Y-yes," the emissary replied while panting.

"Now then, I have a few questions for you. If you lie, I'll kill you on the spot," I continued.

"T-that's not a problem!" they replied.

I asked whether they had other companions who were going to try to kill Father, along with any other questions I could think of. But the slave curses never activated. It seemed that we could consider them true allies.

"T-testing them like that so suddenly was a bit rude, don't you think?" Father asked.

"We can't be too careful, I say! But this proves that they can't betray us. That's a fact. Please take us with you to Siltvelt!"

The emissaries bowed their heads in response. It was

probably safe to trust them, judging by the loyalty and good faith they had shown. They had become our slaves to earn our trust.

If I could be made a slave, I would happily become a slave for Filo-tan! Actually, I was already not only the Love Hunter, but a love slave as well. HA! HA! HA!

"Now then, Mr. Kitamura, the question is whether or not we should try to level Mr. Iwatani now or wait until later," Éclair said.

"Ah, we have some information that should be relevant," the emissary offered.

He raised his hand. His animal-like ears were bouncing up and down in true demi-human fashion. It reminded me of the slaves at Father's village.

"What might that be?" I asked.

"The queen of Melromarc has officially taken you off of the wanted list. You should be able to go into the towns and villages now."

Oh? So this is what Father was talking about in the future when he said the queen could be trusted. She was much more reasonable than Trash. She was Fiancée's mother, after all.

"Then we can move about freely now?" asked Father.

"I'm not so sure about that . . ." Éclair replied.

Her eyes were full of uncertainty. It was more complex than that, after all. Even if the adventurers and bounty hunters stopped coming after us, the Church of the Three Heroes would likely keep trying. A large majority of the Melromarc soldiers belonged to the church, so we would have to consider soldiers dangerous too.

"Even if we're no longer on the wanted list, it's still highly likely that assassins will come after us. We need to be careful," I said.

When I really thought about it, it was a mystery how Father had managed to survive the first time, before I'd traveled back in time. He'd climbed his way to success under such adverse conditions. He really was an amazing person, after all.

I imagined part of it might have been all of the stunts I'd pulled on the first day. Because of that, the Church of the Three Heroes had viewed Father as insignificant and assumed he would just end up dead out on the streets or in the fields. Perhaps that was it.

During the first month or so, Father's equipment had been pretty pitiful. Big sis hadn't been all that strong either. I remember I was already over level 40 around that time. I think I was level 47. But Father was strong enough to pin me down and drive me into a corner. What level would he have been? I wanted to say around level 30, if I had to guess. But Father had spent a lot of time raising obscure stats. He might have actually been closer to level 20.

Heroes and their group members got experience point

boosts. If the Church of the Three Heroes was watching Father under the assumption that things worked the same as they would for normal adventurers, he might very well have seemed like a level 10-ish nothing to them. If that were the case, maybe they just wrote him off as insignificant and ignored him. It's possible that they were just focusing on helping the other heroes progress before dealing with Father.

"What level are you all?" I asked the emissary.

"My apologies, but we were only chosen because we happened to be staying nearby. We're not that strong. I'm level 35, and my companions are 29 and 28."

Their levels weren't very reassuring. I wasn't sure what level Éclair was, but I doubted she was any higher than 60 or so. Father was level 1, so taking him somewhere dangerous could be an issue. I would have to leave his side if we wanted to power-level him like during the last cycle. Things could get ugly if he were ambushed when I wasn't there.

If we wanted to get away from feeling like we were playing in time attack mode, we would need to escape to a place where the Church of the Three Heroes couldn't reach us.

"It would be nice if there were a place where we could lie low," Éclair said.

She glanced over at the emissaries.

"Because of the waves, the best place to hide around here would probably be . . . the Seaetto territory, I believe."

"You mean the former territory that my father was in charge of. That could be difficult."

So lying low would be difficult. It would be possible to hide out in a mountain hut or something, but that would be rough too.

"For now, it looks like prioritizing leaving Melromarc is our best option," I said.

"I guess so. An adventure in another world felt like a dream at first, but this has turned out to be a real nightmare," Father grumbled.

He was complaining. I understood how he felt. When I first came to this world, pigs were the only thing on my mind. Thinking about how much of a fool I was made me want to cry bitter tears, I say! But Father thrust all of these miserable feelings aside and rose to success! This time I was here to help him, so it would probably be more bearable than before.

"Understood. Let's take this low-traffic road then."

And so, we continued our journey and kept Father protected.

The next day came. Father was in the middle of cooking up some meat from the monsters we had defeated the day before.

"And on it goes! Are you sure it's okay for me to be doing the cooking? I'm really not all that great at it."

"There's no need to be modest, Father!"

"He's right. It seems like you're quite the cook," added Éclair.

"Indeed. Just as expected of the Shield Hero," said the emissary.

"Oink oink!"

"Oiiink!"

The demi-human and swine seemed to be enjoying the flavors as well.

"You think so?"

Father carried on the conversation while using the sword he'd borrowed from Éclair as a cleaver to cut up to the meat.

I could see it! I could see that with each nonchalant cut, he was slicing against the grain to make the meat easy to chew. I could see that he was making incisions to speed up the cooking time. He was even unconsciously draining the blood as he went. Father had a natural talent for cooking.

Not to mention, he put the leftover meat in a bag and sat it in the corner of the carriage to marinate so that it would be tender and flavorful later. He didn't waste the bones either but used them to make soup instead. It would be impossible to say his cooking wasn't delicious!

"Oh, if I had some herbs I could improve the flavor a bit, I'm sure. It still tastes a bit gamey," Father mentioned.

"What? You're saying it's possible to make it taste better than this?" Éclair exclaimed.

She had a look of surprise on her face. The emissaries started looking all around, trying to find grasses and herbs.

"Now you're being too easy on him. Father's cooking was even more delicious than this in the future!"

"E-even more than this?!"

"I'm not sure what good comparing me to a different me will do . . ."

"I'm sure you'll catch up in no time once you get used to cooking here!"

He was Father, after all! One of the power-up methods activated a stat called EP that made using life force easy. If he made good use of that, upping his game would be a breeze!

"First things first. We need to cross the border if we're going to get to Siltvelt. We can probably assume that won't be too much of a problem if we're no longer on the wanted list."

After we finished eating, Éclair opened up a map for everyone to see. But therein lay the problem. Last time, Father had died two days after I saw him off. As far as I could tell from the map, that would have been right around the time he reached the border. If something was going to happen, it would probably be around the same time. I still couldn't ignore the possibility that the Siltvelt emissaries might have actually been the cause, so I was keeping a close eye on them too.

"We won't be able to leave the country by boat due to rough sea, as a result of the waves of destruction. We'll probably have to settle for going by land," Éclair continued.

"We should be extra cautious, I say!"

"You're right, but still . . ."

"That's especially true for anywhere along the border! Our enemies may be gathering there."

"Hmm . . ."

Éclair seemed to be thinking about something. I once tracked Father after being deceived by Trash, the crimson swine, and the Church of the Three Heroes. I remember a whole lot of people gathered at the checkpoint tower back then. It had only been a few days since being summoned this time, so they would only be able to gather so many people. Even so, it was highly likely that they were keeping an eye on the borders.

"We could try crossing over the mountains instead of using the checkpoint. But if they have security measures in place even in the mountains, it would be pointless. It would just slow us down, if anything," said Éclair.

"Yeah. And it would be harder to make an escape, which could be a problem," Father replied.

"Not really. If it's escaping we're talking about, I'm sure Mr. Kitamura's teleportation ability should be able to take care of that," she said.

"In that case, really our only option is to just go for it, don't you think? If it doesn't work out, we can just flee, right?" Father asked.

"We can't be absolutely certain of that," I replied.

"Huh? Really?"

Éclair and Father seemed to have gotten the wrong idea. There were issues with the portal skills.

"In the future, Ren and Itsuki were almost eliminated by the Church of the Three Heroes once, when it had gotten out of control. Why do you think they weren't able to escape then?" I asked.

"No idea. Are there restrictions on the portal skills?" Father inquired.

I nodded in response to Father's question. That was exactly it. The portal skills had several limitations. I believe Father had discovered them after doing some testing of his own. It was an odd twist of fate when you thought about it.

"First of all, you have to bind to a location to be able to teleport there. In general, any place inside of a building is a no-go. And it's not possible to teleport from a location with a barrier in place."

"A barrier?"

"Dragon territory, for example. Filolials and a few other select monsters sometimes use them to claim their territory as well. As for areas where humans reside, there are often barriers in place near churches. It also applies to regions affected by a wave, while the wave is occurring."

"I see. And what does any of that have to do with getting away?" Father asked.

"Why do you think Ren and Itsuki failed to escape? There's more, I say!"

"I'm guessing they were taken by surprise and didn't have time to use their skills."

"I can't deny that possibility. But we also know that casting large-scale ceremonial magic will restrict portal usage within the area of effect."

The truth is, I had used Portal Spear the instant the high priest attacked us. Like a fool, I had tried to protect the crimson swine and the other pigs. I was confused when it didn't work at the time, but later we found out through testing that the portal skills couldn't be used when affected by ceremonial magic.

"Large-scale ceremonial magic?" asked Father.

"It's a type of magic often used during war. That makes sense. It's only natural they would use such a thing if they were seriously trying to kill either of you," Éclair said.

"If they use a ceremonial magic spell called Sanctuary on us, it's safe to assume we won't be able to run," I said.

Sanctuary was similar to barrier magic. The spell could nullify most debuff-type attacks and remove curses. The effect continued for a short while, which would make it impossible to flee using teleportation.

"Then what should we do?" Father asked.

"Leave it to me, I say! With my power, we should be able to deal with almost anything!"

"So we're going to resort to brute force, after all. I thought you might have a secret plan or something," mumbled Éclair.

"Attacking the problem head-on is the most effective solution, I say!"

Éclair and Father both let out a long sigh for some reason. Before I knew it, the two of them seemed to have really hit it off. That was just like Father! He'd cultivated their friendship in such a short time!

"Alright, I guess we'll just try going straight through for now. If anything happens, we'll be counting on you, Motoyasu," Father said.

"You can count on me!"

And so we continued our journey to Siltvelt.

We had finally approached the checkpoint tower at the border of Melromarc and the country that separated it from Siltvelt. We were currently checking things out from a spot in the forest that allowed us to observe the tower from a distance.

"What do you think?" I asked.

From what I could see, there was nothing more than the usual merchants passing through. Nothing felt off, but Éclair furrowed her brows and responded in a whisper.

"Everything seems normal at first glance, but there are more guards on the lookout than I would have expected. I have a feeling there are more people inside the tower than usual too.

You can tell if you check the windows carefully."

I checked all of the places Éclair had pointed out. She was right. Now that she had mentioned it, there did seem to be more people than usual. It wasn't as many as there had been the first time around, when Father was a wanted criminal, but it was still a lot.

"R-really?" Father stuttered.

"I'd like to think it's just my imagination, but that's probably wishful thinking," Éclair whispered.

The Siltvelt emissary was nodding too.

"How about switching to a wagon and hiding the Shield Hero when we pass?" he asked.

"Smuggle him out, in other words? It's not a bad idea, but it could be quite dangerous if we got caught, considering Mr. Iwatani's current level," Éclair replied.

"That's true. They'll probably be checking cargo carefully, after all," Father said.

"You're right. What should we do?" the emissary wondered out loud.

Father and the others were talking it over and seemed to be stumped. This was my time to shine!

"I'll go ahead and check things out. You all stay hidden here!"

"Huh? You're going by yourself? Isn't that dangerous?"

I humbly acknowledge your sincerity, Father! A waterfall of tears spontaneously began pouring down my cheeks.

"M-Motoyasu?! Why are you crying?"

"I'm fine, I say! I was just moved by your kindness is all!"

"Did I say something nice?"

Éclair sighed for some reason.

"Mr. Iwatani, I'm starting to think it's about time we got used to Mr. Kitamura's quirkiness."

"Oh, yeah. I guess you're right. I was just wondering if he would be okay going by himself."

"I don't think that will be a problem. As far as I can tell, Mr. Kitamura has an unfathomable amount of power. Not to mention an unfathomable personality."

I had trouble hearing Éclair's last comment. Father must have heard her fine, because he was nodding in agreement. Now that I thought about it, I seemed to remember Father and big sis whispering to each other a lot like that too. It made me feel uncomfortable when I'd first noticed it, but thinking back on it now, I'm sure it was an important part of their friendship.

"Rather than him going alone, wouldn't it be better if we just all went together and blasted right through?" Father suggested.

"That's certainly worth considering too. But from what Mr. Kitamura has said, his teleportation ability can take us to places he's already been, right? In that case, if he made it through the checkpoint, then he could set a teleport location there and return for us."

"I see! So even if they are on the lookout for me, it shouldn't be a problem as long as Motoyasu can make it through."

Indeed, that would work. It seemed like my saved portal bindings would remain even if the loop was reset again, so I might just use that plan next time if it happened.

"All we have to do is avoid being found and protect Mr. Iwatani while Mr. Kitamura goes and takes care of crossing," Éclair told the Siltvelt emissary.

"Understood," he replied while nodding.

It pained me to leave Father's side, even if only for a moment, but it was time for battle! I would call it the Battle of the Melromarc Tower. I would flaunt my achievements on the battlefield to prove to Father just how loyal I was!

"I shall return! If anything should happen here, just give me a clear sign and I'll come racing back!"

"Got it."

"Leave it to us."

I went walking toward the border checkpoint by myself. As I neared the tower, I could see the guards starting to make a fuss. Soldiers came pouring out from inside the tower.

"Spear Hero! Where's the Shield Demon?!"

A representative of the soldiers called out to me loudly. I was pretty sure he was the knight commander that I had met several times in the first world I'd been summoned to. I'd stopped seeing him eventually. I wondered what he was doing in a place like this.

"That's none of my business. I'm just here to cross the border, I say!"

"Nobody's letting you through! Be a good boy and tell us where the Shield Demon is! If you don't . . ."

Some magic-using soldiers at the rear began reciting the incantation for a large-scale ceremonial magic spell. I could tangibly feel a dense magical field begin to form in the surrounding area. That was something I learned how to do around the time I became able to use life force and energy boost.

"Come on! Spill the beans if you value your life!"

"Do you really think I'd tell you?"

There was no doubt that this was the riffraff that had killed Father after the first loop. The Siltvelt emissaries must have attempted to cross the border unsuspectingly, and then this bunch found them and killed them.

Father hadn't attempted to flee to another country in the initial world. Maybe that's why he had managed to survive. That showed just how much these bastards must have hated the idea of Father going to Siltvelt.

"I'll say it one more time. Let me pass. Or I'll kill you. I'm willing to let this slide if you allow me to pass!"

"Ha! You're a fool, Spear Hero! Prepare to meet your doom!"

"Collective Ceremonial Magic! Judg—"

While I was talking to the knight commander, I had been chanting a spell that I learned from Father in the past. As long as the opponent wasn't an extremely skilled magic-user, the spell would be effective even against ceremonial magic.

"I, the Love Hunter, command the heavens and earth! Transect the way of the universe and rejoin it again to expel the pus from within! Power of the Earth Vein! Merge with this magic power of mine! Merge with the power of the heroes and forge a unified force! As the source of your power, the Love Hunter commands you! Let the way of all things be revealed once more! Absorb that power which is wicked, that it may become my own!"

"All Liberation Absorb X!"

When I finished the incantation, I raised my spear up into the sky. Their ceremonial magic caused enormous rainclouds to form overhead. Then, with a loud thunderclap, a massive bolt of lightning came flashing down directly toward me.

This attack was probably what had killed Father during the last loop. I suddenly realized I was gritting my teeth hard. In that case, I would just have to avenge that Father's death.

"Hahaha! Foolish Spear Hero!"

The knight commander was laughing loudly. I turned toward him and grinned. The lightning hit me. And in that same instant, the magic power it was made of was sucked straight into my spear.

"Hahaha . . . ha?"

I could feel the magic power flowing throughout my body.

Then again, I didn't use much magic power to start with, so restoring it was pointless.

"I-impossible! Judgment just disappeared into thin air?!" the knight commander spluttered.

The knight commander glared at me with a look of disbelief on his face. How truly foolish he was! Didn't he know that their defeat became inevitable the moment they decided to oppose Father? If anyone, it was these incompetent fools that required judgment!

"You vastly underestimate the power of the heroes, I say! Dealing with an attack like that is child's play!"

The magic power that I had absorbed would just dissipate eventually, so I decided I might as well take care of them with some magic instead of using a skill.

"*I, the Love Hunter, command the heavens and earth! Transect the way of the universe and rejoin it again to expel the pus from within! Power of the Earth Vein! Merge with this magic power of mine! Merge with the power of the heroes and forge a unified force! As the source of your power, the Love Hunter commands you! Let the way of all things be revealed once more! Mow down this pack of fools with a storm of flames!*"

"W-what are you waiting for?! Hurry up and kill the Spear Hero!" he shouted.

The knight commander haughtily barked orders at the soldiers. They let out a war cry and began charging toward me. But it was too late, I say!

"Liberation Firestorm V!"

I switched my spear to my left hand. I let the magic materialize in my right hand, which I then held out toward the soldiers in front of me before activating the attack. A massive vortex of flames leapt out of my right hand. This was Liberation-level magic. I had learned it from Father. Only usable by heroes, it was the most powerful type of magic there was!

"W-what is that?!"

"Gaaahhhhh!"

"Urgaaaahhh!"

Their shrieks and cries echoed throughout the air as the Melromarc soldiers were swallowed up by the storm of flames. That went for the knight commander too. He tried to use the soldiers as a shield and run away, but it was too late. He was sucked up into the vortex along with the others as it quickly swept over them. Finally, the storm of flames smashed through the tower with a loud roar and then dissipated.

"I guess that should do it."

No sign of the tower remained. Perhaps this would make those fools understand. Picking a fight with Father equaled death.

The scorched bodies of soldiers came raining down out of the sky. The state of the surrounding area was horrifying. I had no idea where the knight commander was. I was guessing most of them were still alive, since I'd held back. I buried my foot into the chest of a dying soldier lying on the ground and made an announcement.

"This is your punishment for trying to kill the Shield Hero! Give Trash and the high priest a message for me! Tell them not to stick their nose in our business unless they want to die, I say! Ha! Ha! Ha! Ha! Ha!"

I was still laughing boisterously when Éclair and the emissaries came rushing up along with the carriage carrying Father. They had bewilderment written all over their faces.

"We saw a huge vortex of flames, so we came in a hurry but . . . What in the world happened here?" Éclair asked.

"Didn't we decide you would stay hidden until I made sure everything was safe?" I said.

"Mr. Iwatani was worried about you," she replied.

"He was?! How deeply moving! The tears—"

"Not right now! Did you do all of this, Motoyasu?"

"I did, indeed!"

"Heroes can become that strong?!" Father said.

Father was at a loss for words. What was he talking about? I was sure Father could manage much more impressive feats than this without even blinking. In all actuality, he'd overcome similar situations repeatedly and protected his companions each time.

That brought back fond memories of the fight against the high priest. I had been Father's enemy at the time, and yet he protected even me! And despite that, I still spoke badly of him afterward. If I could return to the past, I would kill the me of then, I say!

"I'm guessing some of them are dead . . . obviously. Don't you think maybe you went too far?" Father asked.

"When we were watching from a distance, I noticed the knight commander was here. That must mean they intended to kill Mr. Iwatani. And I guess that led to fighting you, Mr. Kitamura. How pitiful," said Éclair.

"You've got to stomp out the embers lest you get caught in a wildfire, I say! Now then, let us continue to our next destination!"

"Y-yeah. I have a feeling you're actually the scariest person there is, Motoyasu. You know how in manga, characters will say something like, 'I'm glad he's on our side'? This is the perfect time to use that line."

What was Father talking about? These fools had most likely cast their ceremonial magic on him during the previous cycle of the time loop. There was absolutely no need to sympathize with them.

"Come! We're off, I say!"

And just like that, we managed to successfully smash through the border unharmed.

Chapter Nine: Filolial Farmer

It had been two days since we smashed through the border. We were currently making our way along the road that led from Melromarc to Siltvelt. According to Éclair, it was a blood-stained road that saw frequent use during times of war between the two countries.

There were other towns and smaller countries interspersed along the road too. But our encounters with assassins had dropped drastically. I guess it was difficult for them to operate outside of Melromarc, after all. For the kind of scum trying to kill Father, it would be hard to make a move while we were in another country.

Father stuck his head out the window of the carriage and asked a question.

"How long does it take to get to Siltvelt by carriage?"

"It normally takes at least three weeks with a horse pulling the carriage," Éclair answered.

"It must be really far away," he muttered.

"I've heard it only takes two weeks if a filolial pulls the carriage!" I said proudly.

"Can filolials really go that much faster than horses? Either way, wouldn't it be faster to just fly on a dragon?" Éclair asked.

She was spouting off nonsense now. Dragons were natural enemies of filolials. That meant they were my natural enemies too. I would never be able to stomach riding on such a detestable thing. Just thinking about it disgusted me. I would rather crawl along the ground on my hands and knees than do that.

That made me realize that I hadn't seen any filolials for quite a while. I mean, I'd caught sight of several as we passed by, but I hadn't touched or smelled any. Oh, how I yearned to breathe the scent of a majestic filolial! I had a filolial feather that I'd found on the ground in my pocket. I pulled it out and held it up to the tip of my nose. Ah, the lingering scent of a filolial!

"I miss being with filolials!"

"Y-you really do like filolials, don't you?" Father asked.

We continued chatting and making our way along the road when a farm came into sight. Oh?! It appeared to be a filolial farm too! I leaned over the fence and peered inside.

"Gweh! Gweh!"

I could see filolials loafing around leisurely in the distance! I sighed.

"You really do like filolials, don't you, Mr. Kitamura?"

"Do they not have filolials for sale somewhere?" I wondered out loud.

I was really starting to approach my limit. It was becoming unbearable, I say! Oh, filolials! I was itching to breathe their scent!

"Hmm, if you really want one that bad, I'm sure it would be fine if you bought one while we're on the road," suggested Éclair.

"Would that really be okay?!"

"S-sure . . ." she replied.

Éclair had made a fantastic suggestion! The Siltvelt emissary nodded too. He had a worried look on his face, though.

"That sounds good and all, but . . . I'm exhausted from riding in this carriage for so long. All I've been doing is sitting around inside of here the whole time," Father said.

"Since we've come this far, we probably don't need to worry about pursuers so much. How about stopping at a nearby town to restock our supplies and give the Shield Hero a break?" the emissary suggested.

"You think that would be safe?" I asked.

The Siltvelt emissary nodded. Relaxing our guard could be dangerous, but our efforts would be meaningless if they came at the expense of our well-being. Not to mention, Father was level 1. Spending a bit of time raising his level was probably a good idea, both ability-wise and from a physical health perspective as well.

"There's an establishment owned by a friend from Siltvelt. I believe it should be safe for us there," the emissary explained.

"Understood. In that case, I'm going to go and try to convince someone at this filolial farm to give me a filolial egg!"

"Is there something wrong with a grown filolial?" Father asked.

"It's best if I hatch and raise it myself, I say!"

"Really? Well, we can probably afford to set aside a little bit of time for that. Considering it's you, I'm sure you'll have no problem raising one."

"Of course! I'll raise a mighty fine filolial! Okay then, I'll go buy an egg and be right back!"

I had Father and the others wait for me there and headed toward the little farm office building. I knocked on the door. There was no response. Maybe they were out.

"Mr. Kitamura!"

I heard Éclair shouting and turned around. She was pointing over at the filolial stable. No one was at the office, so it only made sense to go check there.

"Gweh! Gweh!"

The sounds of the filolials drew me instinctively toward the stable. Once there, I peeked inside. A well-built man who fit the rugged-farmer image perfectly was feeding the filolials some hay. I guessed he was the owner.

"Who are you?"

"A customer, I say!"

"And? What is it you're after, Mr. Customer?"

"I'd like you to give me a filolial egg, I say!"

The filolials were looking at me. Their eyes were brimming

with curiosity. There were plenty of ways to go about fostering an intimate relationship with them, but first impressions were always important!

"Why do you want a filolial?"

Why? I had no reason in particular. As long as filolials existed, I would raise them. Logic and reasoning had no place in the matter. If I had to come up with something, I'd say it was simply a rule of the universe.

"Because filolials are precious and indispensable creatures, I say! Do you need a reason to breathe?"

"What kind of nonsense is that? I'm asking what you're going to use the filolial egg for."

"I love all filolials equally, I say! Indeed, I love them as if they were my own children. Whether they be fast or slow, strong or weak, clever or dull, I love them all equally!"

"Like I said . . . Oh, hell. That's not what I want to know."

The farmer rested his pitchfork on his shoulder and let out a frustrated sigh. Was there a reason to be frustrated?

"Did I say something strange?"

"Are you really fond of filolials? You're not going to eat the egg or something, are you?"

"Of course I'm fond of them! What kind of monster would eat filolial eggs?!"

Just what was he thinking I wanted to use the filolial egg for? Did he think I was going to boil it just before it hatched and eat it like balut?! I had no interest in such hideousness, I say!

"Okay, then. Can you tell me what species this—"

"A filitelt, right? No, wait. It's a mix between that and a filobred. If you go back a generation further, there's some fisauzan in there. I'm guessing there's some fidermeo mixed in the paternal bloodline too."

The filolials in the stable were all species that were bred for their speed—the kinds that were common in Zeltoble's filolial races. The farm apparently specialized in breeding thoroughbreds.

"That one is quick, but it seems to be having some issues with its legs. Rather than simply trying to make a certain weight, you should focus more on quality nutrition to avoid injury," I added.

The filolial would fetch a high price if sold.

"B-bingo. Being able to guess the lineage with a single glance is really something . . ."

"That's the power of love, I say!"

I could tell that the filolials trusted the farmer from the way they looked at him. It made me want to trust him too. I reached out slowly and petted the filolial's neck. Petting the neck always made them happy.

"Gwehhhh . . ."

"Oh? Not bad for a first encounter. You must not be a bad guy, after all."

The farmer grinned at me. Anyone passionate about filolials couldn't be a bad person. I grinned back at the farmer. Oh, magnificent filolials!

"I treasure all filolials equally, be they cheap or expensive. There's nothing more to it, I say!"

"I'm not really sure what to think, but your passion is clear. I've decided to give you an especially good egg."

"I want more than one, so I'd appreciate if you could also tell me where I can buy more eggs. I don't mind if they're cheap eggs!"

"How many do you plan on raising?!"

"As many as I can! All of them, I say!"

The farmer facepalmed.

"You're fine with cheap eggs, huh?"

"I don't judge an egg by the price humans put on it!"

"You're an interesting fellow. How much money do you have to spend?"

I showed the farmer all of the money I had on me. We hadn't gotten any money from Trash this time, so it wasn't that much. But we'd defeated numerous Melromarc soldiers and assassins along the way, and I had taken the money they had on them. I was sure it was enough to buy several eggs.

"I'd like you to give me however many filolial eggs this will buy."

"Let's see . . ."

The farmer looked inside of the money pouch and nodded several times.

"This should cover the premium egg, and then I'll throw in two more cheap eggs that I was planning on passing off to the monster trainer. How does that sound?"

"That will do just fine, I say!"

The farmer took me to a nearby shed where he kept the filolial eggs. He chose one egg that was set aside from the others at the back of the shed, as if it were special, and then he picked the two extras from a pile near the entrance. He brought the eggs back to me.

"I supply all the nearby farms with the eggs they resell anyway, so you're lucky you came here first. I'll throw the incubator in too. You take good care of these."

"Your generosity is appreciated!"

"I'd love to see how they turn out. Drop back by later if you have the time."

"Roger that! Once I've raised them to be legendary filolials, I'll be back to show you!"

I purchased the three filolial eggs from the farmer. Excellent! I really liked this farm. I decided to save it as a portal location. Also, I found this out later on, but this farmer was apparently the area's filolial farm tycoon. He supplied people far and wide with filolials. He was a true paragon of a filolial farmer!

"Oh, hey. You're back."

After buying the filolials, I met back up with Father and the others.

"How did it go? Were you able to buy a good egg?" Father asked.

"There is no such thing as good or bad when it comes to filolials, I say!"

I showed Father the filolial eggs. They all looked exactly the same. I wondered just what kind of filolials they would turn out to be. I couldn't wait to find out!

"Nice. So those are going to hatch into those bird-like monsters?"

"They are, indeed!"

"You bought three? I guess if they're that fast, it won't hurt to have a few. But it will probably take some time before they can be used," said Éclair.

"They haven't even hatched yet, after all," Father replied.

"I'll raise them in no time!"

Éclair seemed to not really understand how filolials worked! It was true that raising them would take some time without my level adjustments, but I could raise them to be powerful, irreplaceable allies in only a matter of days! By the time three days had passed, they would probably be able to understand human language too.

"How long will it take?" Father asked.

"To use them for transportation? It would take an experienced soldier at least two weeks to raise one," Éclair replied.

"Once they've hatched, two days will be more than enough, I say!"

"No way. Surely that's too fast. Do heroes have some kind of special ability for that?" she asked.

I nodded at Éclair. That's right. Filolials—along with the rest of the monsters in this world—grew quite fast when they were leveled up rapidly. Father had verified this at the territory he'd managed. His monsters were impressively well-trained.

"I guess we'll find out soon enough. He already bought the eggs, after all," Father said.

"Just watch! You'll see!"

"Y-yeah. Okay, we should head to the town," Éclair replied.

We all headed to the nearest town. It seemed to be a merchant town. It felt like a trading post more than anything. It was in a neighboring country of Melromarc that I'd only been to a time or two. I think it was the country where there was supposedly a famine in the northern region.

The Siltvelt emissary guided us down an alley and we stopped in front of a tavern. There was a sign out front with writing used in demi-human countries on it.

"A demi-human tavern? Of course. It's the perfect place to hide Mr. Iwatani since he's the Shield Hero," said Éclair.

"Yes. There is a room in the back where he can feel free to relax."

"So I can get out now, right?" Father asked.

He stepped down out of the carriage and stretched.

"Phew! I don't get motion sickness, but it's still really cramped in there."

He had been sitting inside the carriage the whole time, after all. It was no surprise that he was exhausted.

"This way, please."

The Siltvelt emissary went inside of the tavern and started talking with the owner.

"We've come to an agreement. Please, make yourself at home."

The owner opened a door that led to the rear and stepped out of the way. The tavern was on the ground floor of a three-story stone building. We made our way to a room on the third floor. The building even had a secret room that was accessed using a hidden switch on the stone wall. There were supposedly similar facilities in all areas of the town. It was close to Melromarc, which was considered a hostile country, after all.

Just to be safe, Father was instructed not to stand near the window. He was sitting on the bed and looked incredibly bored.

"It's not as cramped as the inside of that carriage, but I guess I'm still just stuck here hiding in the end," he said.

"That you are. If there's anything you'd like, I'll be happy to go buy it for you, I say!"

"Hmm . . . They gave me something to eat already. If I had to say, I'd really like to take a bath."

"Do ordinary homes in this town have baths?" Éclair asked.

"I'm afraid not, but it would be possible to improvise by filling a wooden barrel with hot water," the emissary replied.

"Kind of like an oil drum bath? That would be just fine," Father said.

"I'm sure some devout believers would be happy to buy your bathwater. It could be a source of extra funds while we're on the road. What do you think?" asked the emissary.

"Definitely not! Please don't sell it!"

Oh? Could we really sell Father's bathwater? That reminded me. There was a hot springs resort on the Cal Mira islands, where there was an event that offered increased experience points. The hot springs had become a major tourist destination after Father bathed there.

"A bath? Who is going to guard Father while he bathes?" I asked.

"Huh? I'll keep watch, of course," Éclair replied.

"Y-you're going to watch me bathe?!"

Father's face was bright red. Éclair realized what Father was thinking and scrambled to clarify herself.

"T-that's not what I meant, Mr. Iwatani! I'm simply going to keep an eye out for security purposes! I guarantee you I'm no pervert!"

"Ha! Ha! Ha! I'll take care of guarding Father while he bathes. Éclair, why don't you take this opportunity to go out into the town and take a bath yourself, while I watch Father?"

"Hmm . . . I certainly wouldn't have to worry, knowing how strong you are. I'll take you up on that offer. But don't come looking for me, even if something happens and I don't make it back."

"Don't worry. My companions here will see to your safety, Miss Seaetto," the emissary said.

"Oink!"

One of the pigs accompanying the Siltvelt emissary took a step forward and said something to Éclair.

"I see. In that case, we'll go clean up too while you're bathing, Mr. Iwatani," Éclair announced.

"O-okay."

Father looked away from Éclair. He seemed to be having trouble deciding where to look.

"Mr. Iwatani, you seem to have misunderstood my intentions. I'm not really . . ." Éclair stammered.

What were they talking about?

"Yeah, I get it now. Sorry. It's just what popped into my head, but clearly I don't need to worry about that," Father corrected.

"Right. Feel free to just think of me as a companion," she said.

"I will. You are a precious companion, after all. That kind of thing is something I'll think about once things are more stable."

Hm? The pig that was standing next to Éclair seemed to be acting embarrassed for some reason. Éclair and the pig left the room. It was quieter now. The Siltvelt emissary had gone out to arrange for the hot water.

"Oh, sorry about that, Motoyasu. It's not like there's anything between us. I was making that clear just in case. Because, well, you know . . ." Father started to explain.

What had I missed?

"Whether it's Éclair or anyone else . . . People treat me special just because I'm the Shield Hero, right? That's why I want to avoid romance, harems, and all of that. I want to be in a relationship with someone who really understands me and wants to be with me because of who I am."

Hmm . . . That wasn't really the kind of response I would have expected from the Father I knew. I was pretty sure he was like me and hated pigs. There was even a ban on romantic relationships in his village. It was difficult for normal people to tell pigs and women apart, after all.

"They were telling me that, when we get to Siltvelt, I'll get lots of marriage proposals and I can marry a beautiful woman," he said.

I just stared at Father silently and he started talking about a bunch of different things. Apparently, the Siltvelt emissary and his companions had been trying to put all sorts of ideas into Father's head.

"That's dangerous business," I told him.

"Yeah. The princess of Melromarc was really pretty too. I have to assume they have ulterior motives."

"I knew you'd understand, Father! You have to watch out for that crimson swine more than anyone, I say! But you should be wary of pigs that try to flirt with you in other countries too."

As far as I could remember, Father had mentioned almost getting caught up in a mess of marriage proposals when he went to Siltvelt in the first world. He told me his underlings fought valiantly and protected him honorably. That deserved respect.

"I've never had a girlfriend before, so I was tempted to let myself get excited. But I know I have to be careful," he went on.

Father was impressive, as usual. I admired his ability to learn so quickly, I say!

"From what you've said, this world is pretty dangerous. The same probably goes for Siltvelt too, right?" he asked.

"Probably so."

From what I'd heard, when Siltvelt found out that Father only took slaves under his wing, they started arranging to have young girls from noble families sent to him as slaves. I think that was what happened anyway.

I know what I did remember. Attractiveness had played a part in determining a woman's value since ancient times. Having a nice face meant a woman was well-liked. In other words, if a woman was physically attractive, you could expect a good-looking child as a result of a physical relationship with her. Somewhere in the back of my mind, I'd made a note that the same attitude was firmly ingrained in the people of this world. Having an attractive face was a good thing.

But women that approached someone based on looks alone were pigs, I say! Similarly, there were a lot of pigs that approached someone based solely on that person's success. I'd finally learned that after coming to this world—after the Spirit Tortoise incident.

Back then, I was popular with the women because I was the Spear Hero. They stroked my ego and I let it go to my head. But then I found out just how cold and cruel this world was. I found out just how easily those pigs that I'd considered friends would betray me. I'll never be able to forget how I felt when that happened.

But when I was still full of myself, it was Filo-tan who harshly rebuked me, for my own sake. And when I fell into despair, after it became painfully clear to me how cruel this world was, it was again Filo-tan who cheered me up. When I finally realized that her berating had all been for my sake, the flame of true love was ignited in my heart, I say! Indeed, it was at that moment that I knew I could go on living as long as I had Filo-tan's love!

That's right—not *everything* about this world was horrible, I say!

"Father, unless it's for that precious someone who means the world to you, you mustn't spread your legs, I say!"

"Spread my legs? I'm a guy, you know. But yeah. I understand what you're trying to say. I have to be careful. People will try to use me just because I'm a hero. I have to make sure that doesn't happen."

Father never ceased to impress. He'd thought about my words carefully and fully grasped their meaning!

After a short while, the Siltvelt emissary returned to let us know that he'd secured some hot water. They'd partitioned off a section of the washing area and set up the wooden barrel there. Father was bathing in the barrel.

"How is the water? I can warm it up with some magic if you like," I offered.

"No, it's fine. Are you not going to get in?"

"I'll wait until you've finished. Here, let me wash your back!"

"Oh, umm, okay."

I finished washing Father's back and he got back in the bath. He sighed quietly. It sounded like he was a bit worn out.

"I plan on teaching you how to get stronger now so that even if assassins come for you, you'll be able to take care of them yourself."

"Yeah. Hopefully I can become as strong as you. I'll do my best."

"That's right! Then you won't have to run and hide like this. You can face the assassins head-on and destroy them, I say!"

"Yeah, that would be nice. So what's the plan?"

"It's what we discussed earlier. We'll set things in motion tomorrow, I say!"

"???"

Father didn't seem to know what I was talking about. I realized later that the discussion I was referring to had occurred in the previous loop.

"That was a nice bath. Now then . . ."

Éclair started discussing something with the Siltvelt emissary. It was around sunset. Apparently, Éclair had sensed the presence of an assassin near the tavern, on the way back from her bath. There were demi-human adventurers standing guard out in front of the tavern and some burly demi-human adventurers staying at the tavern too. It was unlikely anyone would try to attack from the front. Still, it never hurt to be cautious.

Father was in the kitchen cooking dinner. He said it was in

return for the demi-humans' hospitality. The tavern guests and I were all drooling as the dishes were placed before us.

"This is really all I can do . . ."

Father belittled himself. But seeing him make an effort got the demi-humans fired up.

"Our mission is to protect the Shield Hero! Everyone! Protect the Shield Hero with your lives!"

"Yeah!"

Father was toiling away busily in the kitchen. He looked like he wasn't quite sure how to feel about the demi-humans' cheers. All of his movements were executed with such skill. Impressive as always! Somebody had called him the Cooking Hero in the first world, and with movements like those, he lived up to the name.

"I worked part-time at an izakaya once, so that helps," he said.

"You worked at lots of different jobs, didn't you, Father?"

I once overheard him saying he'd worked in a food court. He'd also mentioned working multiple jobs at once.

"You could say that. Are you going to drink with the others, Motoyasu?"

"I'll pass. Speaking of which, I don't remember you liking drinking, Father."

"Yeah. I've actually never been able to get drunk, so I don't really like drinking. Everyone around you gets smashed and it turns into chaos. People always talk about the same things, and pretending like I'm interested just gets exhausting."

Now that he mentioned it, I remembered hearing that Father couldn't get drunk. That brought back memories. There was this one time when I heard Father didn't get drunk even if he ate rucolu fruit. I didn't believe it was such a big deal, so I tried eating one and passed out. I felt like hell now even just thinking about how drunk I was after that. Add to that the nightmarish experience of being nursed back to health by a pig, and I started to feel like I would throw up.

"Alright, I'll throw together some snacks to go with the drinks. You all just enjoy yourselves in the meantime," he said.

I stayed and watched Father until he finished cooking. After that, we both went and joined Éclair, who was talking with the emissary.

"How goes the meeting?" I asked.

"Well, we're thinking that using your portal skill might be the best option," Éclair replied.

"That seems reasonable. I was thinking about going out and leveling up the filolials tomorrow, so I'll use that chance to save a portal location for us, I say."

"Please do, Mr. Kitamura."

"And so I shall!"

"Also, after discussing things with the Siltvelt emissary, we decided that tomorrow we'll use the sewers to switch our hideout to one of the other buildings in the town."

"We're going through the sewers?" asked Father.

"Yeah. They've already made the arrangements. We have to make sure the assassins have no chance of tracking us," Éclair replied.

She cast a wary gaze toward the window. We could hear the sounds of people fighting outside.

"It's the Church of the Three Heroes. I guess it only makes sense, but they apparently really don't want you to go to Siltvelt, Mr. Iwatani."

"They're trying to make it seem like random adventurers just being rambunctious, but we have no doubt it's them," said the emissary.

Some demi-humans from the tavern and the town's vigilante corps had quelled several disturbances involving seemingly drunk adventurers. They did seem to be occurring abnormally frequently. Three or four times now, I'd heard someone outside shout, "What's with this tavern?! It stinks of demi-humans!" It was impossible not to notice when they kept doing it repeatedly. It would have been nice if they'd added a little variety to how they tried to pick a fight.

On top of that, they must have paid someone in the vigilante corps off, because someone had apparently used a weird excuse to try to force their way into the back of the tavern. I guess even if we had left Melromarc, this was the kind of thing we could expect in a neighboring country.

"Well, even if the assassins do attack him, I plan on making Father strong enough to take care of them himself," I announced.

"Can you do that?" asked Éclair.

"The preparations to begin doing so will be complete by the day after tomorrow, I say!"

"Understood. We'll make the move to the new location after you head out tomorrow, then. It could be dangerous, but we have no choice."

In order to make Father stronger, I had to leave his side. How incredibly troublesome! But once we took care of that problem, piddling assassins would pose no threat to Father, I say! Having fought both against and alongside Father numerous times, that was something I could say with confidence!

That evening, for the first time in a while, I got to fall asleep while relishing the scent of my filolial eggs.

"Hey, Motoyasu. There's a crack in one of the eggs. They're probably going to hatch soon, don't you think?"

We'd been attacked four times during the night. They'd even resorted to arson in the end, before we drove them away. Now it was morning and the sun was shining bright.

They really made me want to use my portal to head back to Melromarc and slaughter Trash and every last member of the Church of the Three Heroes. Father and Éclair wouldn't let me, though, so I just had to restrain myself.

I looked over at the eggs just as one of them began to hatch. I was pretty sure it was the one that the filolial farmer mentioned being expensive.

"Chirp!"

The egg hatched and the little filolial let out a spirited chirp! It was a white filolial.

"Wow, it's white as snow," said Father.

I picked the filolial up in the palm of my hand and looked it over. It was a female. Female filolials were slightly more common than males, by the way.

"What shall we name her?" I asked.

Actually, "Shiro" was the name that had popped into my head, but I'd named one of my filolials that before traveling back in time. I wasn't sure if I should use the same name again. The Shiro I knew had been a male, so it couldn't be the same filolial. I had a feeling that meant I shouldn't use the name.

"Well, it's a filolial, so there's 'Filo.' But that's the name of your special someone," Father said.

Indeed. That's why I had to pick a different name.

"A white filolial . . ." Éclair whispered to herself.

She was staring at the freshly hatched filolial chick.

"Does it make you imagine something romantic, like a prince on a white horse, Eclair? Or what would the trope be in this world?" Father asked.

"A hero on a bird with white feathers. There's also the hero on a white gryphon griffin and the hero on the white dragon," she replied.

"So it's always a hero, huh?"

"Pretty much. But now that dream is . . ."

I got the feeling that Éclair was thinking something rude. I wondered if she wanted to say that Father was lacking in some way.

"How rude. Father riding a filolial is a glorious sight, I say!"

"That's not it. I was thinking about you when I said that, Mr. Kitamura!"

"Haha . . . Sorry, but I don't think I can defend you, Motoyasu," Father chuckled.

We went on chatting and another one of the eggs started to crack.

"Chirp!"

The next one was a yellow filolial. They were all so cute!

"Chirp!"

Éclair picked it up and handed it to me. It was a male.

"Hmm, what should we do about the names?" I wondered out loud.

"Chirp! Chirp!"

"Would naming him something like 'Yellow' be too lame?" I asked.

"So he's a male, then? I was thinking 'Lemon' because of the color, but I'd feel sorry for any guy named 'Lemon,'" Father said.

The final egg hatched while we were still discussing the names.

"Chirp!"

It was a pink filolial that kicked through the shell of the final egg.

"Chirp!"

Father picked up the pink filolial chick and handed it to me. It was a female.

"I think you mentioned that I should absorb some of the eggshell into my shield, right?"

"I did, indeed!"

"Thanks. Ugh. It says my level isn't high enough."

Only being level 1 had lots of disadvantages, after all. We needed to level him up soon. After watching Father clean up the broken eggshells, I looked at the three filolials.

"I know you already asked this, but what should we name them?" Father asked.

"What, indeed . . ."

"Naming them based on their colors would make things simple. Do you have some kind of preference?" he asked.

"Shiro and Lemon have been used already."

"Do you mean in the future? In that case, maybe something like 'Blanc' or 'Haku' could work for the white one."

Fantastic! I hadn't used either of those names yet. That just left the other two. I held the pink filolial up and christened it.

"Pink!"

"Now you're just using the exact name of the color! That's no good. Plus, think about how 'pink' is used metaphorically. I'd feel bad for her if we named her that."

"Yeah. I think you should pick another name, Mr. Kitamura."

"Then I'd like you to choose, Father. I'm sure that would make Pink happy."

"Me? Umm, let's see . . ."

Father was looking at the filolials and thinking. Just like he had for Filo-tan, I was sure he would choose a sublime, lovely, fantastic name!

"The white one is white as snow, so let's use the Japanese word for snow and name her 'Yuki.' The yellow one looks like the stereotypical yellow chick, so we could go with 'Chick' for—"

"We can't use 'Chick.'"

I was pretty sure that the second filolial Father had raised had been named Chick. She wasn't my angel, but I still wasn't willing to compromise on that one.

"Umm . . . Well, the Japanese character for 'yellow' can be read 'Kou,' so we'll go with that. As for the pink one . . . Either 'Momo,' from peach, or 'Sakura.'"

Fantabulous! Father had done it again! The names he chose were simply superb! I was worried he was going to say Filo-tan

#2 or something. I remembered big sis complaining about how Father just added numbers to names he already knew, because he couldn't be bothered to remember a new name.

"I like the way 'Sakura' rolls off the tongue," said Éclair.

"Father has spoken! I christen thee Yuki, Kou, and Sakura!"

"Chirp!"

All three of the filolials responded in unison with a lively chirp. Now then, what else was there left to do? I placed a filolial on each shoulder and one on my head.

"Okay! I'm going to go level the filolials and then I'll be back, I say!"

"See you later, Motoyasu."

And so I left the tavern and headed out.

Chapter Ten: Hallucinations

"Eh? Who the hell are you? If you want to use this road—"

I was walking down a back alley when some shady character suddenly tried to pick a fight with me. He was probably a Melromarc assassin. Even if he wasn't, that wouldn't change the fact that he was some fool trying to get in my way.

"You're a nuisance, I say! Paralyzing Lance!"

Father and Éclair had asked me to do my best to hold back, so I stabbed the fool in the forehead using a skill that inflicted a status effect. It made a nice, crisp crunching sound, like biting into a lollipop.

"Gah?!"

He must have been paralyzed from head to toe, because his eyes rolled back into his head and he fell over twitching and foaming at the mouth.

Sheesh. Those Church of the Three Heroes fools never learned their lesson. This was what happened when they tried to pick a fight with Father, I say! Hm? I thought I could hear Father trying to refute that in my head. I'm sure it was just my imagination, though!

"Now then! We're off!"

I only had until tomorrow night! I had to get in as much

leveling as possible by then and pick up plenty of souvenirs for Father too! Just like the last time, I headed deep into the mountains to a region where powerful monsters lived. It seemed like this time I ended up in an area with lots of griffin and dinosaur-type monsters, rather than dragons.

"Shooting Star Spear X! Brionac X! Ha! Ha! Ha! So fragile! Too fragile, I say!"

"Chirp!"

All three filolials were shadowboxing, as if to cheer me on. Doing my best to make them strong was priority number one!

All of this sure brought back good memories. It reminded me of leveling Crim, Marine, and Midori. The three of them were the first filolials I'd raised to be angels. I'd been wandering around aimlessly searching for Filo-tan when a monster trainer approached and spoke to me. I responded by mumbling Filo-tan's name, and the monster trainer offered me a free filolial egg and told me where to find his shop.

Fast-forward a bit and Crim, Marine, and Midori were born. I leveled them up and they all said they wanted to race, so we started street racing on a mountain pass. Father and the others scolded me for doing that, though, so I stopped. But I'll never forget how it made me feel like the wind!

"Everyone! You're all going to grow big and strong, I say!"

"Chirp!"

I went on leveling in the mountains with Yuki, Kou, and

Sakura by my side. After a while, the monsters began fleeing from us in droves, but I didn't care! I'd chase them to the ends of the earth and make a bloodbath of them all, I say!

But I was keeping the ecosystem in mind when I hunted too. Completely wiping out the monsters wouldn't be a good thing. Father had warned me to think more about the ecosystem back in the first world. Still, I needed to get plenty of souvenirs for Father here, and food for the filolials too! It only made sense to go on fighting until I got sleepy.

I continued hunting monsters deep in the mountains for some time. Everything was going as planned, but all of the materials and other stuff I was gathering had started to become unwieldy. I would need to arrange to transport it back on a wagon.

I went on hunting, and before I knew it, the sun had begun to set. I wondered if Father and the others were doing okay. There was no sign of the time loop resetting, so it was probably safe to assume that they hadn't had any problems. I still couldn't help but worry about Father. Despite that, I spent the night out in the fields with the filolials. They'd already grown enough that they were starting to look like big, fat dinner rolls. They were level 34 now. That was fair progress, considering we didn't have to return to Father yet.

"Cheep!"

"Cheep!"

"Cheep! Cheep!"

The three of them looked so cute as they slept. And then, out of the blue, a huge griffin came flying up and landed in front of me.

"I've been informed that someone or something has been causing trouble here within my vast territory, so I came to see for myself. To think that—"

"Brionac X!"

"Gah?!"

The massive griffin was mumbling about something or other, but I paid no heed and put a swift end to him. Without any semblance of grace, the griffin fell over dead right in the middle of his sentence. Griffins were another natural enemy of filolials. I hadn't known that there were talking griffins, but that was of no concern to me. He sure was a big one. We'd be having a real feast tomorrow!

"You could have woken everyone up, I say!"

I wondered what to do about the corpse. For the time being, I cut the meat up and checked the remaining parts for drop items. Oh? There was some armor that looked useful. I considered equipping it. But I much preferred the idea of gathering up filolial feathers and making a suit of filolial feather armor, I say! I decided to give the griffin armor to Éclair or Father after I returned.

Just past noon on the second day, all three of the filolials had finally reached level 40.

"Gweh?"

"Gweh! Gweh!"

"Gweeeh!"

They'd all gotten rather large and were squawking energetically. Yuki had the refined delicacy of a snowflake, and Kou had the dazzling splendor of a lightning bolt racing across the sky. As for Sakura, she mirrored the soft colors of the cherry blossoms. She was so close! If only her pink had been on a base of white, she would have been Filo-tan! She was Filo-tan with the pink and white swapped.

"Okay, everyone! Let's get back to Father, I say!"

"Gweh!" they all squawked in unison.

I got us a wagon and loaded it up with the mountain of materials I'd gathered. The filolials pulled the wagon and we headed back out of the mountains.

Just as we'd discussed beforehand, I had the filolials wait outside of the town and headed for the building where we were supposed to meet. It was a restaurant. On the way there, I noticed that something seemed off about the town. I could see black smoke rising from several different locations. I wondered if they were fires. What a dangerous town!

I arrived at the restaurant we had agreed upon.

"Good day, I say!"

I entered the restaurant. There was a pig inside that began

talking to me. I had no idea what the pig was saying, but I was assuming that Father and the others had notified them of our plans beforehand. Then a man that worked there came out to meet me.

"Welcome. Judging from that spear, you must be the Spear Hero. This way, please."

The man wasn't a demi-human. He was a human. Perhaps the restaurant was meant to look like it was run by humans on the surface. I considered that and several other possibilities as we proceeded to the back of the building. There, a slightly exhausted-looking Father was waiting along with Éclair and the Siltvelt emissaries.

"Oh, it's you, Mr. Kitamura. How did things go?" asked Éclair.

"Everything is in order, I say!"

"I see."

"Things seem like a dangerous mess out there," I continued.

"Yeah, we've been told there have been cases of arson and other disturbances all across the town," she replied.

"Is this all because of the Church of the Three Heroes?" Father asked.

There was a hint of guilt in his voice.

"I would imagine so. The town's governor is doing his best to run around and put out the fires, but the town is apparently on the verge of ceasing to function. That's primarily due to disturbances being caused by groups of thugs claiming to be adventurers."

"Such a poor excuse for a religion, I say!"

"You've sure got that right. Even extremists usually have a limit to how far they'll take their troublemaking. I lost count of how many times they set fire to the tavern we were staying at before we parted ways with you. They had to close it temporarily for the time being."

That sounded like a real disaster.

"It's probably best if they close this restaurant after we leave too," she continued.

"Yes, we've already requested funds for compensation to help make that possible," said the Siltvelt emissary while nodding.

It was possible that some thugs had tailed me and got wind of the place, after all. Just as the thought crossed my mind, I heard an adventurer outside the restaurant begin shouting the same old "this place stinks" line. Hmph, I guess there was no helping it. I stepped out from the back of the restaurant and made my way toward the entrance.

"What are you going to do, Mr. Kitamura?"

"We'll be leaving shortly anyway. It's time they learned the hard way just how foolish they are, I say!"

"S-somebody stop Motoyasu!" shouted Father.

"You're the only one who can do that, Mr. Iwatani!"

Father and Éclair started quibbling for some reason.

"Motoyasu! Please don't make this mess any worse than it already is!" Father said.

"Ha! Ha! Ha! You're too kind, Father! It brings tears to my eyes, I say!"

His compassion was overwhelming. He was the father of an angel, Filo-tan, and his immense compassion was truly fitting of a god!

"But this is different, I say!"

I wasn't compassionate like Father. This pack of fools wouldn't think twice about doing things like this if I didn't make them pay for their actions.

"He won't stop! Eclair!"

"Mr. Kitamura! Please! Let's just move on to—"

I left the overly benevolent Father behind and made my way to the front counter. When I got there, a foolish . . . Oh? It was the thug that I'd paralyzed recently with my Paralyzing Lance. He turned pale as soon as he saw me. The look on his face was perfect! I had no doubt he'd been traumatized.

"I guess you haven't learned your lesson, have you?"

"G-go to hell! The Shield Demon is here, isn't he?! If I kill him, I'll get a massive bounty! So get out of my—"

"Be thankful that Father is compassionate, I say! Illusion Lance!"

Once again, I thrust my spear into his forehead. And once again, it made a nice, crisp crunching sound.

"Gah!"

The idiot fell over with a thud, and the idiot that had been standing behind him gulped.

"Heh . . . heh, heh . . . I . . . I did it! I'm gonna be rich! Ahahaha!"

The effects of Illusion Lance had started to kick in. Just like the name implied, the skill made the person it was used on experience an illusion that suited them. It placed them in a trance, basically. The man's pupils were fully dilated. He started drooling and stumbling around with an empty look in his eyes and a creepy grin on his face.

"Eek!"

The other thug turned white as a sheet when he saw how strange his companion was acting. What should I do with him? I decided the usual would do.

"Paralyze Lance, I say!"

"Gaaahhh! Urgaahh! Argh!"

He'd turned and tried to run, so I went ahead and upgraded the size of his butthole for him. Ha! Ha! Ha! Ha! Running away in the face of the enemy meant death, I say! He was still twitching from the lingering effects of the paralysis. I kicked both of them out the front door of the restaurant. There were several thugs who looked like members of the Church of the Three Heroes out front, but they just stood there speechless when they saw the adventurers come tumbling out.

With a clap of my hands, I turned around and headed back to the back of the restaurant.

"Oh no . . . We're too late . . ."

"What's wrong?" I asked.

"Did you actually hold back, Mr. Kitamura?"

"I held back more than enough, I say! If I hadn't, they would all be meeting their maker right about now."

"So that was him holding back . . ."

"I can't help but think it might have been better for them if he'd just killed them."

Father and Éclair were whispering to each other again.

"Mr. Iwatani, you should be careful about what you say. Mr. Kitamura has a tendency to misinterpret your words and cause all kinds of trouble."

"Yeah. I'll do my best to be more careful."

The two of them went on chatting and it started getting noisy outside. I looked out to see the vigilante corps fighting with some self-proclaimed adventurers, who were actually members of the Church of the Three Heroes.

"I guess we should probably get moving," said Father.

"Understood!" I replied.

After Father formed a party and invited everyone, we went out the rear exit of the building and I immediately used Portal Spear. In the blink of an eye, the scenery around us changed to that of the mountain path where the filolials had been waiting for us.

"Whoa! That was crazy! Hearing about it is one thing, but experiencing it really is wild," said Father.

He was looking around at the surroundings. The Siltvelt emissaries were doing the same.

"Gweh!"

Yuki and the other filolials spread their wings and welcomed us back.

"They got that big in only two days?" asked Éclair.

"That's incredible. Hey, do you remember me?" Father asked Sakura.

Sakura gave a quick nod in response and then started to rub her head against Father's chest.

"Ahaha . . . You're a lot bigger, but you're just as cute as always."

Father was grinning and petting Sakura on the head. The scene was picture-perfect. The Father I knew almost never let himself be seen looking like that. I seared the image of him lovingly petting Sakura into my brain for safekeeping.

"What level are they now?" asked Éclair.

"Level 40, I say!"

"Level 40?! In only two days?!" she exclaimed.

"That was super quick. Is that normal?" Father asked.

"That's unbelievably fast!" said the emissary.

Éclair and the Siltvelt emissary seemed really surprised. But it was no lie, I say!

"Also, I brought you some souvenirs, Father!"

I showed Father the equipment drops and all of the materials on the wagon the filolials had been pulling. It was a pretty impressive catch for two days' work, if I say so myself!

"What is all of this?!" Father asked.

"That's the result of two days' work, I say! There was actually a lot more, but it wouldn't all fit on the wagon."

"Wow . . . There's tons of different materials here."

"Go ahead and absorb them into your shield."

"I have a feeling it's just going to keep telling me my level is too low or I haven't unlocked the appropriate tree, but okay. I'll just use the amounts needed to satisfy the conditions to unlock each shield," Father explained.

Father went about absorbing the different materials into his shield.

"I recommend you use this sword, Éclair," I suggested.

"I really wish you would learn to pronounce my name correctly, Mr. Kitamura. But where did you find a sword, anyway?"

"I'm sure it was one of those drop things. It's an ability of the heroes' weapons, right? You can get different equipment when you absorb monsters into your weapon," Father replied.

"That is correct!"

I'd gotten the sword when I defeated a monster deep in the mountains. It seemed appropriate for Éclair, so I gave it to her.

I think it was named Griffin Edge. Rather than a straight blade, it was shaped like a feather and had a sharp edge. I was sure she could still use it, though. Éclair took the blade, groaned, and looked it over carefully.

"It appears to be a very fine sword. I'm worried I won't be able to do it justice," she said.

"I also managed to secure some armor for you, Father!"

I showed Father the armor that I'd gotten when I defeated the huge griffin.

"Umm, thanks. It looks super heavy, though."

"Come now, Father. Lift your arms up. I'll help you put it on."

"Umm, yeah, okay."

I put the armor on Father. He fell forward like a sack of bricks.

"So . . . heavy . . ."

Oh? I guess his stats were still too low to equip the armor. Oh well. I took the armor off of him and put it back on the wagon.

"It appears we need to level you up a bit first."

"Y-yeah. I wouldn't want to waste the equipment you worked so hard to get," said Father.

"We have a lot more cargo now. I imagine we lost our tail when we teleported, but we should probably get going soon just to be safe," said Éclair.

"Understood! Come, everyone, on to the wagon! We're off, I say!"

"I'd really rather we turn it into a carriage first, but I guess that can wait until we've gotten a bit further away," mumbled Éclair.

Father and Éclair looked like they had decided to give up— what, I wasn't sure. They climbed onto the wagon, followed by the Siltvelt emissaries.

"Gweh!"

I climbed onto Yuki, who had assumed the leader role among the filolials, and I raised my spear into the air.

"And we're off, I say!"

"Gweh!"

The pitter-patter of the filolials' feet filled the air as they burst into motion, leaving nothing but a cloud of dust behind. We continued on our journey!

Chapter Eleven: Camping Out

It'd been half a day since we departed, carried by the filolials—Yuki, Kou, and Sakura. Our journey to Siltvelt was going smoothly so far.

"Ugh . . ."

"Are you okay, Eclair?" Father asked.

We'd just stopped at a riverbank and began setting up camp for the night. But Éclair and the Siltvelt emissaries had gotten dizzy from riding on the wagon and could barely even move. The filolials rode like a dream! I could imagine how trying to grasp the sheer bliss of it might make someone's head spin. It was an out-of-this-world experience.

"It truly is a mystery how you heroes manage to act normal after being shaken around like that," Éclair said with a groan.

I couldn't say I understood how she felt, though. The shaking of the filolials was the epitome of happiness! Feeling lightheaded was just a result of filolials being so intoxicating. Ha! Ha! Ha!

"I've never really had to deal with motion sickness," Father replied.

"Okay then, we'll camp here tonight, I say!"

"Alright. I guess I'll take care of cooking us a meal," Father offered.

"And I shall convert our wagon into a carriage!"

We laid Éclair and the Siltvelt emissaries on the riverbank to rest, built a fire, and then went to work.

"Gweh! Gweh!"

Yuki and the other filolials were playing happily on the riverbank. They'd been looking on excitedly when I first started converting the wagon, but they must have gotten bored. Watching them play warmed my soul.

"And then I'll add a bit of this . . ."

Father was in good spirits. He started to make some kind of stew in a big pot. It smelled fantastic. Drawn by the aroma, Yuki and the other filolials started making their way over to Father.

"You mustn't interfere with Father's cooking, I say!"

"Gweh!"

Yuki responded with a spirited squawk and the filolials all stood there drooling and watching Father eagerly. They were clearly hungry.

"Are they going to eat with us?" Father asked.

"They shall, indeed! Filolials are omnivorous, so these magnificent creatures will eat anything, I say!"

"Oh, really? I guess I'll need to make more then."

Before Father even finished speaking, he pulled some monster meat off of the wagon and began cutting it up. Oh! He must have been getting more comfortable with prepping, because his movements started to look just like those of the Father I remembered.

"There were some herbs in the materials you gathered, and I have some medicinal materials that I should be able to use for seasoning too," Father explained.

Father skillfully coated the meat in cooking spices and then began tying it up with cooking twine. I wondered what he was planning on making.

"There are really a bunch of steps that I'm skipping. It won't taste quite as good, but whatever," he went on.

He stacked some stones up in the form of a stove and built a fire at the bottom. It looked like a smoker. Was he going to smoke the meat?

"It's a really quick-and-dirty setup, but this will be a good way to preserve the meat too."

"Gweh!"

The filolials appeared to be nodding in response to Father's words.

"What else? Hey, Motoyasu, do you think you could slice through a boulder crosswise? It'd be great if you could make a thin slab for me," Father asked.

"Consider it done, I say!"

I found a big boulder on the riverbank and sliced it up to form a slab. Father took the slab and set up a table. No, that wasn't it. It was a stone griddle. He built another fire under the griddle and began grilling some meat on it.

"I guess that should do for now."

The smell of the meat grilling caught the attention of Éclair and the emissaries. They got up and came over, looking much livelier.

"I was able to do something a bit different this time, since Motoyasu brought so much stuff back with him. I used lots of seasonings. Try just sprinkling a bit of salt on and eating it like that."

"Wow!"

"Gweeeh!"

Everyone started gobbling up the food that Father had prepared.

"You really do have a knack for cooking, Mr. Iwatani!" said Éclair.

"All I did was grill some meat. That doesn't take any talent. This meat is really stringy, so it might be a bit difficult to chew. Wild game sure is difficult to cook."

"Well, it's far more delicious than anything we could make. I have no complaints," she replied.

Everyone went on chatting and eventually it started getting late. We set up shifts so that someone would always be on the lookout while the others slept. Thanks to my foolishness, Father had probably spent many nights like this the first time, before I got stuck in a time loop. The thought of it made me want to cry.

"Gwehhh . . ."

I was petting Yuki, fully aware that I had a ridiculously huge grin on my face. Filolials really were the greatest thing in existence, I say! Their very presence alone brought happiness and good fortune.

"I hear cracking noises every time the filolials move. Are they alright?" Father asked.

"They're fine, I say! That's the sound of their bodies developing."

"Are you saying they're still growing?!" asked Éclair.

She had been drifting off to sleep but sat up suddenly. What was she so surprised about? The answer to her question was obvious.

"They are, indeed! They have plenty of growing left to do, I say!"

"They must not be like the filolials I'm familiar with . . ."

"Filolials display a special pattern of development when raised by a hero," I explained.

"I-I see . . ."

Unable to hide her surprise, Éclair lay back down.

"Nothing really strikes me as odd anymore," Father whispered while petting Sakura.

There was nothing odd about it, I say! The filolials would complete their magnificent evolution into angels soon. How delightful! It seemed like Sakura had taken a real liking to Father. Nothing could be more heartwarming than that! Ha! Ha! Ha!

"Gweh . . ."

Father was sitting down, and Sakura laid her head on his lap. She began snoring and he petted her on the head lovingly. Was this how the Father I knew had treated filolials? My memories of the future were hazy and full of gaps, so I couldn't deny the possibility.

Hmm . . . I did seem to remember him looking really happy and petting something once, but I couldn't recall the details. I had a feeling big sis was involved, but . . . Surely it must have been a filolial! The memory was hazy, but I couldn't imagine anyone or anything other than a filolial being that important to someone!

"You ran a lot today. I'm sure you're exhausted. Thank you," Father soothed.

"Gweh . . . gweh . . ."

Father spoke to Sakura so fondly.

"I think you and the filolials should go out leveling tomorrow, I say!"

"You mean power-leveling, right? Do you think it's okay to do that here?"

"We lost our tail, so I'm sure it will be fine!"

"I see."

"I want you and the filolials to do your best!"

"Going on what you've said, I can imagine leveling up ridiculously quickly. It's kind of scary."

Father looked at Sakura and smiled. Ah, seeing the two of them like that made me start crying for some reason.

Oh, Filo-tan! Wherefore art thou? I was sure she was still but an egg, hidden away somewhere inside of that monster trainer's tent. When all of this was over—more specifically, once we had ensured Father's safety—I would go running to her, I say! I just needed her to wait a short while longer!

And so our night, spent on the riverbank with the filolials, wore on.

Morning came. We decided that Yuki, Sakura, Éclair, and one of the pigs would take Father out to level. I had other things to do and Kou would be coming with me as my transportation. Éclair climbed on Yuki's back, and Father mounted Sakura.

"Gweh!"

"Yeah, they've grown a lot," said Father.

"I'm guessing they're about fifty percent bigger than normal filolials. It feels like I'm really high up in the air," Éclair replied.

The two of them were mumbling. The Siltvelt emissary was helping me convert the wagon into a carriage. I'd gathered plenty of materials, so we probably had everything we needed.

I noticed the filolials had established their positioning, or something of a pecking order, amongst themselves. Yuki seemed to be the overall leader and gave Kou and Sakura their orders. Today, Yuki would take the lead to help protect Father.

Sakura would act as his personal bodyguard. They had only hatched several days prior, and yet they were already carefully coordinating. Filolials never ceased to amaze!

"Do your best, I say!"

"Gweh!"

I gave them a word of encouragement and Yuki saluted, as if to say, "Roger!" Sakura attempted to do the same, but she was being extra careful to avoid making any sudden movements so that Father wouldn't fall off her back.

"What are you going to do today, Motoyasu?" Father asked.

"I'm going to take care of some preparations for the filolials, I say!"

"Preparations? Is something going to happen?"

"It shall, indeed! If everything goes as expected, the filolials will become angels tonight!"

"Huh? Are they going to die?"

Father was standing there speechless with a sad look on his face.

"Well, I guess that's understandable considering how fast they've grown. Their lives are like an intense flame that burns brightly but only lasts for an instant," said Éclair.

"They did get this big in only three days, after all. That's too bad," Father replied.

He and Éclair were gazing at the filolials with sad looks on their faces.

"That's not it, I say!"

Father had apparently misunderstood. Death? That sure was a violent misinterpretation. And Éclair sure was rude! Had Father really been satisfied with her assessment?! My answer clearly needed further explanation!

"By angels, I meant that the filolials will literally take on the form of an angel. I must secure certain equipment to prepare for that."

"Oh, I see. I was really surprised for a moment there. What equipment?" asked Father.

"A machine that can turn magic power into clothing, I say!"

"Oh, I've heard of those. They're used in Siltvelt and Shieldfreeden to make clothes for demi-humans who have the ability to shapeshift," said Éclair.

She seemed to know what I was talking about.

"Let's just hope that they sell them in one of the towns around here," she said.

"I shall be searching the nearby towns!"

In the first world, I'd asked the monster trainer for advice and he told me about the equipment. He even ordered one of the machines for me. But that wasn't going to be possible in the current time loop. I would need to go to the nearby towns and look for a machine myself.

"Would you like me to help you secure the items you need?" asked the emissary.

"Can you do that?" I asked.

Come to think of it, Siltvelt was a country of demi-humans. There were probably a lot of shapeshifting demi-humans there too. The emissary had a lot of unique connections, so he just might prove helpful. I might even end up being able to make clothes far superior to those I'd made in Melromarc—splendid clothes that showed off the magnificence of the filolials perfectly! The thought of it made me giddy!

"That will give me an opportunity to reach out to our contacts back in Siltvelt as well, although I have already done so several times now," the emissary explained.

"Yeah. We really need to do something about these people chasing us. No matter how many of them we defeat, more just keep showing up. Things would be much less dangerous if we had the Siltvelt military protecting Mr. Iwatani," said Éclair.

Her words couldn't have been truer.

"We shouldn't have to worry about that quite so much if Father can make it through today, I say! Once he levels up a bit, it won't be so easy to hurt him."

"Y-yeah. I'll do my best."

"Yuki and Sakura, both of you be sure to protect Father!"

"Gweh!"

Yuki and Sakura lifted their wings and squawked energetically. The magnificent creatures were dependable *and* adorable!

"Then let the fun begin, I say!"

When I gave the signal, Yuki and Sakura squawked loudly one more time and launched into a sprint.

"Whoa! They're so fast!" Father exclaimed.

"I'm going to fall! Can't we go just a bit slow—" Éclair started to say.

I watched Yuki and Sakura sprint away into the distance with Father and Éclair on their backs. It was a glorious sight! Then I climbed into the makeshift carriage with the Siltvelt emissary.

"And we're off! To the nearest town, I say!"

"Gwehhh!"

I pulled on the reins and Kou broke out into a lively sprint. There was nothing quite like that exhilarating feeling of the wind on your face when flying along at breakneck speeds.

The Siltvelt emissary and I made our way to a nearby town. According to my map, it seemed to belong to a small country situated between Melromarc and Siltvelt. I'd been told there was no dragon hourglass there, unfortunately.

"Are you familiar with this country, Spear Hero?"

"I am not."

I only really knew about Melromarc, Faubrey, and Zeltoble. I'd stopped by several other places in my travels, but I had never been to this area, unfortunately. I might have gotten a hint or two if I tried to remember what I knew from my gaming, but Father had told me all about how knowledge from games couldn't be trusted. It would be best to go check things out with my own two eyes.

"I see. This country is rather weak due to its short history and small size. Since it's located in a region where there are frequent struggles between humans and demi-humans, Siltvelt and its enemy, Melromarc, fight over who controls it whenever the two countries are at war."

That made sense. So the country probably wasn't very well-off. That made me wonder if they had issues with food supplies. From what I could see, the place appeared to be rather desolate.

"Is it known for any specific products or anything?"

I figured if it was known for a certain food, I could take some back as a souvenir for Yuki and Sakura.

"None that I've ever heard of. The country's development was driven by trade, so it's a good place to buy products from other countries."

"Hmm . . ."

I bet that was it. Melromarc residents would purchase items that could only be found in Siltvelt via this country or something. So basically, it was a second-rate version of Zeltoble.

I thought back to my time gaming. Had there been a town in this area? Ah, yes, it was coming back to me. I recalled a town in the region that was where the locals—well, actually, it was more like a way station for travelers. It wasn't that there was nothing to do there, but the only thing of any note was a nearby dungeon. But this world wasn't a game, so I didn't need to go chasing dungeons. I could have gone and checked it out to try to get some rare items or equipment, but Father and the others didn't need any new equipment at the moment.

"Do you think they have equipment to turn magic power into clothes here?" I asked.

"I'm not sure, but I plan to inquire with my contact here," the emissary responded.

"Understood."

The emissary and I made our way to his contact's base of operations. Fortunately, it turned out we were able to acquire the equipment I needed.

"You'll need to have the thread woven into fabric. That will require a specialist," the contact told us.

"Indeed. Can I have that done in this town?" I asked.

"Yes, as long as you can pay, there is a shop that can produce the fabric in no time."

That would take care of everything I needed!

"Now I just need to get a sewing kit. I will take care of making the clothes once I have the fabric!"

"You're going to make the clothes yourself?" the emissary asked.

"Is there something strange about that?"

The emissary clearly had no idea who'd been in charge of sewing clothes for the filolials. Making clothes was my specialty, I say! With my aptitude for crafting things and an eye for style that I developed by looking at fashion magazines back in my world, this was the one thing I was proud to say I excelled at more than Father! I wasn't ashamed to admit that it was I, Motoyasu, who had handmade the filolials' clothing.

I'd also made a life-sized Filo-tan stuffed doll. It had turned out brilliantly, if I do say so myself. It was certainly worthy of sharing my bed with me every night, I say! Hm? That reminded me. There had been someone else skilled at sewing in Father's village. She'd declared me her rival when she saw how impressive the clothes I made were. But I couldn't recall her name or what she looked like. I could remember the clothes, but not the maker.

It didn't matter, anyway. This took care of the preparations for being able to produce clothing for the filolials. I decided to buy some large cloaks that I wouldn't mind getting torn. The filolials could make do with those until I finished making their clothes.

"Gw . . . Kweh!"

Kou completed the transformation to his filolial king form. He looked absolutely adorable! The Siltvelt emissary looked at him with a confused look on his face.

"He looks like . . . the filolial king . . . from the legends. He looks like the bird god."

"Indeed, that is what he is!"

"What?!"

The emissary stumbled over backward in surprise. What was he so shocked about?

"Filolials are all godly birds, I say!"

"Oh, yes. I'm sure they are."

"Kwehhh . . ."

I rubbed Kou on the front of his neck and thought about what to do next. I'd already gotten everything I needed. All that was left was to wait for Father and the others to return. Was there nothing else for us to do then? The Siltvelt emissary had been talking to his contact and suddenly furrowed his brow.

"What is it?" I asked.

"Oh, it's nothing. I've just been told that Melromarc has begun to exhibit some ominous behavior."

"They've already sent numerous assassins after us, I say!"

"They claim to have no involvement with that. But now they have issued a complaint to Siltvelt about the Shield Hero destroying a checkpoint tower on the border."

The nerve! It was them who had responded with hostility and attacked. I'd simply turned the tables on them and now they were trying to pick a fight over that. They were contemptible, through and through! If Father would have allowed it, I would've used my portal to infiltrate Melromarc and kill Trash and his minions right then and there, I say!

"The Siltvelt nobility is currently attending an international assembly called to address the issue of the waves. They are attempting to inform the fox of Melromarc of the truth."

"Does Siltvelt plan to invade and conquer Melromarc?"

"It would be a truly difficult feat to overcome the fox of Melromarc and the one they call His Excellency, the Wise. Any rash attempt to invade would not only draw the ire of the alliance, but potentially make an enemy of the whole world."

Trash still had some influence, it seemed. Indeed, I could remember the crimson swine bragging about Melromarc employing sly tactics to make a mockery of Siltvelt in the past.

"Just as you and the Shield Hero have said, protecting the world from the waves is what is truly important. I would like to think that Siltvelt understands that as well, but . . ."

"Ha! Ha! Ha! You need not worry, I say! For I, Motoyasu, shall defeat any and all enemies of Father's!"

"I don't doubt you're capable of that, having personally seen the extent of your power. However, the Siltvelt nobility has not, and so they are not confident in making a move. I would like to ask that you please remain patient for a while longer."

I guess there were troublesome formalities that needed to be taken care of.

"Furthermore, it's a fact that our country is in turmoil due to the waves. Just as the legends say, we must assist the Shield Hero in fighting against them."

"You're right. Addressing that issue is more important than starting a war, I say!"

"Our foremost priority is to deliver the Shield Hero to Siltvelt safely. The country's nobility will decide what happens after that."

The emissary clenched his fist as he spoke.

"Is there anything else we need to do here?" I asked.

"I've finished my business here. However . . ."

The emissary glanced over toward the shadows cast by a nearby building. I felt like I could sense the presence of someone hiding there.

"Should I go and take care of them?" I asked.

"We can't be certain it's a Melromarc assassin, so we should let them go for now. We're slowly gathering more and more supporters, in any case."

"Understood. Then I shall return us to the place where we split up with the others, I say! Portal Spear!"

I used my portal to teleport us and shake our tail and then waited for Father's return.

"We're back!"

"Kweh!"

It was just before sunset. I was waiting at the riverbank where we'd decided to meet back up when Father and the others finally returned. It looked like Yuki and Sakura had both completed the transformations into their filolial queen forms.

"So umm, their appearances suddenly changed in the middle of leveling, but that's okay, right?" Father asked.

"It is, indeed! In fact, to say that this is their true form wouldn't be an overstatement."

"Oh, really? I guess it's kind of like how monsters can evolve in some monster tamer games," Father said.

Father climbed down off Sakura as we continued chatting. As soon as he was off, he started rubbing the inside of his thighs, like they were sore.

"Man . . . My thighs were rubbing the whole time. That's really tough when you're not used to riding."

"Would you like me to cast some healing magic on your legs?" I asked.

"Oh, no, I'll be fine. I had the Siltvelt emissary use some on me earlier."

"Oh really?"

The Siltvelt pig tumbled off of Yuki and fell on the ground. Éclair was covering her mouth with one hand and leaning on Yuki for support. All of the color had drained from her face.

"N-no more . . ." she mumbled.

She then fell to her knees with a thud. She looked like she was on the verge of death.

"We were gaining experience at an incredible rate, and all we had to do was watch the filolials plow through monsters. But

I can't endure any more of this," she said.

"Yeah, I can't say it was a very comfortable ride," Father replied.

"You're not normal, Mr. Iwatani. I don't see how you can be unfazed by that ride," Éclair said.

"What can I say?"

Father was scratching his head awkwardly. It was only natural he would be unfazed, I say! Father had raised Filo-tan. He was like the head of the filolials. He wasn't the kind of weakling that would be bothered by a bit of shaking, I say!

"How were the fruits of war today?" I asked.

"We made pretty good progress, I think. I'm level 28 now. Isn't that incredible? Éclair and the emissary said they leveled up a bit too."

"That's excellent. I'd like to get your level a bit higher, if possible, though!"

"Yeah, but I should probably work on powering up my shield and stuff too, right?"

"I suppose you're right."

Come to think of it, I needed to take Father to the weapon shop in town. If he didn't copy more weapons, he was going to have a hard time building up his collection of equipment.

"Hey, Motoyasu. Is it okay if I go ahead and power up a shield I can already use?"

"No problem at all, I say! If you need any materials, I'll get them for you. We won't have to worry about assassins nearly as much once you raise your defense, after all."

"Thanks. Alright, then I'll go ahead and work on powering up a shield I can use that seems to have good stats."

There was no guarantee the weapon shop in that town would have a good selection of shields. Father probably wouldn't be able to use "awakening" yet. That was Ren's power-up method. He would probably be trying to implement some of Itsuki's and my power-up methods, such as refinement, spirit enchants, item enchants, or the job gauge. That alone would be enough to allow him to withstand attacks from the average adventurer or soldier.

"You've finally grown a bit stronger, Father."

"I'm still nowhere near as strong as you, of course. I can't use magic at all, either. I need to unlock some skills."

"It's still a big step forward, I say!"

"Yeah. I feel like I've suddenly grown incredibly strong, even though I know that's not true."

I wanted to get Father to level 40 by sometime tomorrow. I tweaked the filolials' stats to make some small improvements, and then we all decided to head to town to find an inn. We laid Éclair and the pig down in the carriage to rest and made our way to a different town than the one I'd gone to earlier that day.

Father sighed.

"It'll be nice if we can finally spend some time just relaxing today," he said.

He was sitting on the bed in our room at the inn and complaining. It was true that we'd had a hectic past few days, constantly being chased by assassins.

Judging from its appearance, this town seemed quieter than the one we'd stayed at previously. There probably weren't any groups of thugs here that would be attacking the inn out of nowhere. Still, we had a bodyguard hired by Siltvelt standing guard out front. I wondered if the bodyguard would accompany Father tomorrow. Éclair and the pig were in their room asleep. The emissary had gone out to buy some medicine. He said their motion sickness had been so bad that they needed medical treatment. Either way, Yuki and Sakura would be plenty of protection for now.

"Okay, I'm going out to the inn's stable," I said.

"Huh? You're not going to sleep in the room?" Father asked.

"My work for the day is not done, I say!"

"What are you going to do?"

"I should probably take you to see for yourself this time."

I took Father out to the inn stable. The filolials were waiting there restlessly.

"Sorry to keep you waiting!" I told them.

"Kweh!"

They squawked cheerfully when they noticed I'd arrived. As a reward for their hard work that day, I fed them some of the meat Father had smoked.

"So what were you going to show me?"

"It should happen any moment now."

The filolials were squawking excitedly. I turned to them and whispered.

"I believe you should be able to turn into angels any time now, my lovely filolials. Please show Father your new form."

They looked at each other and then stood tall and . . . they began to transform.

"Huh?"

There was a faint glow as the filolials transformed into their angel forms. Father was looking on speechless.

The colors of their feathers, when they had been in their filolial forms, coincided with the colors of their hair and the wings on their backs. They were all around the same size. No, wait. Yuki seemed to be a bit taller than the others. She had a look of determination on her face that gave her an air of authority. Kou gave off an impression of being a young man full of curiosity. And Sakura . . . She seemed to be the happy-go-lucky type, I guess. Something about her made her look a bit drowsy.

"Motoyasu!"

"Motoyasuuuu!"

"That's me, I say!"

They each called out my name. Well, aside from Kou. They

were all so adorable! Father was opening and closing his mouth, but nothing was coming out.

"I mean . . . You told me it would happen. But seeing it with my own eyes still blew me away. It makes me want to go tell Eclair all about it," he finally said.

"Éclair is off in la-la land. She probably wouldn't even be listening," I told him.

"Yeah. That's true. But 'la-la land'? She has motion sickness is all."

"Naofumiiiii!"

Sakura turned and ran over to Father.

"You must be Sakura."

"Yup! I'm Sakuraaa!"

Sakura hugged Father. She was completely nude, aside from the lush, pink hair flowing over her shoulders.

"Whoa!"

Father's eyes opened wide. He hugged Sakura back and petted her on the head. Sakura looked up at him and grinned.

"Tee hee hee!"

"This is the first time we've gotten to talk like this, isn't it?" Father said.

"Yup. But you know, I've wanted to talk to you ever since I first met you! Thank you for always petting my head!"

"Oh, umm, sure."

Father was glancing off in the other direction, like he wasn't sure where to look.

"Are you not going to have them wear clothes, Motoyasu?" he asked.

"That's what I procured that equipment for, I say! Come now, my lovely filolials! There's a tool here that we'll use to make your clothes. I need you to turn the handle."

"But whyyy?"

"Because wearing clothes will make all of you even more attractive, I say!"

"Does that mean I should wear clothes, Motoyasu?" asked Yuki.

"I don't mind being naked!" exclaimed Kou.

"That's not an option!" Father shouted.

"Do you want me to wear clothes, Naofumi?" Sakura asked.

She loved getting attention. Seeing her act so intimate with Father reminded me of Filo-tan. But her hair and eyes were a different color than Filo-tan's. She acted rather laid-back, and even her movements were somewhat sluggish. Her hair was wound up in the shape of a flower in one spot on the side of her head. It was attractive, but the texture of her hair wasn't quite the same as Filo's. Sakura's defining characteristic was that all of the little details fell just short of Filo-tan.

"Umm, yeah. I think it would be good if you wore clothes."

Sakura nodded in response to Father's answer.

"Okay, then I'll wear clooothes!"

"I'll go first, then," said Yuki.

"Huh?! But I wanna go fiiirst!" Sakura replied.

"You'll wait your turn," said Yuki.

"Boooo!"

Yuki made Sakura wait. She clearly held the role of leader.

"Hm?"

Kou was just standing there. I realized he still hadn't called me by my name. I walked over to him and gave him a gentle smile. And then he said it.

"Kitamura."

"That's me, I say!"

"Umm . . . Why's he calling you by your last name?" Father asked.

Kou grabbed the handle of the machine while we were talking and started turning it before Yuki could.

"Ahahaha! This is fun!" he said.

"Hey! No one told you to turn the handle, Kou!" shouted Yuki.

She scolded him. The whole scene made me chuckle.

"If they look like that, then I guess they can sleep in the room with us now, right?" asked Father.

"I suppose so," I said.

After making sure that the thread was being spun correctly, I had the three of them put on some pajamas for the time being.

"Listen up, you three. You be good little filolials and sleep in Father's room. It's your job to keep him safe, I say!"

"We know that," Yuki replied.

She sure was clever.

"Yup. I wanna sleep with Naofumi toooo!"

"Alright. You can sleep with me as long as you behave yourself."

"Yaaay!"

Sakura hopped up and down excitedly and Father petted her on the head. I remembered he was good with children. My original filolials had been very fond of him too. I could remember him sleeping soundly once while he was surrounded by a bunch of filolials that were practically screaming.

Kou was turning the handle of the machine quickly and it spun his magic power into thread. Yuki went next. The way she turned the handle looked very graceful. The filolials were full of personality, and the differences showed even when doing something like spinning thread.

"Now then, Sakura, you're next," said Yuki.

"Okaaay!"

Sakura grasped the handle of the machine and began to turn it. But she moved at a languid pace and turned it very slowly.

"Sakura, are you not going to turn it any faster than that?" asked Yuki.

"Huh?"

Sakura looked over at Father.

"Do yooouuu want me to turn it faster, Naofumi?"

"It's not like it really takes that long. Turn it however fast you like."

"Reeeaally? Okay, I'm gonna turn it slooow then."

Sakura began spinning her thread again. Kou sighed.

"I'm getting sleepy," he said.

"I'm tired too," Yuki agreed.

Sakura went on spinning her thread. Yuki and Kou started yawning a lot and kept complaining about how tired they were. Father motioned to me to go ahead and take them back to the room, so I told them to come with me.

"I'll leave Sakura's thread here once she's done spinning it. You three go ahead and get some sleep while we finish up."

"Understood. Sakura, if anything happens, it's up to you to protect Father, I say!"

"Gooot iiiit!"

Sakura seemed to be having fun spinning her thread. She was alternating between turning the handle slowly and quickly, like it was a game. Father was watching her with a warm look in his eyes.

"Okay, we're heading back to the room, I say!"

Seeing the two of them like that made me feel all warm and fuzzy inside. I took Yuki and Kou back to the room and we went to bed.

Sakura

Filolial

A filolial that hatched from a cheap egg. She is happy-go-lucky and loves to receive attention. She reminds Motoyasu of Filo-tan more than any of the other filolials.

Yuki

Filolial

One of Motoyasu's filolials. As a thoroughbred, she is worth more than most filolials. Her innate dignity and strong sense of responsibility helped establish her authoritative position among Motoyasu's filolials.

Kou

Filolial

One of Motoyasu's filolials. Like Sakura, he's just an average filolial that hatched from an egg thrown in as a bonus when Motoyasu bought Yuki. He's intensely curious, innocent, and loves to eat. He can also tend to be a bit slow to catch on at times.

Chapter Twelve: Finesse

It was the following morning.

"So hot . . ."

The sound of Father groaning uncomfortably woke me up. I sat up to find Yuki and Kou snuggled up against me, snoring. Where was Sakura? I turned toward Father to see her in her filolial queen form—her wings wrapped around him. I'd woken Yuki and Kou when I sat up, and they were both blinking their eyes.

"Good morning, Motoyasu."

"Morning, Kitamura."

Yuki and Kou greeted me. It was turning out to be a fine morning!

"I wonder how late Father and Sakura stayed up spinning thread," I mumbled.

I climbed out of the bed and looked over at Father and Sakura. Father was talking in his sleep and complaining about how hot he was. Sakura was still fast asleep and breathing deeply.

"Ugh . . . So hot . . ." Father groaned again.

Father finally woke up and realized what was going on.

"S-Sakura, didn't Motoyasu tell you not to do that?" Father scolded gently.

The floor was making creaking sounds, but I was sure it would be fine!

"Buuut . . ." Sakura started.

"Sakura! It's about time you got up!" Yuki snapped.

"Aww . . ."

When Yuki scolded her, Sakura slowly opened her eyes and yawned. She hugged Father from behind and rubbed her cheek up against his.

"Good mooorning, Naofumiii!"

"Good morning to you too. Being in that form is going to cause trouble for the people around you. You need to change back to your angel form."

"Aww . . . Fiiine," she grumbled.

Sakura did just as Father told her and returned to her angel form. She had obeyed Father! Learning to do that was part of my filolials' education, I say!

"Is this better, Naofumi?"

"Yeah. That's better."

"Can we sleep together again?"

"I was a little bit hotter than I would have liked, but . . . I guess so, as long as we're sleeping outside. Otherwise you're liable to end up falling through the inn floor."

"Okaaay! I can't wait!"

"Ha! Ha! Ha! You sure like Father, don't you, Sakura?" I said.

"Yup! You told me to protect Naofumi, so I'm going to do my beeessst!"

Her spirit was truly admirable! It moved me to tears! I could rest easy knowing that Sakura would be protecting Father. After chatting for a bit longer, Father got up and left the room. He walked over to the room next to ours and knocked on the door.

"Eclair? How are you feeling?" he asked.

He went inside, so I followed him. Éclair had been snoring quietly, but she woke up when we came in.

"Huh? Oh, it's you, Mr. Iwatani."

"How are you? Can you stand?"

"I think . . . I should be fine, now."

I looked over at the Siltvelt emissary and his pigs. They'd woken up too and were looking over at us. But they weren't looking at me or Father. They were looking at Yuki and the other filolials.

"Who are they?" the emissary asked.

"They're angels, I say!"

"You're really terrible at explaining things, Motoyasu. Just stay quiet for a minute and let me explain," said Father.

"Understood!"

I followed Father's orders and took a step back. All I had to do was zip my lips. That was easy enough! Father placed his hand on Sakura's shoulder and began to speak.

"So umm, these three are the filolials that Motoyasu has

been raising. Things would get messy if they transformed here in the room, so you'll have to wait until later to see for yourself. You'll just have to trust me for now."

"What?!"

Éclair yelped in surprise and her voice cracked. The emissaries were shocked too. I guess I could understand. I'd sputtered out some kind of nonsensical sound the first time I saw Filo-tan transform too. And then immediately after, I felt a powerful impact race through my body. It felt like it would last forever. Thinking back on it now, I was certain that encounter had been destiny! Just recalling the incident sent a sharp pain racing through my lower body.

"I know it's hard to believe, but we can show you firsthand soon," I told them.

"U-understood," Éclair replied.

"Alright, everyone, introduce yourselves," Father told the filolials.

The three of them stepped forward and bowed.

"I'm Yuki."

"I'm Kou!"

"I'm Sakuraaa!"

"So they can speak too. The surprises just keep coming," Éclair said.

Once again, Éclair was being rude. Did she think Father looked like the kind of scum that would tell lies? Ha! Ha! Ha!

Father told no lies! Technically speaking, anyway.

"W-well then, we should start getting ready for the day ahead," said the Siltvelt emissary, trying to appear calm as he hobbled off.

After that, we all went to eat breakfast at the tavern next to the inn. We ordered a massive amount of food and everyone ate together. The filolials were all stuffing their faces.

"You three sure eat a lot," Father said.

"Perhaps, but compared to your cooking, the flavor of the food here is slightly inferior. Right, Kou?" Yuki replied.

"Yeah, I think so."

"The food you make is better than this, Naofumi!" Sakura added.

The mountain of food we'd ordered disappeared in a flash. Seeing the way filolials ate always put me in such good spirits!

"This doesn't bode well for our food expenses," Éclair whispered with a perplexed look on her face.

"If it becomes a problem, we can just have Motoyasu and the filolials gather food supplies, I'm sure. Or we could sell off some materials, I guess," Father replied.

"We could definitely do that. We should sell those materials in the carriage to the vendor in town here," said Éclair.

"You think so? Alright, how about I go do that before we leave, to help cover our travel expenses? Haggling is a specialty of mine."

That reminded me. I remembered Father mentioning earning quite a bit from his peddling operations. He had the slaves from that fantastic village of his helping with the operations too. He'd taught them his secrets to getting people to pay handsomely.

"In that case, we'll leave it up to you, Mr. Iwatani," Éclair said.

"Alright. Oh, we didn't even ask Motoyasu. What do you want to do today, Motoyasu? Those people chasing us are probably going to start showing up soon, I'm guessing."

"I'd like to spend a bit more time in this area leveling you. If we get you strong enough, we won't have to worry about assassins anymore, I say!"

"Alright. Then we can go level after I've gotten us some money."

"Ugh . . ." Éclair moaned.

Her face turned pale.

"Are you okay, Eclair? I can just go with the filolials if it's a problem."

"Th-that's unacceptable. Protecting you is the whole reason we're here."

"Yeah, but still . . ."

Father was worried about Éclair. Was it because of the motion sickness?

"People can get used to anything, I say!"

"Y-yeah, I suppose you're right. If we don't get used to it now, we're liable to spend the whole trip sick," she conceded.

The Siltvelt emissary was looking back and forth at me and the pig.

"Oink!"

"I'll go with the Shield Hero this time. You can accompany the Spear Hero instead," he told the pig.

I'd gotten sick too at first. But in the end, riding was more blissful time spent with the filolials. My body got used to it over time, and I stopped getting sick. Ah, I wanted to be able to get sick riding a carriage pulled by filolials again!

"What do you plan to do, Motoyasu?" Father asked.

"I'm going to take the thread, spun from the filolials' magic power, into town to have it woven into fabric. After that, I'll probably use any spare time left over to gather materials for you to power up your shield."

"I don't believe it will take long to have the fabric woven," said the emissary.

"In that case, I could take the filolials' measurements and go ahead and make their clothes."

If I had some spare time, I could use it to make clothes for Yuki and the other filolials. We could always just buy any materials Father needed to power up his weapon, after all.

"Alright, so Motoyasu will be making clothes for the filolials today, I guess. Although we could also just have that done at a clothing shop—or would that be a tailor?" Father asked.

"Don't be ridiculous! It is I who shall make the clothes, I say!"

Sewing clothes for the filolials was my lifework! Without that, I would have no way to express my love for them. Filolials were the greatest creatures of all! To have them wear clothes that I'd poured my heart and soul into . . . Nothing could make me happier, I say!

"Oh, umm, I see. Alright, you're making clothes today, then."

"Indeed!"

My work for the day was decided. I would have the thread the filolials spun woven into fabric and then I'd make their clothes! I took the filolials' measurements before they departed. We'd found out previously that the sizes didn't need to be exact, since the thread was made out of magic power. There would be some leeway even after the clothes were finished.

"This one is worth more than that!" Father snapped.

"Grr . . . Fine! But this is as high as I can go!"

"It's a deal!"

Father was at the vendor's shop in town haggling over prices. This region was outside of Melromarc's jurisdiction, so they conducted trade with Siltvelt here too. The Siltvelt emissary had intervened to help Father assess market values, and a fierce battle to determine the purchase price had followed. Father's eyes seemed to be sparkling.

"You're really something, Mr. Iwatani. You got twice the market value!" Éclair said, showering Father with praise.

"I feel like I could have gotten him to raise the price a bit more if I'd stuck around, but I didn't want to waste too much time. Besides, I ended up buying the materials I needed to power up my shield from him, so we didn't actually make that much profit," Father explained.

"Being a hero makes you naturally good at all kinds of things, I guess," Éclair said.

"That's not it. I'm just really good at this kind of thing, personally, is all. Plus, I couldn't have pulled that off if the emissary hadn't told me the market values."

"You're really something, Naofumi."

Right? Right?! Father was exceptional at handling money. Case in point, he'd taken care of supplying everything from food to work for the filolials I'd brought to his village of slaves. I'd been planning on squeezing out the money for food expenses by defeating monsters and selling the materials and meat, but I quickly came to understand that leaving things to Father was the solution to all problems.

"I'm sure there will be people looking to buy items that the Shield Hero sold, so I don't think the vendor got a bad deal either," said the emissary.

"Yeah, I got that impression. I only raised the price because he didn't look like he minded too much. We both profited, so I think it was a good transaction all in all."

"I guess you can't survive without being skilled at trade in that alternate universe of yours—that country you call Japan. That's definitely a world I've never experienced," said Éclair.

"That's not exactly true. I, uhh, just like doing this kind of thing is all," Father replied.

"Hmph . . . Judging from what I've seen so far, you seem to excel at helping others out, Mr. Iwatani."

"Really? You think so? I got the best part of the deal, you know. Not to mention, I've just been letting Motoyasu and Sakura do everything for me. It's a bummer that this is all I can really do to give something back."

"Mr. Iwatani, modesty can start to sound like sarcasm if you're not careful. Anyway, I feel like I've gotten a better idea of what kind of person you are now," she continued.

Éclair was nodding confidently for some reason. I seemed to remember she was always trying to mimic Father in the future. That was a good attitude to have!

"You're right on the mark, I say! I've heard the finesse with which Father would strip bandits of everything they owned was truly awe-inspiring!"

Father and Éclair both turned their heads in my direction, moving so slowly that I almost expected to hear a loud, drawn-out creaking noise, like a rusty, old metal door might make.

"What?! Would you really go that far, Mr. Iwatani?!" Éclair exclaimed.

"How should I know?! And what the hell?! What's up with the sudden public exposure of my barbaric acts?!"

Oh? Father seemed to have gotten upset all of a sudden. Whenever something like this happened in the future, I seemed to remember Father ignoring the admonitions of big sis and responding with the dignity of a champion, brimming with confidence!

"Motoyasu!" he shouted.

"Let's see. 'Bandits are a resource! If you release them without killing them, you'll be able to reap the harvest again in no time.' I believe those were your words, or so I was told."

"Mr. Iwatani!" Éclair shouted.

"Just what in the world was future me up to?!" he asked.

Oh? The two of them seemed to be getting even more excited. I wasn't sure why.

"You were working slaves like horses, I do believe."

"Yeah, you told me about that. But letting bandits go free? What's the idea behind that? Wouldn't those bandits have caused problems for others?"

"I believe you said that even if you took the bandits into custody, other bandits would just take over and nothing would actually change in the end."

Éclair covered her face with her hands and shook her head in disappointment.

"I can't imagine Mr. Kitamura would be lying to you, Mr.

Iwatani. Seeing the kind of person you are now, I can't even begin to fathom the hellish future you must have gone through to make you say things like that. On the contrary, I feel like I should take this chance to apologize, assuming it was my own country's fault that you ended up so warped," she said.

"And besides, are there really that many bandits in this world?! What a mess!" he replied.

"Indeed. More kept showing up, no matter how many we disposed of," I said.

"'There are more thieves in this world than there are grains of sand on the seashore.' Those are words supposedly whispered by a past hero who tried to eliminate the bandits. While I can't help but be disappointed, I have a feeling we've also been given a glimpse of the resolute strength of your future self, Mr. Iwatani. You must have gone through a lot."

"I don't want to go through a lot!"

Father seemed flustered now and started moaning. I guess I could understand. Before awakening to my destiny as the Love Hunter, I tended to interpret everything in a positive light. On top of that, I even looked down on Father's actions. Sheesh, it was disgusting how much of a fool I was!

"In the end, you collaborated with some merchants to rear your own bandit protégé and started pulling the strings from behind the scenes, I believe," I went on.

"That sounds more like an evil overlord than a hero . . ." Father muttered.

"Well, the Church of the Three Heroes calls you names like that and Shield Demon, but if they're the ones that make you that way, then they really are beyond all help," Éclair groaned.

"I mean, I've read stories where things like that happened, but I really don't want to become one of them," he said.

"But they say that, ultimately, it made things difficult for the bandits and so they ended up dwindling off. You only had your bandits attack crooked merchants, who were inhumane or broke the rules, supposedly," I explained.

"So he was manipulating the corrupt to improve public security. I will admit that is impressive, but it's also the kind of thing I don't want to find myself sympathizing with," Éclair said.

Éclair was such a straight arrow.

"But Éclair, I seem to remember the future you doing her best to learn from Father and other leaders of Melromarc, in order to become a better governor," I retorted.

"You're saying I was trying to learn from advice and behavior like that? I find that hard to believe."

"Yeah, with behavior like that, I wouldn't even be able to argue if someone called me an evil overlord who reared bandit protégés," Father said.

Father nodded as if he agreed with Éclair. But he'd pulled off the incredible feat of getting the bandits under control, I say!

"So I guess your goal really is to become a governor after things settle down, then?" Father asked Éclair.

"Yeah, I suppose it is. I would like to continue in my late father's footsteps and develop a truly great territory."

"I hope you do. I'll be rooting for you."

"Thanks. And I'll be praying that you don't turn out like future you did, Mr. Iwatani."

"Wait a second. Motoyasu, you said you're stuck here in this world in a time loop, right? What about the butterfly effect, the grandfather paradox, and all of that? Aren't things supposed to try to return to the original timeline?" Father asked.

"Is that how it works? I guess that means you'll be going through hell before long . . ." Éclair replied.

"That would suck! Are you telling me I'm going to end up homeless or get tossed out penniless?" he asked.

Father looked over at the Siltvelt emissaries with fear in his eyes. Butterfly effect? I'd seen the term in some science fiction story or something once. Unfortunately, I'd only been interested in online games and pigs back then, so I wasn't familiar with the details.

"Shield Hero! Please rest assured that we will let nothing of the sort happen to you! No matter what!" the emissary said.

"Hmm? Is something wrong, Naofumi?" Sakura asked.

She was standing there confused, unable to grasp the situation.

"Naofumi will go through a terrible experience in the near future and end up being the kind of person who commits hideously evil deeds without a second thought," Yuki explained to the confused Sakura.

"Iwatani the villain!" shouted Kou.

"Yes, he's going to become a villain," Yuki replied.

"Oh really? But I'm still going to protect him. I won't abandon you, Naofumi," Sakura said diligently.

"I'm not going to become a villain! I'd never do those things," he denied.

"Bandit hunting, I say! It's a fantastic way of getting your hands on some money!"

I too had learned the value of hunting bandits to make money. If things went well, it could be even more lucrative than completing subpar job requests. The fact that you didn't have to worry about things like reputation and annoying social constraints was another advantage over those job requests.

"Are we going to hunt bandits? Do those taste good?" Kou asked.

"We're not! Stop saying weird things, Motoyasu! And people are not something you eat, Kou!" Father snapped.

"This conversation could give the filolials all kinds of wrong ideas," said Éclair.

Things were starting to get noisy. Things were starting to get exciting! I was standing there watching them and thinking to myself when Father suddenly addressed me.

"Don't just stand there looking like this has nothing to do with you, Motoyasu!" he said.

"Hold on. If that's how you act in the future . . . Mr. Kitamura's behavior suddenly makes a lot more sense," said Éclair.

"Don't just accept it so easily like that! I don't want to become a villain!" Father shouted.

His voice echoed throughout the whole surrounding area.

"This sucks! I don't want to experience anything like that . . ." he went on.

"Then you just need to get strong enough so that you won't have to, Mr. Iwatani," Éclair added.

"Y-yeah, you're right," Father replied.

After the fuss died down, we decided that Father would take all three filolials and go hunting. I was going to stay in town and make the filolials' clothes.

"Off you go, then!" I shouted.

"We'll be back!" Yuki called back.

"Whoa! Run a bit slower, please! Otherwise, I'm going to—" Éclair began.

"Th-the feathers are grabbing my hand! They . . . They won't let go! Shield Hero!" the emissary called out.

Éclair and the Siltvelt emissary were whining again. They just needed to get used to it. They might not level up, but they would gain experience fighting. They would develop a better understanding of how to operate more efficiently on the battlefield.

Watching the filolials get stronger by the day sure did warm my heart!

"Naofumi, let's goooo!" Sakura exclaimed.

"Umm, yeah, okay."

"Don't worry! I'll protect you no matter what!"

"Thanks, Sakura."

"Tee hee hee!"

Father and Sakura really did get along well.

"Alright, we'll be back later."

"Be careful, I say!"

"We will. I'll do my best to get stronger so that I can protect everyone—like the Shield Hero is supposed to—instead of always relying on you to protect me."

Father waved at me and then he and Sakura left.

Now, then! I was able to pick up the fabric made from the filolials' magic power, before we departed. I took the fabric and returned to our room at the inn. I needed to make three outfits. I would start by deciding on the colors and dyeing the fabric. I had more than enough dyes, so I'd have no problem making clothes that would look great on the filolials, I say!

I was fired up! Excitement level: MAX!

Finally! It was just past noon, I think.

"And they're done, I say!"

I'd finished so quickly that even I wanted to give myself a pat on the back. The clothes were complete, and they were going to look great on the filolials! All filolials looked great in one-piece outfits. But a good design was more than fancy details—the basic elements were important too.

Yuki had white hair, so I'd made a beige one-piece dress for her. I went with overalls for Kou, since they would be easy to move around in. Plus, that's what he'd asked for. The dark blue denim color was sure to look fantastic on him! I made Sakura a pea-green one-piece dress since she got along so well with Father. Imagining the filolials all wearing their new clothes filled me with immense happiness. That said, I didn't have anything left to do now that I'd finished making their clothes.

I looked out the window. When I did, I caught a glimpse of someone hiding in the shadows of the building. There seemed to be more of them now. I had a bad feeling about this. I put the filolials' clothes away in my bags, and then I heard the clatter of footsteps. A large crowd of people had gathered outside of the inn.

"Spear Hero!"

The brawny demi-human who was in charge of security at the inn came running in.

"What is it?" I asked.

"A crowd of what seems to be members of the Church of the Three Heroes has gathered outside. It's not safe for you here. The Shield Hero could also be in danger!"

"Right, you are!"

As we were talking, I felt highly concentrated magic begin to fill the air around us. I remembered Father saying he wanted me to protect everyone, so I opened the door and thrust the demi-human down onto the floor. At the very same moment, there was a loud roar and a massive boulder came rushing down toward us from up in the sky above the inn. If I didn't do something, the inn would be completely destroyed!

"Hmph!"

I stopped the huge rock hurtling toward us with my spear.

"Wh . . . wh-wha . . ."

The demi-human guard lying on the floor was at a loss for words. I was pretty sure not only him but the owner and workers were also still in the inn. What a pain. But I was going to try to keep casualties to a minimum, since that's what Father had told me to do.

"Brionac!"

I fired Brionac at the huge rock and turned it to dust. The second floor of the inn had been halfway destroyed. I stood in the rubble, glaring at the culprits. It was safe to assume that they were members of the Church of the Three Heroes.

Judging from their numbers, they must have cast the

cooperative magic spell Megalith. If there had been enough of them, they could have cast ceremonial magic, but a smaller crowd would be forced to use cooperative magic. Fewer people meant that the spell would be less powerful. I might've had to worry if it'd been someone like big sis's big sis casting the spell, but with riffraff like this, blasting their attack out of the sky was a breeze.

> **Big Sis's Big Sis**
>
> This refers to Sadeena, who is kind of like Raphtalia's adopted big sister. She's a therianthrope who can transform into a killer whale. She usually runs around in her demi-human form messing around and never taking anything seriously. Her specialty is using electricity-type magic and a harpoon to attack. She's easily one of the most powerful among my companions.
>
> She loves alcohol and is a real drunkard. She tends to have a devil-may-care attitude, but she's also a real force when she gets serious. I find myself relying on her often. She'd also lived in the same village that Raphtalia grew up in, and she went searching for the villagers after the village was destroyed and everyone got split up.

But still, could they be any more reckless? Once they realized they couldn't kill me, they all started to run away. These embers needed stomping! If I hadn't finished making the filolials' clothes as quickly as I had, the clothes might have ended up getting torn! On top of that, if they were attacking me, that meant assassins had probably been sent after Father too. Absolutely unforgivable! I'd make them pay for their foolishness with their lives, I say!

"Aiming Lancer X!"

Multi-target lock-on! I selected all of the imbeciles that had just been standing outside the inn. The fools were trying to escape into the crowd of onlookers that had gathered to see what the commotion was about. But there was no escaping from Aiming Lancer, I say!

Fire! I hurled my spear and it split into multiple beams of light that impaled all of the church members who'd attacked the inn with their magic.

"Ahhh!"

Some of the onlookers screamed, but I hadn't harmed anyone other than the culprits. I wasn't going to drag anyone into this who wasn't already involved. Just like I'd promised Filo-tan, I would be honest and kind to all, and I would obey Father's wishes! I would become the Love Hunter, I say!

And so, obviously, I slaughtered every last one of the fools that dared defy Father. Ha! Ha! Ha! Evil would never thrive in this world, I say!

"My spear touches none but demons and devils, I say!"

"I-in . . . incredible. The gods truly have returned," the demi-human guard whispered.

I couldn't have him calling me a god after doing something as piddling as this. It was Father who was the godlike one, after all! And Filo-tan was an angel that dwelled in the heavens, I say! They were a supreme god and angel, and I, Motoyasu, would annihilate any scum that attempted to defile their names! But right now, making sure Father was safe probably should have been my first priority.

"It seems the assassins have completely caught up with us. I have a feeling this will make meeting back up with Father and the others a real pain," I said.

Sheesh. If Father would have allowed it, I would've gone and killed Trash and the high priest of the Church of the Three Heroes right then and there, I say! I made my way out of the half-destroyed inn and started thinking things over.

The fact that I'd been attacked meant that it was possible something had happened to Father and the others too. I felt like I'd taken all the necessary precautions, but it was probably best if I hurried and went after them anyway. I'd leave a message with the demi-human who had been guarding the inn, just in case.

The scum hadn't been able to harm me, but I was worried about Father. Thoughts about the incident from the previous cycle of the time loop started to creep into the back of my mind. I imagined those knights with church ties smirking and torturing Father at the Melromarc border. I was sure that's how it had been.

"Save me! Motoyasu!"

I could practically hear Father crying and calling out for me to save him. Oh? I thought I saw the Father from the first time around waving his hand dismissively, with a look on his face that said "no way." I'm sure it was just my imagination!

I had to protect Father's life no matter what!

"I'm going after Father now. If we happen to miss each other and he shows up back here, can you to tell him to meet me in the next town?" I asked the demi-human guard.

"O-of course!"

I left the town and started following the filolial tracks in search of Father. But after a while, the filolial tracks suddenly grew chaotic and then disappeared just after turning off onto a mountain path.

There was no need for me to waste time toying with monsters here at the moment. I was sure Father had already gotten materials from all the monsters in this area. I continued to track the filolials using their scent until the sun set, but there was no sign of Father. I'd exhausted my options, so I used my portal to return to the town.

Things had begun to settle down a bit back in the town by that time. But I got the impression that the demi-humans there seemed a bit agitated. When I arrived at the half-destroyed inn, I found the guard and owner there cleaning up the mess.

"How are things here?" I asked.

"Oh! Spear Hero! The Shield Hero stopped by quite some time ago," the guard told me.

"Hmm . . . Around how long ago?"

"It wasn't too long after you left. It had just started getting dark."

"I see."

It seemed I had missed them right after leaving. I needed to go after them as soon as possible.

"After the Shield Hero and his party returned, they were attacked by a group of people who I assume were members of the Church of the Three Heroes. The monsters accompanying them defeated the attackers straight away, and then the Shield Hero departed to continue on his journey," the guard explained.

"Understood. Thank you for the report."

It sounded like Father had managed to depart without issue. In that case, the only thing left for me to do was spend the night traveling to the next town.

"Umm, Spear Hero . . ." he continued.

"What is it?"

"Are you going after the Shield Hero now? Shouldn't you have just waited for him at the next town instead of coming back here?"

That wasn't an option . . . that I'd considered. But there was no way I would have been able to sit around waiting anyway. Coming back here might have seemed like a waste of time and effort, but it was better than just waiting around idly, I say!

"We're currently deploying doubles of the Shield Hero to confuse the church assassins. The frequency of attempts on the Shield Hero's life should drop off shortly. Please try not to worry."

"Understood."

That made sense. Siltvelt was placing fake Fathers out on the roads. That just might make our trip a bit less chaotic.

I set off to spend the night traveling to the next town. I'd been running down the road at full speed for several hours when the lights of the next town finally came into view. I began to approach some mountains as I drew closer and I felt a slight drop in the temperature. And then I came to the town gates. The town seemed to be a hot springs resort. I could see steam rising from several different spots on the skyline.

"Halt! Who goes there?" a gatekeeper yelled out.

"The Love Hunter, I say!"

"Huh?! What is that supposed to mean?!"

The gatekeeper pointed his weapon at me warily. How foolish. I considered making him regret that right then and there. I was on an urgent mission to return to Father's side, after all!

"Wait!"

Just then, somebody stuck their head out of the gate and called to the gatekeeper.

"That man is a colleague of ours. Please allow him to pass."

"Umm, okay. If you say so. He seems really suspicious, though."

"His behavior is indeed suspicious. Regardless, I've been told that he is incredibly powerful," the person said.

Who was that? He was a demi-human, but he wasn't the Siltvelt emissary we'd been traveling with.

"Please, this way. The Shield Hero is waiting."

"Does that mean you know Father?"

"Yes. The Shield Hero said there would be a man who referred to him as 'Father.' He asked me to bring you to him."

And that was how I made it through the gate of the hot springs resort. The demi-human took me to the inn where Father was staying. The filolials must have sensed my presence, because the door to the inn swung open and Yuki and Kou came running out.

"Motoyasu!"

"Kitamuraaa!"

"Yuki and Kou! I finally found you!"

"When we returned from hunting, the inn was halfway destroyed. I was really worried about you!" said Yuki.

"Welcome back, Kitamura! Where's my souvenir?" asked Kou.

"I didn't bring any souvenirs, but I finished your outfits long ago!"

I showed the two of them the clothes I'd made for them. Just then, Father, Sakura, and the others came walking out of the inn.

"Motoyasu! We were worried! We left you all alone and then came back to find the inn like that," Father said.

"I sustained no injuries, I say! More importantly, are all of you okay?"

"Yeah. Sakura and the other filolials fought off the people that attacked us," he replied.

"These filolials are ridiculously strong. My presence may no longer be needed here," Éclair said quietly.

Bwahaha! She was right! So very right! Filolials reigned supreme! They were the ultimate species—the strongest species! Pitiful humans could never measure up to the majestic filolials, I say! But it sure was insightful of Éclair to have realized that.

"Mr. Iwatani was really worried about you. He's hardly rested at all since we arrived at the inn. Come, Mr. Kitamura. Both of you should get some rest," Éclair suggested.

"Understood, I say!"

"Fortunately for us, this town seems to be a hot springs resort. It's the perfect place to recover from the fatigue of our travels, don't you think?"

Éclair seemed giddy with anticipation. Hmm . . .

"Kitamuraaa! Clooothes!" Kou prodded.

"You can put them on once you've bathed yourself properly, I say!"

"Okaaay! Everyone, to the baaaaths!"

"Good idea. I'm worn out after today. Let's clean up and relax a bit," Father agreed.

We all decided to take a bath at the hot springs, now that

we'd finally met back up. This time the baths seemed to be made of stone. They had a rough, unpolished feel that was different from the elegant Japanese-style baths at the hot springs on the Cal Mira islands.

> **The Cal Mira Islands**
>
> This is a group of islands not far off the shores of Melromarc. All of us heroes went there to earn experience during the activation, which is a phenomenon that occurs on the islands during which adventurers can level up rapidly by killing monsters. (It's kind of like the events in online games during which the amount of experience gained by players is increased.) The islands are famous for their hot springs.

I'd expected something more grandiose, like the Roman baths, but I guess this region was mostly just a hub of trade. On top of that, frequent wars meant that control of the region was constantly changing, so the more refined aspects of cultures would never take root. Regardless, the baths were still divided by gender. And that could mean only one thing . . . Muhahaha, I say!

"You're lucky, Kou. You get to bathe with Motoyasu," said Yuki.

"Heh heh heh! Kitamura! Let's wash each other's backs!" Kou said.

"Of course, I say!"

Yuki and Sakura enjoyed talking with us guys. But Father had told me in the past that girls belong in the women's bath.

"Éclair, please take Yuki and Sakura with you."

Éclair sighed.

"I give up. Call me whatever you want," she said.

Muhaha . . . Muhahaha! It wasn't long now until we would get a glimpse of heaven, I say! Father noticed the expression on my face and started eyeing me suspiciously.

"Umm, Motoyasu . . . Surely you're not thinking of trying to take a peek, are you?"

"Ha! Ha! Ha! Of course I am! I can't wait to get a glimpse of Yuki and Sakura!"

"How can you admit it so brazenly, Mr. Kitamura?!" Éclair asked.

I wouldn't be able to see Filo-tan here, but as a man, peeping was still my job when at the hot springs, I say! And getting peeped at made the women even more attractive. Experiencing the embarrassment that came with having to hide their naked bodies from the prying eyes of men would only increase Yuki's and Sakura's feminine charm, I say!

As their father, it was my duty to teach them these things. That was nothing to be ashamed of.

"It's impressive that you guessed what he was thinking, Mr. Iwatani," Éclair said.

"Well, his eyes were twinkling unmistakably. I didn't want to believe it, but here we are."

"So that was it."

"But I usually have absolutely no idea what's going through his head."

"Naofumiii . . . Will you be okay without me? Should we bathe together?" Sakura asked.

"Huh? No, it's okay. I have Motoyasu and Kou with me. I'll be fine, so you go bathe with them."

"Okaaay! I'll come find you in a little bit, then!"

"You heard what I just said, right? Eclair, please keep an eye on them."

"Yes, I will. You keep Mr. Kitamura under control too."

"Yeah, got it. I'll try my best, anyway."

Father and Éclair stopped talking to each other for a moment and then they both let out a deep sigh.

"How in the world did I end up looking after a bunch of children?" Éclair mumbled.

"Motoyasu is super helpful, but he gets out of control sometimes and trying to talk sense into him is practically impossible," Father replied.

"Ha! Ha! Ha! You're such a jokester, Father! I'm sincerely doing my very best to help you all, I say!"

For some reason, they both sighed deeply once more before turning around and walking away in opposite directions toward the baths.

Chapter Thirteen: Peeping

"By the way, Father, what level are you now?"

"I'm level 38. I powered up my shield too. I even used the weapon copy system you told me about before we came to this inn, so I feel like I've gotten fairly strong now."

Father was taking off his clothes while speaking. Hmm . . . I looked at his body. Compared to the Father from the first world, he wasn't as muscular as I remembered that Father being the last time I'd seen him. I guess that was only natural, since that Father had struggled to overcome so many hardships.

"I've gotten a bunch of different skills too, so I should be pretty strong, right? The only thing is, I'm not really sure *how* strong, and that kind of scares me. I've never been in a real battle either."

"You're just being modest. You've always been dependable in battle, I say!"

"I don't know. I'm a bit worried, honestly. I've played online games, so I've seen those bigheaded players who have nothing going for them but their high level. They're completely useless when it comes to a real battle."

"I do remember hearing something about you running a notorious guild."

"Oh, did I mention that in the future? Yeah, I was an officer in a guild that ranked maybe third on the server."

"That's right."

"But what does that have to do with anything? I mean, it did teach me a thing or two about forming parties, giving basic commands, like when to attack or withdraw, and providing logistical support. But I really doubt that's going to help me in the real world, here in a parallel universe."

"What are you talking about? Your experience helped you minimize casualties during the waves—a meritorious feat, I say!"

Back when I was still acting like a fool, I was only concerned with attacking the bosses and the cracks in the sky during the waves. Ren and Itsuki were the same. We didn't even consider the damage to the surrounding area or the residents, but Father was different. He was always thinking about how to minimize the number of casualties.

I'm sure that's why there had been so little damage. There was even a group of soldiers that sought to assist Father, regardless of the fact that he was in Melromarc, a country that treated him as an enemy. His command of those soldiers once again helped minimize damage during subsequent waves. I was sure he made use of his experience with inter-guild warfare in numerous other battles too.

I was well aware that it was thanks to Father's instruction

that I had become as powerful as I was. I had no doubt he would show the same resourcefulness and quick wits this time around as well.

"Hmm, are you sure?" he continued. "Something about that seems off. I find it hard to take your word for it on this one. Was I really commanding people? Are you sure I didn't leave that to someone else?"

Father sure was skeptical. He was being extra careful about what he chose to believe. It wasn't the first time I'd seen him do that. Okay, it was true that he'd left the strategizing and commanding up to Trash at one point. But that was an entirely different story.

"Absolutely certain, I say!"

"Well, I guess I'll believe it, if you say it's true. But I don't think that kind of thing would work against an experienced strategist. It's hard to believe that picking up bits and pieces from a game could actually help in the real world."

"Kitamura! Let's wash each other's backs!" Kou suddenly shouted.

"Of course! Allow me, I say!"

Kou began begging, so I started to wash his back. I lathered up some soap and went about carefully washing each feather, right down to the root. This kind of attention to detail would help make filolials even more attractive. Sadly, I was generally only able to do this for the males—Midori and Kou. But I had groomed Crim and Marine after they took baths.

"It ticklessss!" Kou said.

"Now, now, stop wiggling, I say!"

"Okay! Come on, Iwatani! We'll wash your back toooo!"

"Alright then," Father agreed.

We were having a pleasant time washing each other's backs when Sakura came bounding over the fence in her filolial queen form.

"Wait! Sakura! That's the men's bath!"

I could hear Éclair shouting.

"Naofumiiiii!"

"Oh, hey, Sakura. I guess you came, after all."

"Let's bathe togetheeerrrr!"

"Umm, well, let's ask first. Hey, Eclair! Sakura came over to our side. What do you want me to do?"

Father called out to Éclair, but it sounded like she was busy scolding Yuki. She sounded upset.

"Why am I the only one who doesn't get to be with Motoyasu?!" Yuki shouted.

"Because it's not allowed! I have no doubt Mr. Iwatani will scold Sakura and send her back immediately," Éclair explained.

"But I, too, would very much like to bathe with Motoyasu!" Yuki stated.

After hearing their exchange, Father chided Sakura gently.

"Well, there's our answer. Hurry on back to the women's bath."

"Aww . . . Okay, then let's go togetheeerr!"

"Huh?! W-wait!" Father exclaimed.

Sakura threw Father onto her back and leapt back over into the women's bath.

"M-Mr. Iwatani?! Why are you in the women's bath?!" Éclair demanded.

"It's not my fault! Sakura brought me without asking!"

"Yup! I wanna get in with Naofumiii!"

"No! Hurry up and take Mr. Iwatani back to the men's bath!"

"Boo . . ."

"Mr. Iwatani, I'll let it go this time, since you're covering your eyes, but I expect you to have a word with her!"

"O-of course!"

Sakura jumped back over the fence and brought Father back to our side. To think that he would get access to the women's bath . . . Way to go, Father! Now *that* was a real hero!

"Umm, Motoyasu? Why do you look so excited? Whatever you're thinking, it's completely wrong," he reprimanded.

I wondered what Yuki had looked like.

"You still haven't given me a satisfactory answer!" Yuki shouted.

She was still arguing with Éclair. The sound of her voice traveled surprisingly well.

"Yuki, I shall be sneaking a peek at the women's bath shortly, I say!"

"Mr. Kitamura!" Éclair shouted.

Éclair didn't seem happy with my announcement. But that wasn't my problem!

"Getting peeped at makes a lady more attractive, I say! But it must be unexpected to receive the full effect, so you should wait there patiently and look forward to being seen!"

"Understood! Then I shall wash my body and wait patiently for you to peek! And I shall undoubtedly be the most attractive of all, once you have graced me with your peeping!" said Yuki.

"Yuki . . . Is that really all it took to satisfy you and convince you to give up?" Éclair asked.

She was speaking more quietly now. Father scolded Sakura too, and she hesitantly returned to the other side.

"Ha! You openly showed them your naked body, Sakura. That means the increase in attraction will be reduced. I hope you've learned your lesson. You mustn't go to the men's bath," Yuki chided.

"Huh? I'm fine with how I am. I would rather take a bath with Naofumi and Motoyasu than be more attractive."

"I don't understand either of you. Anyway, both of you wash yourselves off properly and get in the water. And make sure you submerge yourselves up to your shoulders!" Éclair demanded.

"Okaaay!"

Yuki and Sakura began washing themselves off quietly.

Over the next several minutes, I focused my attention on the women's bath. I was worried about Father, since his face was slightly flushed.

"The water is so waaaarm. It feels so gooood."

I could hear the sound of bubbles.

"Sakura, don't go to sleep in the bath!" Éclair scolded.

Then there was a loud splash, followed by snoring.

"So what, you think you won't drown if you change to your filolial queen form? Stop coming up with such strange ideas!" she continued.

Éclair was starting to sound like a pesky mother-in-law. It reminded me of big sis for some reason. I'm sure it was because she was always giving Father advice.

"It sounds like Eclair is having a tough time over there," Father said.

"Now then, I suppose it's about time to peek," I told him.

"You were actually serious about peeping?"

"Of course! I must keep my promise to Yuki, I say!"

"I realize I can't stop you even if I try, but I really don't think you should do that. Yuki will be happy as long as you tell her you peeked, even if you don't actually do it," he told me.

"Father, telling lies is wrong, I say!"

"Well, yeah, but using that to justify peeping just doesn't seem right."

"Come now, Kou! I need something to stand on!"

"What do I get for letting you stand on meee?"

"I shall rub your cheeks, I say!"

"Yaaay! Stand on me!"

"Don't let him!" Father snapped.

Kou ignored Father's objection and complied with my request. He changed into his filolial king form and put me on his back.

"Come, Father. Join me for a peek, I say!"

Thinking back, I had no memories of Father joining me for a peek at the paradise known as the women's bath. Generally speaking, he was never very fond of peeping. But things might have been different, since this was a different cycle of the time loop.

"Whoa! H-hey, put me—" Father began.

Kou understood what I was thinking. He grabbed Father by the waist and lifted him up into the air so that he would be able to see over the fence into the women's bath. Éclair's face popped up out of the water all of a sudden.

"Mr. Kitamura, I would like to ask that you comply with social norms. Have you ever thought about how the women— the victims of your peeping—might feel?" she scolded.

"You need not worry! No woman has ever been upset with me for peeping at them in the bath, I say!"

Even if they pretended to be upset, they were always happy in the end! Although, actually, I did feel a bit of uncertainty, since my experience had only been with pigs. But my intuition as the Love Hunter was telling me that I wasn't mistaken.

Éclair sighed and said, "I will admit that you are quite handsome, as long as you keep your mouth closed. Perhaps there aren't many women who would be upset by you looking at them. But that's not the point!"

"Eclair! I'm sorry! I promise I'm not looking!" Father shouted.

Father was desperately covering his eyes with both hands again. He was so shy! He would never become manly at this rate. Just like women became more attractive with being seen, men honed their manliness by looking, I say!

"And now you're forcing Mr. Iwatani to take part in your shenanigans. I don't even know what to say anymore. Do you really want to see naked women that badly, Mr. Kitamura?"

"I'm only interested in seeing Yuki and Sakura, I say! The only problem is that there are occasionally pigs claiming to be women in the women's bath. Seeing naked pigs just makes me want to puke! Yuck!"

". . ."

Éclair was squinting her eyes at me suspiciously. Looking more closely, I noticed she had a towel wrapped around her torso to cover herself. It looked like Yuki did too. As for Sakura . . . She was near the edge of the bath, nodding off in her filolial queen form.

"You *did* brazenly announce that you were going to peek. We were originally the only ones in here, so I took the liberty of preparing in advance."

"What do you think, Motoyasu? Has my attractiveness risen now?" Yuki asked.

"Try to submerge yourself in a slightly more seductive manner, I say!"

"Did you seriously just critique her bathing? You really are something, Motoyasu . . ." Father mumbled.

In order to become a truly exceptional lady, one would need to hone their attractiveness from time to time. Filo-tan had been a ten on the attractiveness scale from the very start, though. There was nothing more appealing than that ditziness of hers! But I wasn't so far gone as to think that everyone needed to be just like Filo-tan. I adored all of my filolials and I would shower them all with affection! That's right! I loved all of my filolial children equally, I say!

Éclair seemed to give up after that. She stopped trying to interfere with my peeping and sunk back down into the water. I shifted my attention back to the men's bath and decided to get back in. Kou put Father down.

Father sighed.

"I can't believe you dragged me into that. What a mess," Father said.

"You're such a sissy, Father."

"I'm fine with being a sissy! I mean, I know that peeping is every man's dream, but you're supposed to do it without being noticed!"

"Mr. Iwatani?" Éclair said.

There was something interrogatory about Éclair's tone of voice. Being questioned must have disconcerted Father, because he hurriedly threw out an explanation.

"I'm not going to peek! I'm just speaking in terms of the conventional wisdom of our world. It's a rite of passage kind of thing. That's all!"

"I see. Well, please talk some sense into Mr. Kitamura. At least if he did things like this without being noticed, it wouldn't turn into such an ordeal. I'm exhausted from having to constantly lecture him about things."

I heard Éclair sigh and then sink back down into the water.

"So like I said, Motoyasu, no peeping. If you wait until they get out and then look at them while their skin is shiny and flushed, it's still satisfying and it's something to get excited about without breaking any rules," he explained.

"I see. So it's like stopping at foreplay," I said.

"Huh? Umm, how is anything I said like foreplay?"

"Because you wouldn't actually get to see their naked bodies," I complained.

"Yeah, but that's the kind of thing that, umm . . . You'll get to do plenty of that once you're in an intimate relationship, like dating someone or being married."

Oh? I was pretty sure I remembered seeing Father go to one of those private baths meant for families with big sis and Filo-tan. Wouldn't he have seen their naked bodies in there? And I also remembered him telling us about big sis showing him her naked body so that he could check on her wounds. But I think I understood his logic. They were like family to him, which is an intimate relationship. It was the same for me and the filolials—they were my children!

"I'm already in an intimate relationship, I say!"

"Huh?"

"I worship the filolials. My relationship with them is basically the same as that of a parent and child. There is no relationship more intimate than that, I say!"

". . ."

Father dropped his shoulders and gazed down at the water like he'd given up.

"Eclair, I'm sorry. I don't think I'm going to be able to talk sense into Motoyasu," he said, defeated.

"It's okay, Mr. Iwatani. You've already said more than enough. Please try to relax a bit now."

I got the feeling that going to the hot springs together had brought us all closer to each other. That was the power of peeping! It strengthened the bonds between people, I say!

"Umm, let's talk about something else. So even if you learn a million skills, that doesn't mean you'll be able to use magic, right?" Father asked.

"That's right. But if you just want to learn one simple magic spell, you can do that by purchasing an expensive crystal ball at a magic shop," I told him.

"But that's not going to give you any kind of deeper understanding of magic, right?"

"You are correct! Indeed, magic learned using a crystal ball is inferior in many ways, including how powerful it is, how much magic power it consumes, and how much control you have over it."

In the beginning, I'd taken the easy way out and used crystal balls to learn magic. But ultimately, Father taught me how to learn spells using magical tomes and I finally realized how convenient magic learned that way could be. It was a perfect example of how taking the easy way out in life just resulted in spinning one's wheels and putting oneself at a disadvantage.

"But learning magic means learning to read the writing of this world and deciphering magical tomes . . ." Father began.

I nodded silently. It was difficult, but it wasn't impossible. Case in point, Father and I had done it, as had the other heroes.

"Leveling up, unlocking skills, and powering up my shields have all gone really smoothly so far. Compared to that, the process is a real pain in the neck, isn't it?"

"That's just how it is, I say!"

"Learning magic sounds really romantic and all, but I guess it's just not the kind of thing you can do overnight."

"You can just learn it bit by bit over time. In the future, you mentioned that it went more quickly than you expected too."

"How long did it take?"

"I believe you could already use magic around the time we defeated the second wave."

"Which means around two and a half months. That's a long time," Father whispered.

He stuck his hands in the water and started squirting water out by squeezing his palms together. He was really good at it too. The water was shooting quite high up into the air.

"Wow! Hey, Iwatani! How are you doing that?!" Kou asked.

"Put your hands together like this and make a little window for the water to squirt out of. It should be a small hole, like you'd make with your mouth if you were going to blow out. Then just squeeze your palms together to create pressure and make it squirt out."

"Put my hands together . . ."

Kou made a clumsy attempt at squirting the water and failed.

"It's so haaard!" he complained.

"You'll get it in no time if you keep practicing. I guess it's the same for magic, huh?"

"Once you learn to read and get a feel for manipulating magic power, using magic is no problem, I say!"

Well, using the Liberation class of spells did require learning the Way of the Dragon Vein, which was a type of magic that couldn't be used without having received a dragon's blessing. I wouldn't have wanted to learn it if Father hadn't ordered me to. Even then I was reluctant to do so, but I couldn't deny the fact that learning it had proven invaluable on numerous occasions.

"We're getting pretty close to Siltvelt. Once we're sure things are safe, we can take our time to study magic and continue to level up to prepare for the waves."

"Yeah, I'll do my best too!" Kou replied.

"As shall I!" I said.

Just then, something came flying toward us at high speed. I jumped out of the water to protect Father, but I'd been just a moment too late. My sudden movement sent large waves rushing across the surface of the water, and the Siltvelt emissary, who had been sitting off to the side quietly, tumbled over into the water.

"Huh?"

I'd been able to deflect the majority of the objects, but one of them had hit Father. It had bounced off and landed to the side, and now Father was looking over at it. Judging from the shape, it appeared to be . . . a thorn? Or a blow dart, perhaps.

"Father! Are you okay?!"

"It just went ping as it bounced off, and nothing else happened. Is that a blow dart?!"

If it was a blow dart . . . Those were often used to assassinate people by coating the tip with deadly poison. A sense of danger came rushing over me when I thought about Father getting shot with something like that.

Several shady characters leapt over the fence and into the men's bath area. It was clear that the attack had been their handiwork.

"That was a paralytic poison! There's no way you can move now, Shield Hero! Prepare to die!"

Father stood up out of the water and held his shield up in front of himself. I thrust my spear at one of the fools who had recklessly attacked us.

"Gah!"

"Let's do this!" Kou shouted.

"Let's, indeed!" I replied.

Kou changed into his filolial king form and kicked one of the morons as hard as he could. It was a good kick that sent the scum flying.

"Should I use magic to nullify the poison?" I asked.

Healing magic and the like had originally been Father's specialty, but I had an aptitude for it as well. Even if it was a fast-acting poison, I would be able to counteract it, I say!

"Quickly! We must treat the wound at once! Where did the dart hit you?" I asked.

"Motoyasu! Relax! It didn't even break the skin. I'm fine."

"Oh?"

Judging by Father's reaction . . .

"I see now. Father, the time has come for you to show them just how strong you've become, I say!"

"Huh? Are you sure I'll be okay?"

"It's a little late to be asking that! Their lethal poison dart was ineffective against you. You have nothing to fear, I say!"

"Here's my chance!" shouted one of the assassins.

Thinking he could take advantage of the fact that I was standing there quietly, the assassin swung his sword at Father. Father held his shield up immediately, but he'd reacted just a tiny bit too slowly, perhaps due to his lack of experience. The assassin leaned to the side and redirected the attack, aiming at Father's torso. But Father successfully defended against the attack by blocking it with his arm. A loud clang echoed out and sparks went flying from the point of contact.

"Umm . . ."

"Shield Demon, this is the end!"

The assassin swung his sword down at Father. Father held his hand up and spread his fingers. Just before the blade cut into his skin, he closed his fingers and grasped it between them, stopping the sword dead in its tracks.

"Wh-what?! Shit! It won't budge!"

"That's strange. If I really focus, everything looks like it's moving in slow motion. Even his voice sounded like it had been slowed down. Is that because of the power-ups?" Father asked.

"It is, indeed!"

As a matter of fact, Father had attempted to implement all of the power-up methods that I'd been able to recall. I was certain two-bit assassins like these wouldn't even be able to scratch him anymore. Ha! Ha! Ha! They were in trouble if they thought he was the same Father they'd encountered before!

"H-he's a monster!" one shouted.

"Now that Father has finished testing his defenses, it's time to pay for your foolishness. Be thankful that Father and his companions are so compassionate, I say!"

I hooked my spear onto the assassin's collar and spun him around a few times before flinging him high up into the air.

"Gaaahhhh!"

"If you don't enjoy that, then don't do foolish things! Ha! Ha! Ha!"

"I never expected to see enemies like this here. We should probably leave this town soon. Eclair? Is everything okay over there?" Father yelled over to Éclair.

Yuki leapt over the fence onto our side. Éclair was sitting on her back with her sword in her hand.

"Yes, we're fine. We wiped the enemies out in the blink of an eye. I'm sorry it took me so long to get here."

"We took care of ours in a matter of seconds. Don't worry about it," Father said.

"My sincere apologies, once again. Escorts from Siltvelt

will have driven away the remaining church members shortly, I believe," said the Siltvelt emissary.

"Good. I'm glad to hear that Siltvelt is responding quickly too. Even if we stay on the lookout, it's always possible that someone will slip through," Éclair replied.

"But that sure is strange. General security was increased after the incident with the Spear Hero, and we asked the demi-humans to tighten the security here at the inn too," he said.

The Siltvelt emissary looked confused. Hmm, it appeared we had an intricate conspiracy on our hands. Perhaps there was nowhere we would be able to relax before we had reached the safety of our destination.

"Well, I sent one of the assassins flying. He should be lying on the ground outside of the baths. We should go tie him up and then force him to spill the beans, I say!"

"I'm glad nothing bad happened," said Éclair.

"Raising my level and powering up my shields made a huge difference. I really felt the effects clearly."

"That's good. Perhaps the assassins will give up after realizing they can't defeat you. Then we could continue our journey in peace," she replied.

We left the hot springs after that. On a related note, we found out the following day how the enemies had managed to show up at the hot springs. It turned out the Church of the Three Heroes wasn't our only enemy.

Chapter Fourteen: Fitoria-tan

"The intruders had demi-human informants?"

That was what we'd found out from our Siltvelt contacts the following day. The emissary had an apologetic tone as he explained the situation to us. It appeared that the Church of the Three Heroes wasn't our only enemy. Éclair had a mystified look on her face.

"Didn't you say security had been increased?" she asked.

"And besides, I thought the demi-humans were our allies. Why would they do that?" Father continued.

"Well, it seems there are some demi-humans with ties to Shieldfreeden who don't want to see Siltvelt take you in. And they're acting accordingly," the emissary replied.

"Hmm, it's true the Shield Hero is revered among the demi-humans. I knew that his presence alone had the potential to trigger fighting, but still . . ." said Éclair.

"It feels like practically the whole world is after me," Father whispered.

He hung his head in dismay. Now that he mentioned it, it did kind of seem that way. In Melromarc, he was considered the god of a hostile country. And in Siltvelt and Shieldfreeden, he was a potential source of conflict between the demi-humans. It wasn't a very good situation to be in.

"Worry not, Father. I, Motoyasu, shall destroy all of your enemies! Even if that means destroying the whole world, I say!"

"Huh? Oh, yeah, thanks. But I think destroying the whole world might be going a bit too far," he replied.

"Mr. Iwatani, these are complex diplomatic issues. Please don't let it get you down," said Éclair.

"I'll protect you no matter what, Naofumi!" Sakura added.

"Thank you, Eclair and Sakura."

Sakura was comforting Father. How heartwarming! It moved me to tears, I say!

"So does that mean there will be fewer Melromarc assassins now, but Shieldfreeden assassins are going to start coming after me instead?" Father asked.

"I'm pretty sure that, officially, Shieldfreeden proclaims freedom and equality for both humans and demi-humans alike," Éclair said.

She was scratching her head and had a troubled expression on her face. My memories about Shieldfreeden were hazy. I couldn't remember whether they were an enemy or an ally. Not to mention, I'd only been concerned with the filolials, so I left all of that business up to Father. All I could do was just follow whatever orders Father gave me, I say!

"I guess there are diplomatic issues like this in every world, aren't there?" Father said.

"The Father in the future would go out of his way to cause

trouble for the opposition. We should go to Siltvelt, I say!"

"Mr. Kitamura, I'm pretty sure you could have worded that better," Éclair said.

"Well, I don't plan on just staying quiet and letting them kill me. If they're going to ask for a fight, then I guess I'll just have to give them one," Father announced.

I could hear a sense of resolve in Father's voice. But . . .

"I wonder if it would have actually been better if I'd never been summoned here," he said.

"What does that mean?" I asked.

"I mean, think about it. People have been after me since the day I was summoned. Based on what you said, I originally got framed and ended up losing my way, right?"

There was a warmth to Father's expression, and yet it seemed to be filled with incredible sorrow.

"Mr. Iwatani . . ." Éclair began.

"Even in the relatively short time span of our journey so far, we've gotten caught up in numerous struggles. I've lost count of how many times I've heard people jeering at us. So I can't help but think . . . Maybe none of this mess would have happened if I hadn't been summoned . . ." he went on.

"That's a mistake, Father! If it weren't for you, I would have never met Filo-tan! I'm confident I would have died a fool, without ever having learned the truth, I say!"

That was an indisputable fact! If it hadn't been for Father,

I would have most likely remained a cocky fool, chasing pig booty and selfishly running amok in this world. I would have died without ever showing even a hint of improvement.

I couldn't remember how I'd died in the initial timeline. But I did remember this: it was Filo-tan and Father who had taught me what true love was, I say! There was a gravity to love now that had not existed before I came to this world. I could say that with confidence!

It was true that this world had tested Father repeatedly— far more than it had ever tested me. And that was exactly why I wanted to help him out.

"It is the ones who are trying to kill you who are in the wrong. None of this is your fault, I say!"

"Motoyasu . . ." he started to say.

"Besides, even if you hadn't been summoned, Melromarc would have undoubtedly come up with another excuse to convince the other heroes to help them invade Siltvelt, I say!"

"He's probably right. It's highly likely that they would have used the heroes as an excuse to start a holy war and invade Siltvelt," said Éclair.

She agreed with my assessment. She looked at Father with kindness in her eyes and placed a hand on his shoulder to comfort him.

"The fault lies with the people of this world, who are trying to erase you for religious reasons, despite being right in the middle of the waves of destruction. Allow me to apologize on behalf of this world," she continued.

Éclair bowed her head to Father. Oh! Now that was a commendable attitude! Even if we were heroes, we were still human. We weren't machines built to save the world. We were living, breathing beings. Father was a hero, but first and foremost he was a man. And I was the Love Hunter! I lived to please Father, I say!

Besides, surely the world couldn't be saved by cold, machinelike people. It needed people who were full of heart—people who were kind, honest, and who kept their word. I wasn't there yet, but I was doing my best to fight for Father, Filo-tan, and the rest of the filolials, I say!

"Thank you, Eclair. Yeah, I guess you're right. Our role as heroes is to fight to save the world from those destructive waves," Father admitted.

"Yes, that's why you and Mr. Kitamura were called to this world. Making a religious issue out of that is wrong. So right now, let's prioritize getting you to Siltvelt safely."

"Yeah. Alright, I guess we should head out, then."

I asked the filolials to pull the carriage, and we resumed our journey to Siltvelt.

"Smooth" was probably the best way to describe how our journey had gone after that. Dealing with assassins had become a breeze, thanks to Father's improved defenses. Every now and then some group would try to cast large-scale ceremonial magic on us, while we were on the road, but I would just nullify it with Liberation Absorb. Then we would defeat the attackers, round them up, and turn them in at the nearest town.

Eventually, even the assassins realized just how strong we heroes were and their attacks grew infrequent. The more reckless attempts had come to an end.

"Kweh!"

I caught sight of some wild filolials. I leaned out of the carriage and gazed at them. Wild filolials had a certain carefree air and a raw attractiveness that domesticated filolials lacked. More than anything, wild filolials had a tendency to value sticking together. There was a magnificence about that cohesiveness that touched me deeply. It was hard to put into words.

"Motoyasu! You don't need to look at them! Look at us instead!" Yuki snapped.

"Ha! Ha! Ha! I treasure all filolials equally, I say!"

"You really do like filolials, don't you? But why not treat Yuki and the others at least a little bit special?" Father asked.

"Filolials are all equally special, I say!"

"But wouldn't that make none of them special?"

"Boo . . ." said Sakura.

"It's no use. Mr. Kitamura clearly doesn't understand," Éclair interjected.

Had I said something strange?

"Hm? What do you think about those filolials, Naofumi?" Sakura asked.

"What do I think about them? Nothing in particular, really. It's just interesting to finally see some wild filolials is all."

"Oh really?"

Sakura and Father sure did get along well.

"Gweh?!"

Oh? The filolials had taken off running and disappeared. I had a feeling I'd seen filolials respond like that before. Maybe it was just my imagination.

"Aww, they ran away," said Father.

"That's wild filolials for you. There are a number of different species, but none of them are very aggressive," Éclair replied.

"Really? Oh yeah, Motoyasu did mention that filolials wouldn't end up looking like his filolials unless a hero raised them, didn't he?"

"I did, indeed!"

"Mr. Kitamura's filolials look completely different. And they can even take on human forms. It's just one surprise after another with them. But it makes sense that being raised by a hero is what makes that possible," said Éclair.

"Did past heroes not raise any filolials, then? It seems like there would be records of something like that," said Father.

"Oh yes, there are countless stories. If we're talking about a hero raising a powerful monster, the Seven Star Whip Hero is a well-known example," she replied.

Hmm . . . I felt like I was on the verge of recalling a nasty memory. Just hearing the word "whip" put me in an unpleasant mood, I say! I had a feeling something tragic had happened, but I couldn't remember. Regardless, it wouldn't hurt to be wary of this whip business.

"Then I guess there might be a lot of monsters that exhibit special patterns of development when raised by heroes," Father said.

"Look how chaotic things have become with just a few filolials. I can't handle any more excitement than this," Éclair exclaimed.

"Haha, it's tough on you since you're the one teaching them proper manners," Father replied.

"You talk like it's just me, but you're having a heck of a time preparing their meals, are you not?"

"Hahaha, I guess you're right."

The mood was delightfully mellow, I say! The Siltvelt emissaries joined in the conversation and seemed to be enjoying themselves too.

And then it happened. It was the following night. We were outside camping, and suddenly what looked like firefly lights began to dance all around us. I could hear the squawking of filolials from far away in the distance.

"Wh-what's that?" Father asked.

"What's going on?" Éclair echoed.

"They say that they're coming to us," Yuki answered.

"What?! Are you telling me there are filolial assassins too?!" Éclair asked.

"That's not it, I say!"

Éclair and Father tightened their guard as our surroundings began to change. But I suddenly remembered what was happening.

There was only one filolial aside from Filo-tan that had ever truly caught my eye, and she would be coming to us shortly. It was all coming back to me, I say! A huge filolial had appeared once when I was street racing with Crim, Marine, and Midori. Her sublime image would forever be burnt into my brain. It was just unfortunate that, before I knew it, she had disappeared.

A horde of filolials gathered around us, squawking.

"Do you know something about this, Mr. Kitamura? What's going to happen?" asked Éclair.

"A huge filolial is coming, I say!"

"Huh? Could you start from the beginning and explain in a bit more detail?"

"The second-most attractive filolial, after Filo-tan, is coming, I say!"

"It's no use. Mr. Iwatani, I can't have a conversation with Mr. Kitamura."

"Yeah, I know. Sakura, can you tell us what these filolials surrounding us are saying?"

"Umm . . . They were saying they're all coming."

"And a huge filolial is coming too? Could that be the legendary queen of the filolials?" asked Éclair.

Her eyes were darting to and fro as she observed our surroundings.

"They're not going to attack us or eat us, right?" Father asked.

"Filolials *are* omnivores. The fact that we can't deny that possibility is distressing," Éclair replied.

After several moments, we were completely surrounded by the filolials. They stood there in the darkness, staring at us. Thanks to the soft glow of the firefly lights, I could tell there were all sorts of different species of filolials. Ahhh . . . I just kept thinking about how it had become a filolial paradise.

And then, finally, a certain filolial appeared and I—

"Keep him away!"

I could hear the huge filolial's voice! Where was she?! It was pitch dark. I couldn't see a thing, I say!

"Get ahold of yourself, Motoyasu!" Father shouted.

This feeling . . . As I began to gather my bearings, I realized that I was blindfolded and Father had me in a full nelson.

"Motoyasu! You're way stronger than me, so I'm going to be in trouble if you lose control!"

Father seemed upset. It brought back good memories.

"That's strange. Why are you restraining me, Father?"

"You pounced on that filolial as soon as she appeared! You latched on to her and screamed, 'It's the huge filolial!'"

"Well, that sure is embarrassing. But resisting such an urge is impossible, I say!"

Father sighed. I could sense the presence of the filolials around me and their scent tickled my nose. I was getting excited!

"Why am I wearing a blindfold, Father?"

"You don't remember? You regained your composure after we first put it on you, but almost immediately after that you leapt right back onto the huge . . . the legendary filolial."

"Sheesh . . . Please show some self-restraint, Mr. Kitamura!" Éclair interjected.

"I think we should be okay now, Fitoria," said Father.

"That was so scary. There's something wrong with the new holy heroes," she said.

"I can hear the huge filolial speaking! That's right. Her name was Fitoria-tan, wasn't it?!" I said aloud.

I heard footsteps scampering away off into the distance. I remembered Filo-tan talking about a filolial named Fitoria-tan once.

"I wish I could say you were wrong. Anyway, I have a good hold on him now so please relax," Father told her.

"Fine. Either way, it doesn't change what I'm here to do," she said.

After that, the huge filolial—the angel named Fitoria-tan—went on to ask Father about everything that had happened.

She sounded slightly annoyed when she replied. "Can I assume you intend to fight against the waves, then?"

"Yeah. Fighting between the humans has caused us a lot of trouble, but I plan to do what I can to overcome the waves. I'd like to work together with Ren and Itsuki eventually too. Motoyasu is an oddball, but he'll definitely be joining me in the fight," Father told her.

"Okay, good. On to the next piece of business, then. I want to fight the filolials that were raised by a hero," she announced.

"Huh? Why?"

"I'd like to know how strong they are. The battles against the waves will be formidable. If they can show me that they are strong, I will give them a fitting reward."

"Ah, so you want them to prove their strength. Mr. Kitamura, you said you remembered something about this. Do you know what she's talking about?" Éclair asked.

"I believe Father did mention this in the future. By proving themselves to Fitoria-tan, they will earn the right to succeed her, I say!"

"So something like a ceremony to pass the torch on to the next generation?"

Exactly. When it came to filolials, Fitoria-tan was *the* filolial. In the world of filolials, she stood at the top. If Filo-tan, Yuki, and Sakura were filolial queens in their own right, then she was the one *true* queen. But gaining the recognition of Fitoria-tan wasn't only about rank.

"At the same time, they will also gain the ability to undergo a special class-up, I say!"

"What? That means they would have the potential to be even more powerful. Giving it a go doesn't sound like a bad idea to me," said Éclair.

"Why does the Spear Hero know so much?" Fitoria-tan asked.

"Well because, apparently, Motoyasu was summoned in a different timeline and came here from the future," Father replied.

"The Timepiece of the Dragon . . ." Fitoria-tan whispered.

"Does that ring a bell?"

"It was far too long ago, so it's hard for me to recall the details. But I do remember that a time will come when the Spear Hero must make a very important decision. If nothing else, please remember that," she explained.

"And remember that, I shall!" I announced.

"Are you taking this seriously? It sounds like something really important. I wonder if you really understand that," said Father.

"More importantly, please remove my blindfold, Father. I would like to embrace Fitoria-tan at once, I say!"

". . ."

Oh? I heard Fitoria-tan's footsteps once again, as she retreated even further off into the distance.

"Umm, sorry about this, Motoyasu," said Father.

Oh? Father covered my ears with his hands. Oh well. I would just have to focus on picking up the little bit of sound that I could still hear!

"Thank you for restraining Mr. Kitamura. If you hadn't, Ms. Fitoria would have fled. Yuki, Kou, and Sakura, it sounds like accepting the duel isn't such a bad idea. What do you think?" Éclair asked them.

"If becoming stronger will earn Motoyasu's approval, then I'll do my best!" said Yuki.

"That sounds fun! I'll do my best too!" said Kou.

"I'm happy with just being able to protect everyone," Sakura said.

"Well, you can't protect everyone if you're not strong, can you? All you have to do is prove that you are able. Do your best!" Father replied.

"Okaaaay!" Sakura shouted.

It sounded like Father had convinced Sakura to participate. But I couldn't see anything! I had the urge to toss all sense of reason to the wind and dive straight at Fitoria-tan, I say!

"?!"

I heard the sound of feathers ruffling.

"Did you do something, Motoyasu? Fitoria looks really grossed out," said Father.

"I want to dive at her, I say!"

"To think your intent alone could make her feathers stand on end . . . You're a bona fide freak, Mr. Kitamura," Éclair told me.

"I want to hurry up and go home," said Fitoria-tan.

I'd heard that line before, I say! Filo-tan used to say something like that all the time! Fitoria-tan's home was *that* place, right? Yes, it was the filolial sanctuary, I say!

"Alright, I assume you'll take turns. How about starting with Yuki, then?" Father suggested.

"Understood," said Yuki.

I couldn't really hear what happened after that. After a few moments, I heard what sounded like the air vibrating. The noise repeated several times. I had the urge to look, but I resisted since Father had told me to do so. It felt like I had been waiting forever, but I persevered. And then, around the same time I grew sleepy and started to nod off, I suddenly heard voices again.

"There was a foolish griffin king who'd been roaming the world and got himself killed by someone not far from here. All of the griffins have been gathering and they're thirsty for revenge. The monsters in this area are on edge, so you heroes should be careful," said Fitoria-tan.

"Alright. Thanks for the advice. See you later," Father replied.

"Farewell," she replied.

After that, Father removed my blindfold. The filolials had already disappeared from the area. I looked around and noticed Yuki, Kou, and Sakura lying on the ground in an exhausted heap.

"That was amazing," Father said.

"Yeah. Yuki and the others fought well, but that legendary filolial was just far too strong," Éclair replied.

"Yeah, and that same strong Fitoria had tried to flee, without looking back, when faced with Motoyasu. Just how strong is he?!" Father wondered.

"Don't say that. It makes me feel so insignificant," Éclair said.

I ran over to Yuki and the others to check on them. They each had a crest feather on the top of their head. Casting healing magic on them didn't seem necessary.

"Fitoria said she acknowledged all of them as potential successors. Apparently the one who improves the most and exhibits the noblest intentions will ultimately take her place," Father explained.

"Fitoria-tan!"

"I thought you were in love with that Filo girl. It would be wrong to cheat on her," said Father.

"The two of them can't be compared, I say! The Father from the future told me to feel free to get close to her."

"I encouraged you to cheat?!"

"Mr. Iwatani, if you had to deal with Mr. Kitamura when he was in this state, blurting out something like that after a while wouldn't be strange at all," Éclair said.

"Oh, yeah, I guess you're right. I must have gotten annoyed and just told him to go for it."

"I, Motoyasu, intend to make all filolials equally happy, I say! I shall cheat on no one! Filo-tan is my number one! Fitoria-tan is my number two! And the rest of the filolials are my number three, I say!"

"And that's not cheating? Oh, whatever. Trying to reason with you is exhausting. Yuki, you're going to need to work on improving your feminine charm if you want to get Mr. Kitamura's attention," Éclair told her.

"I . . . will . . . Eclair."

Yuki's legs wobbled as she stood up. She nodded at Éclair.

"I sure am worn out, but that was a blast!" exclaimed Kou.

He seemed energetic. Sakura was snoring.

"Oh no . . . Sakura, you're going to wake up sore if you sleep in that position," Father said.

He gently shook her awake. The experience had been unfortunate, but the end result had also been different than when Crim, Marine, Midori, and I had met the huge filolial.

Yuki, Kou, and Sakura all had improved stats now.

"Oh yeah. Hey, Motoyasu, Fitoria left this for you. She said it was a souvenir," Father said.

Father handed me one of the huge filolial's crest feathers. Without hesitation, I took a big whiff.

"Umm . . . That's not what it's for. It's supposed to unlock the filolial series if you absorb it into your weapon," he told me.

"No way!"

There was a way to unlock the whole filolial series! Father hadn't told me about that in the future. But how awful! If I absorbed such a splendid piece of treasure into my spear, I might never have the chance to get my hands on another one like it. Of course, it might have been possible if the time loop reset again, but . . . There was no way I could absorb this feather into my spear, I say!

"Are you not going to?"

"I shall keep it as my treasure, I say!"

I took another big whiff and then stuck the feather into the langet of my spear—between the shaft and the metal collar—as decoration. Now I could enjoy the feeling of fighting alongside Fitoria-tan, I say!

The feather was a gift from Fitoria-tan. I was certain that it would protect me, Father, and everyone else! And besides, if Father had unlocked the filolial series, then there was no point in me using the feather to do the same. Yuki and the other filolials would receive the stat adjustments as members of his party.

"Motoyasu . . . I know I keep saying this, but you really are something. That was clear today more than ever," Father said.

Éclair and the Siltvelt emissary nodded affirmatively. Had I done something strange? The way all three of them sighed together really stuck with me.

CHARACTER CHAT CORNER
DO YOU HAVE A TREASURE?

My treasure is a ball. It was the first thing Mr. Naofumi ever bought for me.

Mine is my memories of Filo-tan, I say!

That ball, huh? That brings back memories . . .

What is your treasure, Mr. Naofumi?

Me? I'll just go with my sense of taste. You figure it out.

NAOFUMI LOST HIS SENSE OF TASTE TEMPORARILY, AS A RESULT OF BEING DECEIVED.

U-understood.

What does that mean? Father! Stop ignoring me, I say!

Fitoria

Filolial Queen

Oversees all of the filolials as their queen. Provided Filo with aid in various forms, after acknowledging her potential. She too was raised by a hero and was not always able to change into her human form. She continues to honor that hero's wishes and fights to protect the world from the waves even today. As a result, she sometimes responds in an exceedingly harsh manner when the current heroes act foolishly.

MORE CONNIVING THAN SHE APPEARS.

The huge filolial! The way she gushes nobility makes me weak in the knees, I say!

It's always the same thing with you, isn't it?

Chapter Fifteen: Church of the Faux Heroes

Spending time with Fitoria-tan and the filolials that night had felt like a dream come true. But sadly, time marched on. We were making smooth progress on our way to Siltvelt, and we came to the consensus that we should arrive quicker than expected if things continued going so well.

We'd stopped by a certain town and stayed the night at someone's house there, which the emissary had arranged for. Perhaps it was because we were gradually getting closer to Siltvelt, but it had become much easier to find supporters and secure safe places to stay.

We were right in the middle of getting ready to move on to the next town when it happened.

"Bad news!"

The supporter that the emissary had introduced us to suddenly burst in and yelled out. He had a look of urgency in his eyes.

"Huh? What is it?!" Father asked.

"S-some group claiming to be the 'Church of the Four Heroes' has sealed off the town gates! They've started capturing people left and right in the town square and threatening them!"

I looked out of the window at the town. I could see smoke

rising from several locations where it shouldn't have been.

"Just to make sure we understand the situation, what kind of threats are we talking about?" Éclair asked the man.

She was furrowing her brow.

"Th-the man said, 'We know Shield and Spear Hero imposters are hiding in this town! Impersonating a hero is a grievous sin according to our religion, and we shall deliver judgment in the name of our gods! Furthermore, the people of this town are equally guilty for hiding them! If the imposters are not turned over to us, we'll execute every man, woman, and child here!'"

Expressions of disgust came over the faces of Father, Éclair, and the Siltvelt emissary. All three of them were shaking their heads.

"So now they're pretending to be the Church of the Four Heroes. I don't even know what to say. This is clearly the work of Church of the Three Heroes extremists," said Éclair.

"I guess it's similar to the idea of using a fake name to commit a crime. Only in their case, it's the name of another religion," Father replied.

"I'm sure they realize what they're doing is inhumane. Or perhaps they stand to gain something by claiming to be the Church of the Four Heroes," Éclair supposed.

"This is just a guess, but it's probably something like the group out there is supposed to capture and kill us, and then just as they do, the Church of the Three Heroes will show up and dispose of the extremists. Then they'll claim to have saved the town," Father went on.

Father was impressive, as always! To be able to imagine a scenario like that . . . I couldn't help but admire his insight!

"That makes sense. The imposters claiming to be the Church of the Four Heroes do something terrible, and the Church of the *Three* Heroes brings them to justice. And if it results in you two being erased, that's icing on the cake. But in that case, why wouldn't they just claim to be Siltvelt's Church of the Shield?" asked Éclair.

"I'm sure they have a reason. It would seem really fishy if the people taking control of the town weren't demi-humans in that case. There might be other reasons too," Father replied.

"You're right. Claiming to be the Church the Shield wouldn't work if the members weren't demi-humans or therianthropes. But anyway, sitting around here thinking about these things isn't going to solve anything," Éclair concluded.

Oh? Were we going to launch an attack?

"Jeez . . . I really can't help but wonder if being summoned wasn't for the worst, after all," Father said.

"You need not wonder, Father! All of the blame lies with those cowards!"

"That's right!" Yuki exclaimed.

"Something really stiiinks here! I hate this smell!" said Kou.

"Hm? Umm, I like Naofumiii!" Sakura added.

Our efforts to encourage Father brought a grin to his face.

"You're right. I'll keep pushing forward for the sake of everyone that believes in me."

With a look of determination on his face, Father turned and spoke to the Siltvelt emissaries and the supporter.

"I'm really tired of these disturbances. But it's also a fact that this is happening because of us. I want to minimize the damage done, and I'd like you to help me do that."

"Of course! Anything you need, Shield Hero!"

"Of course!"

"I'm going to go confront the group in the town square. Motoyasu, you come with me."

"I shan't leave your side, I say!"

Yes! Things were starting to get exciting! Father's wish was my command, and nothing could stand in my way, I say!

"What about uussss?" Sakura asked.

"I want Éclair and the three of you to take care of any church member imposters causing trouble around town. I'm pretty sure I'll be fine. Okay?" Father told them.

"With me there, we shall destroy the enemy in a flash, I say!"

"Thanks. I'm counting on you."

Father had given the order! I was finally going to get some action!

"I'd like the rest of you to help Éclair and the filolials."

"B-but . . ."

"Don't worry about me. I'll have Motoyasu with me, and I've gotten a lot stronger too. Their attacks don't scare me."

Father praised me and said this was all thanks to me, I say!

"I'm really tired of dealing with this bunch. Whether it's the Church of the Three Heroes or some other bunch of troublemakers pulling this stunt, if we expose them here, I'm sure it will throw their operation into disarray. I'm not trying to start a witch hunt, but perhaps it will put people on the alert and make it harder for the assassins to operate," Father continued.

He shifted his gaze over to Éclair and the Siltvelt emissary.

"One of the legendary shield's power-up methods that Motoyasu taught me works by trusting others and being trusted by them. I trust you, Eclair, and everyone else who has helped me since coming to this world. The benefit goes both ways. That makes both of us that much stronger. I want you to use that strength to go help those people."

"So that's what that was. I thought I felt strength unexpectedly swelling up from somewhere recently. If your trust is a source of power, then I shall make sure it does not go wasted!" Éclair replied.

"Very well. If that is your wish, Shield Hero, then we have no reason to refuse. To our triumph!" shouted the emissary.

"Alright, everyone . . . Let's do this!" Father said.

They all let out a whoop and we left our hideout to begin the retaliation.

"People are about to start dying! Hurry up and show yourselves, Shield and Spear imposters! If you don't . . . we, the Church of the Four Heroes, shall end the life of this small child!"

Father and I made our way out to meet the scumbags who'd gathered up the helpless townspeople in the town square, where they were making their self-righteous announcements. They had built a scaffold for the executions in the square and were planning on executing the townspeople one by one. They were in the process of securing a child in the guillotine stocks, as if to imply the child would die first.

"Wahhhh! Somebody save me! Daddy! Mommy!"

"S-stop . . . this . . ." stammered a man tied up to a post behind them.

His body showed signs of already having been tortured, but they continued to whip him. Next to him was a pig that was also being whipped.

"Stop this! You've harmed enough people already!" Father shouted.

"So you finally show yourselves! It's the vile imposters that claim to be the Shield and Spear Heroes!" said an ugly, rotten-looking man wearing ostentatious religious attire.

Glaring at us, he went on. "You're the ones harming people! People of this town! Now you shall see just how grievous a sin pretending to be a hero is! We will prove to you that these fools are not the heroes we believe in! Come, imposters! The time for your judgment has come!"

Some of the townspeople in the square began throwing rocks and other things and yelling at us.

"Pretending to be heroes is ungodly!"

"Boo!"

"None of this would have happened if you hadn't come here!"

"Did you think this would make you famous?! Vile imposters!"

I tightened my grip on my spear, but Father pat me on the shoulder lightly, as if to say, "Don't worry about them." He kept walking straight toward the man who seemed to be the leader of the imposters who claimed to be the Church of the Four Heroes. I followed behind. But mixed in among the things being thrown at us were countless blow darts. They had no effect on us since our weapons were powered up, but they were still incredibly annoying.

With each step, the crowd before us parted to reveal a path leading directly to the scaffold. The leader was standing on the scaffold and shielding himself with a hostage in restraints. His intent was clearly to render us incapable of retaliation.

"Come on, we're not going to run or hide. Hurry up and let that innocent person go," Father said.

"Ah, yes, that's right! But before that, you're going to do exactly as I say! Stand in the middle of that circle there!" he commanded.

There was a blatantly obvious circle drawn on the ground. All it took was one glance to see that it had been drawn there as part of some scheme.

"Everyone! Now!" he shouted.

Immediately after we stepped into the circle, a massive ball of light appeared above us. It looked like the ceremonial magic spell Last Judgment. The ball of light would condense and then come falling down toward a single point on the earth below. Landing a direct hit with the attack was difficult, but the spell was more formidable than Judgment if used successfully.

The point of impact was undoubtedly the circle we were standing in. The fools really did never learn. We had turned the tables on them time and again, and yet they continued to use the same old tactics. I was getting ready to recite an incantation when the leader called out to us.

"Careful, now! We've heard rumors of some kind of dirty trick that allows you to evade ceremonial magic. If you try anything sneaky . . . There's no guarantee that your friends here won't get hurt!"

In other words, they would kill the hostages if I used

Liberation Absorb. That wasn't my problem! But Father signaled for me to hold off.

"..."

His expression was beginning to look like the Father I remembered from the first world. I knew it! In the end, Father was Father, I say!

"Is this the kind of thing your religion deems righteous?" Father asked.

"Hmph! What right does an imposter, who claims to be a hero, have to say anything about us, the Church of the Four Heroes?!"

"Whether I'm an imposter or not has nothing to do with it! I'm asking if you really understand the implications of what you're doing!"

Father's intensity made even the onlookers gulp.

"You hide behind innocent people, call us out here, and take hostages just to pull a stunt like this—all for your own self-satisfaction. I'm asking if that's what you call your religion!"

"Hmph! You sure are a smooth talker, Shield Hero imposter. You speak of justice in an attempt to mislead these people and grow your own pathetic fold of worshippers! But we cannot allow that! Your wicked believers are guilty of the same sins as you! We act for the sake of the world and our gods! Dissidents like you must be judged in the name of our gods!"

"I'm impressed. You express your selfishness so eloquently," Father replied.

He glared at their ringleader with a look of disgust on his face.

"Ha! If you say you're the real Shield Hero, then why don't you just protect yourself and save all of your believers here with your own two hands? If you can, that is!"

Having said that, their leader cut the rope tied to the blade of the guillotine, right in front of our eyes. And at the same moment, their attack came shooting straight down at us.

"High-level ceremonial magic, Last Judgment!" the man shouted.

Father held his shield up toward the sky with his left hand. He then turned to the guillotine blade—which was only moments away from severing the young boy's head—and whispered, "Air Strike Feather Shield V!"

It was a skill that called forth a shield. Assigning points to the skill and raising its level increased both the shield's toughness and the skill's range. In other words, the guillotine blade struck the shield Father summoned and stopped dead in its tracks. At the same time, the light of Final Judgment impacted Father's shield and came to a halt, continuing to shine but failing to scorch us. It was like the sun on a clear day when it was just bright enough to make you squint.

"What?! He was hit by the light of Final Judgment and survived?!" their leader screamed out in surprise. Did they really think they could defeat Father with such a meager effort? They were such fools, as always.

The townspeople clasped their hands together and began praying to Father when they saw him standing there like he was.

"Amazing . . ."

"He saved the boy's life while guarding against such a severe attack! And he's still standing there unfazed!"

"He truly is our savior, the Shield Hero!"

That was the proper way to worship Father, I say!

"Why are you praying to an imposter, you filthy heretics?!" the leader asked.

"You can't fool us!" others shouted. "Boo!"

Just as I suspected, there were people planted in the crowd to stir up trouble.

"Hmph! That's far from worthy of being called a miracle! The executions are not over!"

The leader drew his sword and swung the blade down at the young boy. Just how disgraceful did these scumbags plan on making themselves look in front of everyone?! I'd promised Father and Filo-tan that I would not allow such reckless violence, I say!

"Don't forget about me! Air Strike Javelin V . . . with a touch of . . . Aiming Lancer X, I say!"

Air Strike Javelin was a skill that required me to throw my spear. I launched it straight at the leader of the Church of the Four Heroes.

"Gaahhh!"

It blasted right through his arm into the blade of the guillotine and blew them both to smithereens. Aiming Lancer went flying at the members of the crowd who had been trying to stir up trouble and skewered each and every one of them.

"These barbarous acts of the imposters are unforgivable!" one of them cried out.

"Don't worry about killing any heretics that get in the way! Everyone! Attack!" the leader shouted.

Father swiftly leapt up onto the scaffold. He grabbed the leader by the collar and tossed him to me, saving the young boy from his impending execution. With complete disregard for the townspeople, the Church of the Four Heroes tried to take advantage of that opening by firing a rain of arrows at us. Father swung his cape and swiped the arrows within its reach down, out of the air. He then raised his hand and cast two more skills.

"Air Strike One-Way Shield IV! Second One-Way Shield V!"

Shields appeared out of thin air to protect the townspeople. The arrows went flying off to the sides when they hit the shields.

"Motoyasu! Help me protect everyone!"

"Understood, I say!"

I could do far more with my powers than simply defeat enemies, I say! Magic could be used like this too!

"*I, the Love Hunter, command the heavens and earth! Transect the way of the universe and rejoin it again to expel the pus from within! Power of the Earth Vein! Merge with this magic power of mine! Merge with the power of the heroes and forge a unified force! As the source of your power, the Love Hunter commands you! Let the way of all things be revealed once more! Bring forth a wall of fire to protect us!*"

"Liberation Firewall V!"

A highly concentrated wall of fire rose up around us to protect us. That's all it took to burn their magical attacks, arrows, throwing weapons, and everything else to ashes, I say!

"You okay?" Father asked the boy.

"Y-yeah."

"Sorry about that. None of this would have happened if I hadn't been summoned here," Father told him.

"Are you guys really . . . heroes?" the boy asked Father after finally being freed from being held hostage.

"We sure are. Even so, we're being chased by all sorts of people. Motoyasu, please treat the wounds of this boy and his parents!"

Father called out to me as he hurriedly untied the restraints of the boy's parents, who'd also been held hostage. Leave it to me, I say!

"I'm not as skilled at it as you are, Father, but healing magic is a specialty of mine, just like you!"

"Yeah, I know I should probably be taking care of it myself, but . . ."

"I know. You still can't use magic. You mustn't be so harsh on yourself, I say!"

Father kept an eye on our surroundings as I cast healing magic on the boy and his parents. He was making sure that none of their attacks made it through the wall of fire.

"Worry not, I say!"

"I worry . . . They're trying to cancel it out with their own magic, you know."

"Ha! Ha! Ha! Their pitiful magic could never interfere with my spells, I say!"

We'd saved the townspeople and they started gathering around us. Their expressions made no attempt to hide their surprise. That's how it was supposed to be, I say!

"The scumbags continue to attack. It's about time to make them pay!"

I had added a certain little something something to my wall of fire. It was an effect similar to the ability of a shield Father used long ago. Flames lashed out from the wall of fire like whips and scorched anyone who attacked it.

"Gaaaaahhh!"

"Wh-what kind of magic is this?!"

"Firewall isn't supposed to have an effect like that!"

"Ahhhhh!"

The attackers were engulfed in flames and the fire began to spread beyond the town square. Ha! Ha! Ha! They were flames of purification, I say!

"Is this going to be okay, Motoyasu?! The buildings are starting to catch on fire!"

"Worry not, I say! I shall extinguish the flames eventually!"

"That doesn't sound like it's okay! But jeez . . . There sure seem to be a lot of them hiding out in the town."

His voice trailed off. He was looking at the church members fleeing from the flames. They were pouring out of the buildings in droves. Seeing just how many people they had managed to gather was actually quite impressive, I say!

"Motoyasu! We've finished taking care of the mob that was keeping the town sealed off!" Yuki shouted.

"We took care of ours too! Siltvelt got wind of the disturbance and deployed an advance team from the army that came to our assistance," Éclair yelled.

She, Yuki, and the others had gone to unseal the town gates. Immediately after they called out to us, I caught sight of them approaching with countless troops in tow. I could hear the echoes of footsteps and triumphant shouts of victory extending far off into the distance. The time had come to put an end to this. I canceled Firewall and proceeded to annihilate the remaining Church of the Four Heroes.

"I'm not done with you yet!" shouted the leader.

"Watch out!" Father shouted.

I thought the leader had died, but he suddenly got up and

ran toward Father, swinging his sword with a crazy look in his eyes. Father jumped in front of the boy and his parents to protect them from the man's attack. A loud shattering sound rang out as the leader's sword hit Father in the forehead and the blade snapped right in half.

"N-no . . . way . . . You're . . . a monster . . ." he stammered.

"Actually, he's a hero, I say!"

"D-damn you!" he shouted.

"You really do need to learn your place. This is the perfect chance for me to teach you, I say!"

There was a loud thud as I thrust my spear forcefully into the ringleader's chest.

"Ga . . . aahhh . . ." he yelled out.

He was stuck to the end of my spear, dangling in midair and groaning. He was a tough bastard.

"You want proof we're real heroes, right? I'll give you the chance to experience that proof firsthand. Be thankful for this!"

Surely even Father, despite his immense kindness, wouldn't be able to sympathize with a man who had taken docile children and adults hostage and then tried to execute them right in front of our eyes. The man had gone well beyond the limits of what was forgivable.

"Now then, die, I say!"

I released the full power of Brionac and launched the attack high up into the sky. I did it partially as a demonstration of what would happen to those who defied Father. A single beam of light shot straight up toward the heavens.

"Gaahhh!"

The leader of the Church of the Four Heroes imposters who had orchestrated this despicable scheme turned instantly into a pile of cinders. He'd most likely been either a priest of the Church of the Three Heroes or an adventurer.

"Incredible! The heroes truly have returned! The rumors of their summoning were true!" the townspeople we had rescued said as they all clasped their hands together and began praying to us.

"This is what happens when you defy Father's authority, I say! Ha! Ha! Ha! Ha!"

"Umm, I'm pretty sure they're praying to you now, Motoyasu."

"Then allow me to rephrase! If Father were serious, an attack like that would be child's play for him! I am but the Love Hunter, I say!"

"Did you hear that?! Oh, glorious Shield Hero! Please save our world!"

The townspeople sure caught on quick! They were praying to Father now, I say!

"Why did you do that?! Oh, good grief . . . Why are you such a goofball?" Father said.

The family that had been taken hostage turned to us and bowed their heads.

"Thanks for saving me!" said the boy.

"You have our thanks!" his father added.

"Oink!"

I had no idea what the pig was trying to say.

"Of course . . . I'm glad you're safe, but there are still enemies here in town, right? Let's hurry up and put an end to this mess! Everyone! Stay close to the Siltvelt soldiers!" Father shouted, issuing his orders to our party members and the demi-human soldiers that had accompanied Éclair here.

"Go search the town and capture the Church of the Four Heroes and their leaders!"

"Yes sir!"

And just like that, we brought a swift end to the disturbance that had been jointly orchestrated by the Church of the Three Heroes and a bunch of Shieldfreeden troublemakers.

Epilogue: Arrival at Siltvelt

It was just past my afternoon snack time. We'd been busy helping with treating the injured townspeople and repairing parts of the town that had been damaged.

"We finally meet! Shield Hero! Spear Hero!"

We were taking a break in the town square when several representatives from Siltvelt approached us.

"We've come from Siltvelt to accompany you back to our country. I'm sure you've had a very trying journey. Come, let us finally get you to the comfort of Siltvelt."

"Yeah, we'd like to, but . . ." Father said as he looked around at the town and all of the damage it had suffered.

"I assure you Siltvelt will spare no effort in assisting with the reconstruction of this town. Getting you heroes into the country as soon as possible is necessary to help ensure that something like this doesn't happen again."

"I guess you're right. Sticking around might just end up causing more trouble for everyone here," Father replied.

He seemed to feel uncomfortable being in the town, even though all of the townspeople were being friendly with us. It was because Father had put his life on the line to save the hostages.

"Are you guys leaving already?" asked the boy from earlier.

"Yeah, sorry. None of this would have happened if we hadn't come here in the first place," Father said.

The boy shook his head.

"It's not your fault! It was . . . those bad guys, right? The Melromarc Church of the Three Heroes!"

We'd already exposed the true identity of the culprits. I'd stabbed several of the enemies we captured with my Illusion Lance and showed them hallucinations. They all spilled the beans straight away. A few of them talked about their dreams of being successful in Shieldfreeden too.

"Luckily there was hardly any damage to the town," Éclair said. "And thankfully, you succeeded in saving the townspeople, Mr. Iwatani. The whole ordeal doesn't seem to have left that bad of a taste in their mouths. The relief efforts and monetary aid have been very generous, as well. Things could have been much worse."

"Just as expected of the heroes! Indeed, it is the Church of the Three Heroes and the countries assisting them that are to blame for this," said the Siltvelt representative.

". . ."

Father looked like he had mixed feelings about it all.

"We're counting on you guys to defeat the bad people that do terrible things like this!" said the boy.

"Yeah . . . we will," Father replied.

"And thanks again! I . . . I want to become a soldier so I can help you guys fight!" the boy continued.

"D-do your best, then . . ." Father muttered.

We decided that we would leave the town before the end of the day. When we departed, all of the townspeople gathered and waved at us. We peeked out of the carriage and waved back at them as we made our way out of the town.

We were being escorted to Siltvelt by several dozen demi-humans and therianthropes. Surely neither the Church of the Three Heroes nor the Shieldfreeden troublemakers would be able to justify trying to attack this many people. Father was gazing off toward the town absentmindedly.

"Was that really okay?" he asked.

"I'm sure the people you saved are grateful," Éclair replied.

Her answer sounded like she might not have understood what Father meant.

"I just think if we hadn't stopped there . . . maybe none of this would have happened in the first place," Father said.

"There's no point in worrying about what-ifs, is there?" she replied.

"But we have Motoyasu, right?"

"You rang?"

"When I was falsely accused and ended up losing my way, did I still get caught up in a mess like this?" Father asked.

"You ran into all sorts of trouble in Melromarc, but I never heard anything about people being held hostage to lure you out."

I'd heard that imposters claiming to be Father had caused trouble all across the country. However, they were proven to be imposters later on.

"I see."

Father was absentmindedly petting Sakura's feathers.

"Mr. Iwatani, you really shouldn't worry too much about it," Éclair said.

"Yeah . . . Hey, Motoyasu," Father began.

"What is it?"

"If there ends up being a next time, I'd like you to make sure we don't cause a mess like this again."

"I should be able to do that. My portal locations are retained even if the time loop resets. If there is a next time, I'll be able to take us to Siltvelt without needing to travel this road."

"That works. Thanks."

"If anything does happen, I'll stomp all over the fools, I say!"

Shortly after, we joined up with the Siltvelt army and proceeded to make our way into Siltvelt without incident.

"Ugh, rain. There's something ominous about those huge rainclouds. I don't like it," Father said.

It was thundering and pouring rain as we continued along the road toward the Siltvelt castle.

"If this were a mystery novel, this rain would probably drive us into some old mansion," I commented.

"Don't say that, Motoyasu. That's scarier than it is funny," Father said.

Yuki seemed to take an interest in our exchange.

"What is a mystery novel?" she asked.

"It's a certain type of story . . . I guess you could say. The stories are generally about a detective character who happens upon some kind of crime and then goes on to capture the culprit," Father explained.

"That sounds like what happened with those bad guys in that town earlier. In our case, Motoyasu would be the detective," she said.

"I guess that might be true, in a sense. But I was thinking of it a bit differently."

"Hm?"

Yuki and Sakura both looked confused.

"Mystery novels are complex, with lots of characters and the relationships between them coming into play. Sometimes the culprit ends up being one of the supposedly good people. If Motoyasu was the detective, then the Church of the Three Heroes' members, who disguised themselves as Church of the Four Heroes' members, would be the first people he suspected, right?"

Of course! They were the only scumbags that would do something so hideous, I say!

"You can't call that a mystery. That would probably classify as an adventure novel or maybe an action novel," Father continued.

"So an important part of mysteries is to make you think then," Yuki replied.

"Yeah."

"That reminds me. This was before I was summoned to this world, but I visited a mysterious mansion once," I said.

I'd gone on a trip with some pigs. It started raining on us and we ended up staying in some stranger's mansion for a while.

"Oh, a story from your past? So? Was there a murder at the mansion?" Father asked.

"No, the pig that lived in the mansion and I just solved several complicated issues is all."

"That sounds like a 'gal game' or a dating sim more than anything. You were the wrong person to ask. Right now, your character would either be the one who committed the murder at the mansion or maybe a bloodthirsty killer on the run," Father said.

"I'd send the culprit straight to the grave with a single blow, I say!"

"You really would. This rain looks like it's only going to get worse."

"Ha! Ha! Ha! Blowing this pathetic rain right out of the sky would be a simple task with my power, I say! Shall I do that?"

"I really wish you wouldn't. I saw some townspeople back there completely engrossed in sketching pictures of the instant you shot that skill off. They're likely to come up with some kind of weird legend about how the rain stopped because of my arrival or something."

"Then I shall use magic, I say! It's your hero's welcome!"

"Were you listening to what I just said? Please don't! Motoyasu!"

There was no arguing with that. Father had told me to stop, so I gave up on using magic. But no matter what misfortunes might be lying in wait for Father in the future, I was going to protect him until the end, I say!

And then . . . finally, we arrived at the Siltvelt castle town.

CHARACTER CHAT CORNER
VOLUME ONE CLOSING WORDS

The journey to Siltvelt sure was tough. Way to stick it out!

It's impressive just how persistent those Melromarc—well, that is to say, Church of the Three Heroes creeps can be.

It would be nice if everything worked out now that they made it to Siltvelt.

I'm not counting on it. But yeah, that journey really was a huge mess.

It's all thanks to you that we were able to arrive safely, Father!

Are you seriously sucking up to me in the chat corner?

It's time to finish this up, but . . . walking a different path really changed the way you turned out, Mr. Naofumi.

In a world like this, yeah. I guess that's how I turn out when everything comes easy.

I think both of you are kindhearted, Mr. Naofumi.

Me? Kindhearted?

No matter what happens, I shall support you, Father! Please look forward to my next adventure, I say!

You're just going to wrap things up all of a sudden? Oh, whatever. See you next time.

The Reprise of the Spear Hero Vol. 1
© Aneko Yusagi 2017
First published by KADOKAWA in 2017 in Japan.
English translation rights arranged by One Peace Books
under the license from KADOKAWA CORPORATION, Japan

ISBN: 978-1-64273-003-6

Written by Aneko Yusagi
Translated by Nathan Takase
Character Design Minami Seira
English Edition Published by One Peace Books 2018

Printed in Canada
3 4 5 6 7 8 9 10

One Peace Books
43-32 22nd Street STE 204 Long Island City New York 11101
www.onepeacebooks.com